A PLAIN DEATH

A Plain Death

An Appleseed Creek Mystery

Amanda Flower

Nashville, Tennessee

Printed in the United States of America

978-1-4336-7697-0

Published by B&H Publishing Group,
Nashville, Tennessee

Dewey Decimal Classification: F
Subject Heading: AMISH—FICTION \ MYSTERY FICTION \
HOMICIDE—FICTION

Publisher's Note: The characters and events in this book are fictional, and any resemblance to actual persons or events is coincidental.

1 2 3 4 5 6 7 8 • 16 15 14 13 12

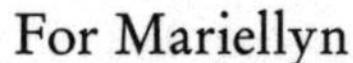
For Mariellyn

Acknowledgments

Special thanks to my fantastic agent Nicole Resciniti. I've always had big dreams, but since we teamed up, my dreams are even bigger.

Thank you to Julie Gwinn and Julie Carobini for their thoughtful comments on this novel.

Gratitude to all my dear friends in Mount Vernon, Ohio. A special thank-you to Brenda and Paul Nixon, John Shelter, Mosie Shetler, and Josh Swartzentruber for sharing their Amish experiences with me.

Love to my family, especially my mother, Rev. Pamela Flower, the best mom a girl could have.

Finally, to my heavenly Father, thank You.

Chapter One

A gust of wind rocked my car and the U-Haul trailer hitched to the back. I yelped, my knuckles white as they gripped the steering wheel.

"Did you fall into a hole or something?" Tanisha's voice rang in my ear.

I lowered the volume on my wireless earpiece. Although my best friend sat in her apartment in Milan, Italy, it sounded like she was right next to me. I wished she were. "No, I'm fine." The wind made its way across the opposing cornfield, its force bowing the stalks in a green wave.

"When can you come visit me?"

"I told you I don't know. I haven't even started my job yet. I don't think it's a good idea to ask for a vacation the very first day."

"I suppose you're right." Tanisha gave a dramatic sigh. "I want you to meet Marcos. He's perfect for you. I've been telling him all about you."

I rolled my eyes. Ever since my boy-crazy friend had become engaged, she thought matchmaking was her new mission in life. Unfortunately, I was the one she thought needed her help.

"Maybe you will meet someone in Appleseed Creek." Her tone brightened. "I know! You will find a nice buggy boy while you're playing country girl."

"Buggy boy?"

"A nice Amish lad. He can make you a computer desk. It will be a match made in heaven." Laughter buoyed Tanisha's voice.

I groaned.

"You can't hide behind a computer forever. It's not healthy."

Before I could think of a decent comeback, my cat, Gigabyte, meowed. He wasn't fond of car rides. He'd yowled his way through the last four counties as I made my way from Cleveland into the middle of nowhere. "Don't worry, Gig. It can't be much longer now." I paused. "I hope."

"Buggy boy or no buggy boy, this move will be great for you," Tanisha insisted. "A fresh start! You'll see. And think about Gig. He's going to have all the mice he can eat."

"He's never even seen a mouse, let alone eaten one."

"You're hopeless." My friend sighed. "By the way, Mom and Dad are sorry they couldn't help you move."

"I know." I forced a smile into my voice. "But I'm happy your parents have a chance to visit you."

"I'm so excited to see them. I can't believe it's been three months."

Tanisha moved to Milan in April to teach English as a second language. Yet I was afraid to move within the same state. I bit the inside of my lip. She didn't remind me of her parents' visit to upset me, but I couldn't imagine *my* father traveling to the other side of the world to see me. He hadn't even attended my graduate school ceremony. My stepmother, Sabrina, said they couldn't make it because of "scheduling problems." Whatever that meant. "And besides," Sabrina said, "we were just there for your college graduation." I didn't remind her that my college graduation had been three years before.

"I wish you could have come with them. Poor Marcos." Tanisha's voice turned sullen.

"I'm sure Marcos will survive." I checked my side mirror for oncoming traffic. There was none. Another gust of wind rocked the car. "Tee, I have to go." My hands ached from gripping the steering wheel.

"Call me tomorrow. *Ciao*."

I removed the earpiece and tossed it on the dashboard.

A low growl came from the carrier in the backseat of my RAV4. Gig's plastic cat carrier sat between my bedding and two small suitcases, one stacked on top of the other. The suitcases didn't hold clothes. My clothing was back in the trailer along with my few pieces of furniture. Instead, the suitcases held what I really cared about: my computer graveyard.

It's not a true graveyard, of course, but the remnants of computers past: motherboards, old VGA cables, USB connectors, hard drives, and obsolete floppy disk drives, all carefully packed inside of those two suitcases. I couldn't bear to part with them. I'd owned some of the hardware since I was a young child and discovered my love of all things tech.

That love of technology led me to this very spot in the middle of Ohio's rural countryside, although this detour—and I did consider it a detour—was never part of the plan. "Okay, God," I whispered. "Two years. Get me out of here in two years."

"Recalculating!" My GPS squawked again. Apparently I wasn't the only one who thought we were headed for the middle of nowhere. My GPS, the one I had affectionately named "Pepper"—since she had such a peppery attitude—had recalculated every ten minutes since I'd exited Interstate 71 South.

"Recalculating!"

Gig yowled his disgust. He and Pepper were not friends. In fact, Gig wasn't a fan of any of my high-tech toys. It was not unusual for me to return to my apartment after a long night of studying at the university's library to find Gig had chewed through a wire or two. The most recent victim had been the AC adapter to my netbook.

"I should really turn her off," I told Gig. "She's not much help to us out here."

Gig growled in agreement.

I reached to hit the power button and my hand froze. A small rise came into view. "Uh-oh, another hill, Gig. Hold onto your tail!" I pressed down hard on the gas pedal to give us the extra boost to pull the trailer up the small hill. The car shook with the effort. My stomach clenched.

As the car crested the hill, I slowed. About a mile ahead of me, a beat-up, green pickup crawled along the edge line. A slim woman wearing an ankle-length skirt and a long blonde braid walked beside the pickup. Something about the way she pointedly ignored the truck set off warning bells in my head.

I sped up.

Then, I slowed down. *Is she in trouble? What if I'm misreading this? Oh Lord, what should I do?*

As my car drew closer, it appeared neither the girl nor the driver knew of my presence.

I looked down the highway. No one for miles. I checked my side mirrors. Not a car in sight. The girl and the passengers of that pickup were the only ones on the road besides me.

What would Tanisha do in this situation? She would run in headfirst, that's what. But that was Tanisha, not me. I could be misjudging the entire scene.

The pickup stopped, but the girl kept walking.

The passenger door opened and a huge man got out. He stepped into the girl's path and grabbed her arm. She jerked it away from him.

I lowered my passenger side window as I approached the pickup. Male laughter sent a chill down my spine. A voice from inside the pickup called, "Come on, honey, we'll give you a ride back home!"

The girl tightened her grip around the handle of her canvas tote bag.

Beep! Beep! My car's horn sounded friendlier than I would have liked. Would anyone in that pickup be frightened by that honk? I pulled alongside the truck. A clear view inside the cabin illuminated the driver. He and the huge man were young, probably somewhere close to my own age of twenty-four. I checked my side mirrors for other cars. Seeing none, I stopped. "Something wrong? Do you guys need help?"

The driver, a thin, wiry guy with a scruffy goatee, turned to me. A set of Army dog tags hung from his neck. "Hello, there." He grinned at me, tobacco juice trailing down his lower lip. "Why would you think we needed help?"

The girl watched me from the other side of the truck, her large eyes the size of dessert plates. A lump formed in my throat. "You were driving so slowly I thought something must be wrong with your truck. I have a cell phone and can call for help." I held up my cell to illustrate only to find the phone had no service. So much for calling the cavalry.

Lord, help me to know what to do.

The driver's eyes narrowed into slits. "We don't need any help from you."

The ogre standing in the girl's way peered through the truck's open windows at me. Unlike the driver, the passenger was clean shaven and had a baby face. He was, however, enormous. "We were giving our friend a lift." His mouth twisted into a scowl. "It's not safe for a little Amish girl out on the road all by herself. She doesn't know how the real world works." He tried to grab her arm again.

I glanced back at the girl and found her staring at me, those eyes even wider. Despite the warm summer breeze through my open windows, I shivered. *Please help, Lord.*

"I can give her a lift. I have more room in my car than you have in the truck." I hoped my voice wasn't shaking.

The girl pursed her lips and furrowed her brow.

The ogre lunged for her, and she jumped out of the way. Unable to stop his momentum, he fell to the ground with a grunt. His friend laughed. The girl ran around the pickup, threw open my passenger side door, and jumped into the car. As soon as I heard the door slam shut, I hit the power locks.

The ogre struggled to his feet.

"What are you trying to prove, Red?" the driver growled. Tobacco juice flecked onto his cheek.

I glared at him. I hated being called "Red." I suspected most redheads hated it, too. I shifted the car into drive.

His passenger climbed back into the truck, his dark expression making the hair on the back of my neck stand on end.

"Nice U-haul." The driver spat. "Are you moving? It'd be a shame to start off in a new place on the wrong foot."

I didn't reply, but stepped on the gas and pulled my car around the truck. As we drove away, I raised the power windows.

The pickup followed us for a couple of miles, and I gripped the steering wheel hard the entire time. All I could think about was the "no service" warning of my cell phone. The girl and I were silent until the driver of the truck finally gunned his engine and sped around us. Within seconds, we were the only ones on the road.

I let out a breath that I hadn't known I'd been holding, and glanced over at the girl. She clenched her small hands folded on top of the tote bag in her lap. "Are you okay?"

"Yes." She tapped her feet on the floorboard. "Thank you for helping."

"Don't mention it," I said. "I'm Chloe Humphrey. What's your name?"

"Becky Troyer."

"Can I take you home?"

A cloud settled on her pretty face, and she shook her head. "No."

I took my eyes off the road and glanced at her. "No? Where can I take you?"

She gave me a bright smile. "Wherever you're headed."

I blinked at her. "I . . . well . . ."

"Recalculating!" Pepper sounded more irritated than ever.

Gig hissed.

Becky jumped in her seat and hit her head on the car's ceiling. She rubbed her head. "What was that?"

"The hiss? That was my cat Gigabyte." I paused. "He's not in the best mood. He's been in his carrier for a while."

She turned for a glimpse of Gig. In the rearview mirror, I saw his blue eyes reflect light from the back of the cage. "He doesn't look like any cat I've ever seen."

"He's a Siamese."

"Oh," Becky said, as if that was explanation enough, though I suspected it wasn't. "Where did that voice come from? Whoever it was sounded angry."

"It's my GPS." I pointed to the unit on the windshield. "It's trying to direct me, but it's lost. I guess that means I'm lost, too."

Becky's smile lit up her heart-shaped face. Without a speck of makeup on she was beautiful, and her complexion would be the envy of any skin care campaign. "Where are you going?"

I picked up a piece of computer paper from my lap and handed it to her. "Appleseed Creek. There's the address." I pointed to the top of the page.

"Grover Lane? I know where this is. I can show you. You don't need the GSP thing."

"It's GPS." I smiled. "And if you can get me there, I'd appreciate it."

Becky turned around in her seat, straining against the seatbelt across her chest as she looked behind us.

"Don't worry. They're gone." I said it, but did I believe it? My eyes flicked to the rearview mirror every few seconds too, searching for the green pickup.

"I know." She took in the luggage crammed into my car, and the U-haul hitched to the back. "Are you moving?"

I nodded and took a deep breath. "Yes."

"Me, too." The ache in her response reminded me of my own.

Chapter Two

As we approached Appleseed Creek, the farmhouses moved closer and closer together and finally gave way to gas stations, storefronts, and townhomes.

"Turn left here," Becky said.

I followed her directions, the RAV4 and trailer jostling from blacktop to exposed brick.

"We're going to have to drive around the square to get to your house," Becky said. "Do you think you will be able to make it with the trailer?"

I tapped a rhythm on the steering wheel with my fingers. "I guess I don't have any other choice."

The brick road widened as we approached the square. I took in the flat-faced storefronts, a cheese shop, a bakery, and a yarn store. I wasn't in Cleveland anymore. It was the last full week of July, and tourists strolled along the sidewalk from shop to shop, tasting the free cheese samples and buying yarn. A large tour bus dominated the corner ahead of me. The driver stood outside the bus smoking a cigarette, as if he wasn't planning to move any time soon.

My fingers continued to drill the steering wheel. "Do you think I have room to get around that bus?"

Becky tapped the glass. "Can you put the window down?"

I did as she asked, and Becky stuck her head out the window. "I think you can make it. It'll be tight."

Slowly, I maneuvered the car and trailer around the bus. In my head, I heard the grating sound of metal-on-metal as we inched by. The driver glared at me but stepped out of the way. Clear of the bus, I turned onto the square, a brick-paved circle in the center of Appleseed Creek. Century-old oak trees dotted the park in the middle of the square. On the bright, green grass, Amish families sold baked goods and homemade preserves from wooden booths to tourists in Bermuda shorts and T-shirts.

Becky scooted down in her seat until her head sank below the window.

"Are you okay?"

"I'm fine." She continued with her instructions. "You want to take Quaker Street. Grover is off Quaker."

I turned onto Quaker.

"Grover is the third street on the right."

I leaned over the steering wheel anxious to see the street where I would spend the next two years of my life. *Only two years. Right, God?* Surely God was unfazed by my Appleseed Creek timeline. However, it didn't hurt to be specific.

With the square behind us, Becky sat up straight again. "Turn here."

The car and trailer rocked onto Grover, a brick one-way street barely wide enough to host a motorcycle, or so it seemed.

"There's your house," Becky said.

She pointed at a white two-story house. At least what was left of the paint was white. Most of it was cracked and had flaked onto the overgrown bushes below the first-story windows. The wraparound porch, a big selling point for me when I discovered the house online, appeared dangerous. Rusted nails held the warped, untreated boards in place. Now I knew why the rent was so low.

I put a brave smile on my face and pulled into the short driveway. "Home sweet home."

Becky hopped out of the car, and I followed. The back end of the trailer hung over the sidewalk. Hopefully I wasn't breaking any town ordinances. Next time I'd hire movers.

I glanced at Becky's outfit, a long, gray canvas skirt and blouse covered with tiny blue flowers. Her dress wasn't Amish per se, more like Amish-*ish*. Growing up in Ohio, I'd seen many Amish people. The women wore plain navy dresses and bonnets on their heads. Becky's head was uncovered. When I was a little girl, a trip to Holmes County was an annual pilgrimage with my parents. We'd visit the shops to buy homemade trinkets and stop at a local restaurant to eat too much Amish food.

That was before the accident, and before Dad met Sabrina and created a new family without me.

I shook thoughts of Sabrina from my head. She couldn't be farther away, sitting in some California spa drinking sparkling water while getting a pedicure.

Becky could be Mennonite, I decided.

After some pushing and pulling, I pried Gigabyte's cage from the back of the RAV4. He yowled at a pitch and volume that only a true Siamese could achieve. "We're home, Gig."

Another yowl came from the carrier.

Becky, who stood at the base of the front steps, glanced back at me. "Is your cat hurt?"

"He's fine," I said. "It must be all the clean country air. He's not used to it. He's a city cat."

She cocked her head and her braid fell off her shoulder. It was as if she were trying to decide something about me.

The porch's first step groaned under my weight. The second step gave ever so slightly. Speed was the safest option, so I skipped up the final three steps and gave a sigh of relief when the porch floor, although uneven, felt firm under my flip-flops.

Becky skipped up the steps, too. The landlord told me the key would be under a flowerpot, and a large terracotta pot sat beside the front door. Something brown and withered languished beyond recognition inside the vessel. I tipped the pot on its side and found the silver key lying underneath. "I guess security's not a big concern around here." I couldn't imagine anyone in my old neighborhood in University Circle hiding their house key in such an obvious place. At least, not if they wanted their television and computer to be there when they got home from work.

I inserted the key into the lock and turned the doorknob. As I did, it broke off in my hand. A *thunk* sounded inside the house as the second half of the doorknob fell to the floor. I stared at the half doorknob in my hand and peered through the gaping hole its absence left. "Now what am I supposed to do?" My voice jumped an octave. Small town or not, no way would I be able to sleep in a house with a hole in the front door.

Becky nudged the door with her foot and swung it open. The interior was dark. In front of us, the stairs—if I could believe anything the real estate website told me—led to three bedrooms on the second floor. To our left was the living room, and in the dim light, I made out a fireplace.

Becky stepped into the house and threw open the drapes that covered the living room's huge picture window. "Call someone on your little phone to fix the door."

Mr. Green, Tanisha's father, came to mind, but he was in Italy. Then I thought of Tanisha's fiancé, Cole, but he was in Florida. I was on my own.

"There's no one I can call." Panic began to rise within me. "The owner of the house lives in Cincinnati. He's not going to come all the way here to fix the doorknob."

What was I doing here? Who was I to think I could move away from everything and everyone? My hand, now clenched into a fist around Gig's cat carrier handle, began to ache. And what about Gig? He could get outside with the door open like that. He could get eaten by wolves or something. Okay, not wolves. There hadn't been any wolves in Ohio since the nineteenth century, but he could get hit by a car.

"Don't worry. I'll call my *bruder*." Becky stared at me with blue eyes. "He's a carpenter and will fix the door for us."

I blinked at her. "Your *bruder*?"

She blushed, her pink cheeks making her even prettier. She must be popular on the square dance circuit or wherever young Amish went to meet each other in Appleseed Creek. "I'm sorry. My brother." She pronounced "brother" carefully and drew out the two syllables.

"That would be wonderful, Becky." I tried not to worry about the "for us" part. I chewed the inside of my lip. Did Becky think she was moving in?

I handed her my smartphone. She stared at the screen and handed it back to me. "I'll tell you the number and you dial."

I left Becky talking to her brother on the porch and stepped into the living room, its wooden floors beautifully worn. I imagined generations pacing across those floorboards. The fireplace was marble, and dark wood crown molding surrounded the ceiling. The house had been a showpiece once. Could I make it one again? I shook my head. Why did I allow myself to think like that? I was renting. I would only be in Appleseed Creek for two years. Two years was not worth the work. Restoring this house would take a lifetime.

Becky entered the room. "He will be here later this afternoon. It's on his way home from work." She had a peculiar pinched look on her face, as if she'd just bitten into a lemon.

"You said he was a carpenter." Becky followed me into the kitchen where I opened and shut all the cabinets. Every one of them needed a good scrub down before I would put any of my dishes in them.

"He has his own workshop, but is working on a project at the college this summer."

"Do you mean Harshberger College?"

She ran her hand along the Formica counter. "Do you know it?"

"It's the reason I'm here."

"You're a student?" Becky opened and closed a kitchen drawer.

I shook my head. I suspected Becky wouldn't be the last person in Appleseed Creek to assume I was a college student. "I start working there tomorrow as the Director of Computer Services."

"That sounds important."

It was important, but I pushed worries of the next day out of my head. Today's worries were sufficient. A larger concern came to mind. "Becky, who were those two men on the side of the road?"

"They were only *Englischers*, who think they are tough by teasing an Amish girl. They were joyriding." She said "joyriding" as if testing out the word.

I glanced at her. "So, you are Amish?"

A determined expression settled over her face "I was. I'm not anymore."

Chapter Three

Three hours later, I knelt on the floor in my new bedroom putting my bed frame together. Taking the bed apart had been easy. Putting it back together was a bit more difficult. As I worked, my thoughts wandered to the two men in the pickup. *Who were they? What did they want with Becky? Would I see them again?* I hoped not.

I slid the bolt into the eye socket, but it wouldn't move into a locked position. I gave the metal frame three good yanks, and finally, the bolt slid into place, nicking the index finger on my right hand in the process. "Ow!" I popped the pinched finger into my mouth.

"Chloe? My brother is here."

I turned my head and found myself staring at jean-clad legs and work boots. I scrambled into a standing position, my face coming within inches of a man's. Startled, I took one huge step backward and stumbled over the bed frame, but righted myself before falling to the dusty hardwood floor below.

Both Becky and her brother jumped forward to help me. My

hands fluttered in front of me as heat raced up the back of my neck. I wrapped my arms around my waist to still myself.

Becky wore a huge grin on her face. "Chloe, this is my brother, Timothy." She tugged her brother's sleeve. "Chloe starts working at the college tomorrow. You should stop in and see her while you're there."

Timothy smiled, and his eyes lit up.

My knees weakened, but I told myself it was from the humiliation of the near fall. Becky's brother was as handsome as she was beautiful. He had the same white-blond hair and blue eyes. His muscles flexed under his shirt as he put an arm around his sister's shoulder.

Buggy boy! Tanisha's teasing voice played in my head. She'd be thrilled with this latest development. My face grew warm. *Lord, why did You have to make me blush so easily?*.

Timothy broke into my thoughts. "Which building will you be working in?"

"I don't know. I haven't seen the campus yet. The college interviewed me over the phone." My words tumbled out in a rush. *Pull it together, Chloe.*

Timothy examined the half-assembled bed frame. "Do you need help?"

"No, no, I got it." I tucked the injured hand behind my back.

His blue eyes twinkled. "If you say so."

My gaze flicked over to his left hand. No ring. My face grew even warmer. *Why did I do that?* Had Becky and Timothy noticed my glance? How embarrassing! Tanisha would get an earful for putting that buggy boy idea into my head.

"Th-thank you for coming to fix the door. I don't know what I would have done otherwise."

"It's no trouble." He frowned at his sister. "I was glad to know my sister is safe."

Becky didn't look at him, but that peculiar pinched expression crossed her pretty face again.

Timothy sighed. "I'd better get to work. It was nice to meet you, Chloe."

"You too." Out of habit, I held out my hand for a handshake.

After staring at my extended hand for what felt like a decade, he shook it. I pulled my hand away as if I had been shocked.

I had only been in Appleseed Creek for a few hours, and already I'd made a fool of myself in front of the first attractive man I'd met. As I sat on the floor for round two with the bed frame, I tried to shake off my embarrassment.

Thirty minutes later, the bed frame was together with my box springs and mattress on top of it. As I struggled with the fitted sheet, angry voices floated through the open window. I gave up the battle and tiptoed over to the window. Becky and Timothy were in a heated argument below. I could not understand a word, as they spoke Pennsylvania Dutch.

Becky crossed her arms. "I've made up my mind."

Her brother sighed, as if in defeat.

I stepped away from the window, guilty for eavesdropping. But was it really eavesdropping if I didn't understand most of the conversation?

Becky entered my bedroom. "Timothy finished fixing the doorknob. Would you like to see it?"

I nodded, then followed her down the stairs while running my fingers through my hair.

Timothy stood by the closed front door. A new shiny doorknob took the place of the gaping hole. "Give it a try."

I turned the knob, relieved that it felt sturdy in my grasp. As I pulled the door open, an enormous brown and black dog rushed in and jumped up on my shoulders. I screamed and stumbled back into Timothy, who caught me before I hit the floor.

Gigabyte hissed; the sound of his nails scratching the wood floors as he made his escape echoed throughout the house.

Timothy extended his free arm toward the animal. "Bad dog, Mabel! Down!"

The dog fell on all fours.

I caught my breath.

Timothy let go of me and took hold of Mabel's collar. "I'm sorry. She usually doesn't behave like that."

Mabel whimpered. The dog had a short ruff that resembled a collie, but the pointed ears and disposition of a German shepherd.

Timothy pointed to the floor. "Lay down."

She obeyed.

Becky's eyes grew wide . "Are you afraid of dogs, Chloe?"

I shook my head. "I was taken off guard. I didn't expect her to be there."

"I didn't expect her to be there either. She was supposed to wait in the truck." Timothy's face turned red all the way to the hairline. If anything, his embarrassment made him even more handsome.

He cleared his throat, and in the awkward silence that followed, Timothy began demonstrating his handiwork by opening and closing the door. "I added a deadbolt because you didn't have one." His voice turned softer. "Appleseed Creek is a safe town, but you can never be too careful."

"Thank you. How much do I owe you for the parts and the labor too? I'd like to pay you for your trouble." I moved toward my purse on the lonc armchair in my living room. The measly collection of furniture from my one-bedroom apartment back home seemed pathetic in such a large house.

His jaw twitched. "Not necessary. I should go. It's my turn to cook dinner tonight at home."

At home? Was he married? I swallowed. Maybe Amish men didn't wear wedding rings. "I hope we didn't keep you from your family."

Becky stepped forward. "Timothy doesn't live on the farm anymore. He lives with *freinden* in a house in town. It's a street or two over from here."

"Oh." I tried to keep a ridiculous smile from forming on my face.

Timothy glanced outside. "Is that your U-Haul in the driveway?"

I nodded.

"If you're finished with it, I can return it on my way home."

"Thank you!" After driving for three hours, I wasn't looking forward to climbing back into my little SUV again to return the trailer.

He smiled. "Mind keeping an eye on Mabel as I hitch it up to the truck?"

I reached for the dog.

A few minutes later, the U-Haul was hitched to Timothy's pickup. Becky and I sat on the crooked front porch steps, Mabel laying across our laps.

Timothy laughed as he approached us. "She thinks she's a lapdog."

I scratched under her ruff. "I don't mind. She's a good girl."

He wiped his hands. "*Schweschder*," he said to Becky. "Think about what I have said."

She pushed Mabel off our laps and stood.

Mabel gave a little woof of displeasure.

Becky raised her chin a fraction. "You made your decision, and I have a right to make mine."

Timothy sighed and slapped his hand to his thigh. "Come, Mabel. Good-bye, Chloe. Take care of my sister. She can be a handful." The pair jumped into the pickup and drove away with the U-Haul hitched to the back.

Later that evening, Becky and I ate fast food on the hard floor of my nearly empty living room. Gig rubbed my leg, and I broke off a little piece of hamburger to give him. I popped a french fry into my mouth, wondering if I should ask Becky about the argument I'd overheard between her and Timothy, and if she planned to stay the night. She'd didn't appear to have plans to leave.

"I saw your Bible and books in one of the boxes," Becky said. "I hope you don't mind me looking at them."

"I don't."

"You are a Christian, then?"

I nodded.

She smiled. "*Gut*. That's what I thought and told my brother so. He wasn't happy when I said I met you on the side of the highway."

I felt my face flush again. I hated to guess what Timothy thought of me. "Did you tell him about the two men?"

She put her strawberry milkshake on the floor. "No, he would worry. My brother forgets I am nineteen years old. I am an adult." She took a big bite out of her hamburger. Ketchup ran down her chin.

I handed her a napkin. "What do you mean?" I gave Gig another piece of hamburger. He deserved it after his harrowing journey in the car.

"He thinks I should go home, back to the farm. My family wants me to give up my *rumspringa* and marry Bishop Glick's son."

"But you don't want to."

"No. Isaac is a *gut* man and will make someone a *gut* husband, but I want to study art. I won't be able to do that if I marry him. I've been taking classes the last year." She twisted the napkin in her hands. "I haven't told my parents about the lessons, but I can't give them up, not yet." She stood and retrieved her canvas bag from where she'd left it beside the stairs. "I have something to show you." She removed a black portfolio from her bag, opened it, and took out several sheets of watercolor paper. The first painting was of an Amish girl and a brown horse.

"The girl is my *schweschder*, my sister, Ruth. She's twelve."

The painting looked lifelike, as if I could reach through the paper and pet the mare's head. Becky had captured the special twinkle in her younger sister's eyes, too, a twinkle much like her own. "Becky, this is beautiful."

She smiled and showed me another painting, this one of a young man leaning against an Amish buggy. He had dark hair, brown eyes, and a patient expression on his face. "This is Isaac."

"He's handsome."

She blushed. "He doesn't understand what I want to be." She put the paintings away.

"You can't paint if you are Amish?"

"I can paint, but not like I want to." Her eyes lit up. "I want to study art—Picasso, Monet, all the masters. I want to learn about their work. I want to learn about light, reflection, and depth and how to be a true artist. I could never do that at home. Education is discouraged there. If I married, I would immediately have to think about raising a family. I'm not ready for that."

"Where have you been living?"

"At home. I left today. I had an argument with my parents about Isaac. I'm glad we saw my eldest *bruder*. He will tell my *mamm* and *daed* I'm safe. I don't want them to worry." She tucked her portfolio back into her canvas bag. "Is that your *mamm*?" She pointed to the lone photograph on the mantle.

I nodded. It was a picture of my mother not long before the accident. In it, she stood on a pebble-covered Lake Erie beach. It was a rare sunny day on the lake, and the golden highlights in her red hair reflected the bright sunlight. My hair was the same shade of red, but I doubted it was ever as beautiful.

"You must miss her."

"I do."

"Will she visit you?"

I bit the inside of my lip. The accident happened ten years ago, but it never got any easier to explain. "She passed away."

Becky paled. "I'm so sorry."

"It was a long time ago." I waited for the next question. It was always the same one. "What happened?" Then I would say, "It was a car accident." And then they would ask for more details. Details I didn't want to share.

To my surprise, Becky asked something different. "Where is the rest of your family?"

Her question caught me off guard. Where was my family? Was

it in Italy with Tanisha and her parents? Or was it in California with my father, Sabrina, and their children?

Becky knitted her brows. "Did I say something that upset you?"

I shook my head. "I'm tired. That's all." I tossed the remains of our dinner into the garbage. "You're welcome to stay here for the night. You were a huge help to me today." I didn't add that we would be talking about her permanent housing plans tomorrow.

"And you to me." She gave me her beautiful smile. "We will be good *frienden*. That means friends."

"I'd like that. There is a box of blankets and sheets in the second bedroom."

She thanked me, and I picked up Gigabyte and climbed up the creaky stairs to bed.

Alone in my new bedroom, I tried to put Timothy Troyer out of mind. Married or not, no way should I consider any kind of attachment to him. He was Amish. I was a computer geek. It would never work. I blamed matchmaking Tanisha for my lapse in judgment. Besides, I planned to be in Appleseed Creek for a short time, two years max. I was here to get the real-life work experience that every other institution and company said I lacked. In two years, I'd find a job in civilization.

I changed into my pajamas and sat on the edge of my newly made bed to call my father. It was only a little after seven in the evening in San Diego.

As usual I got his voicemail. I swallowed. "Hi, Dad. I'm in Appleseed Creek now. I moved into my new house today. It's nice enough. I start working at the college tomorrow—"

Beep! A female automated-voice much like Pepper's came over the line. *The mailbox you are trying to reach is full. Please hang up and try again.*

I tapped my smartphone's screen and hung up, then moved to the window and peered out onto my narrow one-way street. The lights in the homes along the street were out, their owners safely tucked away in bed. Large oak trees lining the tree lawn blocked the streetlamps' dim glow. Cicadas hummed their nightly songs, and birds twittered in the tree branches, waiting for sleep. I'd imagined country life would be like this—quiet, serene, safe.

The jarring sounds of a car backfiring broke the evening's tranquility. A pickup roared up the street, and I watched as its red taillights disappeared around the corner. Although I hoped it was my imagination, there was no doubt in my mind that the pickup was green.

Chapter Four

The next morning, the smell of fresh bacon wafted up the stairs. I found Becky in the kitchen, flipping pancakes on the stovetop. Gig purred as he wove in and around her bare feet. Undoubtedly, he hoped she'd drop a piece of bacon onto the floor for his breakfast. If Becky lived here much longer and kept cooking like this, I would be replaced in his feline affections.

"Sit, sit," Becky said. "I made you breakfast." She had tied a white apron over her skirt and flower-printed blouse. It was the same outfit she'd worn the day before.

I sat at the small dinette table in the corner of the kitchen. Usually, the most I had for breakfast was a piece of toast and a glass of orange juice. Becky had made enough food for a five-course meal: eggs, pancakes, toast, bacon, and sausage. "Where did this come from?" I asked. She set a heaping plate in front of me. I swallowed. I'd never be able to eat so much food, especially when I was already nervous about my first day at Harshberger College.

"Timothy brought it this morning. He noticed we didn't have any food in the house and didn't want us to starve."

My stomach did a little flip. Now I really wouldn't be able to eat. "That was nice," I managed to squeak.

She set a plate for herself across from me. "My *bruder* is thoughtful." She straightened her shoulders. "Chloe, I need to talk to you about something."

I set my fork on the edge of my plate.

"I want to live here. I can pay rent."

"How? Do you have a job?"

She shook her head. "No, but I can get one."

I picked up my fork. "I don't know, Becky. I just got here. I don't know anyone, or anything about Appleseed Creek." The green pickup came to mind again, but I shoved the thought aside. I needed to get a grip. Nothing bad could happen in a town like Appleseed Creek.

"That's why you need *freinden* like me."

"You're welcome to stay for a few days, but any longer than that, I'll have to think about it." I forked a bite of pancake. It melted in my mouth.

"I'll get a job today, Chloe. I know it. Meet me downtown after you are through at the college. I plan to be there all day knocking on doors, looking for work."

I wasn't sure that was the best way to find employment. I'd search online for job postings. However, I could see why that wouldn't work for Becky.

"I'll meet you," I said. "But I still have to think about you living here full time."

Becky frowned. "I understand." She rose and started clearing the kitchen counter. "Meet me outside Amish Bread Bakery. It's right on the square."

I drove to Harshberger still wondering what to do about Becky. It seemed cruel to ask her to leave when she had nowhere else to go. Tanisha's family took me in when I needed a home. Could I do the same for someone else?

I pushed Becky from my mind. I had a meeting with the college dean at nine o'clock. From half a block away, a large stone sign announced Harshberger College. I drove onto the campus's main road, which divided the grounds in two. All the buildings matched in a tan brick façade, except for one that looked like it had once been a horse barn. The thwack, thwack of hammers split the silence as I passed the barn building. I leaned out of my open driver's side window and looked up to find the silhouettes of Amish men moving back and forth across the roof.

I parked in the small lot in front of the administrative building. *A little courage would be great right now, Lord.* I stood a little straighter and prepared myself to join the professional world.

In front of the glass door, I adjusted my blazer in my reflection. Straight red hair fell to my shoulders, freckles ran across the bridge of my nose, and anxious hazel eyes stared back at me. Tanisha's mom always said I was as "cute as a button." But did anyone actually want to look like a button? I wasn't beautiful, not like Becky. Instead, I resembled Little Orphan Annie playing dress up.

I followed the signs pointing to the dean's office. In the reception area, two men stood in front of the secretary's desk. One was more than six feet tall with a dark JFK Jr. pompadour, polished good looks, and the physique of a serious athlete. The second was a small round man wearing glasses and a big smile.

"I couldn't be happier with the college's reception to my idea," the taller man said. He smacked the shorter man on the back.

The smaller man stumbled forward and caught himself on the edge of the desk. "You've been so generous, Grayson. Harshberger and Appleseed Creek are in your debt."

"I know how much my father loved this place. It only seemed right I would come to Harshberger first."

"He was an institution here and is still greatly missed."

A smile worthy of a toothpaste commercial spread across the taller man's face. He spotted me standing in the doorway. "Charlie, you have a student here to see you."

I felt my face turn the color of my hair. "I'm sorry to interrupt. I'm Chloe Humphrey. I'm here to meet with Dean Klink."

"Chloe!" The shorter man hurried over and gave me a brisk handshake. "I'm Dean Charlie Klink. This is Grayson Mathews, an Appleseed Creek legend. He's the only one to leave our little town, play football for Ohio State, and turn pro."

"Oh, nice to meet you," I said. I might have been more impressed if I knew anything about football.

Mathews laughed. "I only played pro for five years. It wasn't exactly a long career."

"Grayson, Chloe isn't a student. She's our new Director of Computer Services. Chloe, welcome, welcome. We are so glad you're finally here!"

Mathews examined me. "Did you graduate college when you were fourteen?" His sparkling white smile took the bite out of his words.

"Chloe is a whiz, Grayson. Trust me. I knew the moment I received her credentials she was the person to turn computer services around. So many great things are in store for the college this year."

My face grew hot.

"Well, I'll let the two of you do your business." Mathews turned to Dean Klink. "It was nice talking to you, Charlie. We'll be in touch."

As Mathews left the office, a curvy woman with a bouffant hairstyle sauntered into the room carrying a file. Dean Klink nodded in her direction. "This is my secretary, Irene. Irene, this is Chloe."

Irene gave me one brisk nod and sat behind her computer.

"I'm so glad you are here, Chloe," the dean said a second time.

"Thank you so much for this opportunity—"

He waved away the little thank-you speech I'd prepared with a flick of his chubby wrist. "No, thank *you*. You will take technology on campus to the next level. I just know it! Did you find a nice place to live?"

I nodded. More or less that was true. The house needed a lot of work, though. *Perhaps Timothy could help with that . . .*

He grinned. "Excellent! Did you have trouble settling into your new home?"

"No, everything went fine." If you discounted my run-in with the locals in a green pickup, my unwitting adoption of a runaway Amish girl, and embarrassing myself in front of her attractive brother, everything had gone fine.

He clapped his hands together. "Now, right to business." He handed me a piece of paper. "This is our agenda for the day. The first day is always the most overwhelming. You will do exciting things like get your parking pass and meet with the computer services department to set up your e-mail. What am I thinking? You are the computer services department. You'll be up and running in that respect in no time." He laughed as if he'd just told the funniest joke ever.

"Your office is in Dennis, one of our academic buildings. It holds faculty offices and classrooms. Since we are in summer, it's all but empty now. We'll head there now and give you a chance to settle in." He tucked a pen into the pocket of his short-sleeve white button-down shirt. "Irene, I'll be back in a jiffy."

Irene nodded. Unlike her boss, she wasn't the talkative sort. Perhaps she'd given up trying.

The dean continued. "You may have noticed some workmen on the barn when you arrived on campus. They're fixing the barn's roof and making other general repairs to all the buildings. We want everything to be shipshape when the students arrive at the end of next month."

"When do classes start?"

"The last Wednesday of August. That may be only a little over a month from now, but the days will pass quickly. That's why we are so anxious for you to start. We want topnotch technology for our students." He jiggled with excitement. "I'm thrilled about the expertise you bring to campus. I know the students and faculty will benefit from it."

"Thank you, Dean Klink."

He waved a hand. "Please call me Charlie. I don't stand by fancy titles. We are all people who should be treated equally. It's a value that Harshberger was founded on."

Despite his height, Dean Klink—I mean, Charlie—set a brisk pace across the main green, and I increased my own stride to keep up.

The closer we came to the barn, the more deafening the sound of pounding nails. The noise didn't discourage the dean's enthusiasm as he shouted out the names of buildings. Two Amish men sorted through a wooden toolbox. Mabel lay on the ground next to them. I tucked my hair behind my ears. Timothy must be close by, but I wasn't prepared to see him today.

"How is it coming along this morning?" Dean Klink asked the men.

The one with the full gray beard smiled at us. "Very *gut*. We should be finished with the roof today."

"Excellent. Excellent."

The younger man closed the toolbox's lid and stood up. I drew in a sharp breath. *Isaac Glick.* In her painting, Becky had captured him perfectly. He smiled shyly at me, his brown eyes kind. I suspected he'd have no trouble finding any number of Amish girls ready and willing to take Becky's place in his affections.

Dean Klink peered at me, his forehead wrinkled. "Are you all right, Chloe?"

I mumbled something about breathing in all the fresh country air.

"Yes, it is a change for you." He smiled at the men. "Chloe is new to Harshberger. She's our Director of Computer Services."

The man with the gray beard smiled.

"This is Bishop Glick, Chloe, and his son."

"Nice to meet you." *Does Becky know Isaac and his father are working with Timothy?*

A familiar voice called from the side of the barn. "I found the nails you wanted, Bishop." Timothy pulled up short. Unlike his friends, who wore plain dark trousers, white shirts, and suspenders, he wore blue jeans and a plaid work shirt.

Mabel jumped up and ran to Timothy, who bent and scratched her between the ears. Her long plume of a tail wagged back and forth with such force I was afraid her back end might take off like a helicopter.

If he worked with other Amish men, why had he left the district? Was he like Becky? Was there something he'd like to learn from the outside world, but couldn't with his own people?

Dean Klink clapped, startling me out of my thoughts. "There's our expert carpenter now. Timothy, I'd like to introduce you to Chloe Humphrey."

He stared at me. "We've already met." From his neutral tone I couldn't tell if he was happy or disappointed by our acquaintance.

Chapter Five

The computer services department was housed in the back corner of Dennis's main floor, closest to the emergency stairwell. The department consisted of a main workroom divided into three staff cubicles and a small conference area. My office was tucked into a small area in the back.

When Dean Klink and I entered the department, we found the conference table covered with a computer graveyard worthy of my collection. Two men sat hunched over a table sorting through the pieces.

"Clark, Miller, look who I brought." Charlie's jovial voice cut the silence. "This is Chloe Humphrey."

Jonathan Clark shook my hand. "Nice to meet you." The tall African-American man spoke in a baritone voice. He was the first nonwhite person I had seen since arriving in Appleseed Creek. I was surprised I hadn't noticed this before, considering I had lived with Tanisha's African-American family throughout high school.

Darren Miller was as short as Clark was tall. He tugged at spiky, dark blond hair and fidgeted in his desk chair until I extended my hand to him. He shook it, and when he did, nervous energy reverberated through his fingertips. *Would he be patient enough for computer programming?*

"You have one more member of your staff. His name is Joel Schrock." Charlie's eyes darted around the room. "Joel must have stepped away from his desk."

Clark and Miller shared a look.

Charlie opened my office door, then placed the key ring on my desk. "Those are for you. They include keys to Dennis, the two campus computer labs—they are down the hall—your office, the server room, and a few other places I can't remember. Just ask Joel. He's worked for Harshberger a long time. He knows the ins and outs of the entire campus. He'll be your go-to man."

"Thank you."

"We are so happy to have you on board, Chloe. Harshberger is small but mighty."

He considered his watch. "Oh dear, I have an academic review meeting in twenty minutes. I'm sure you won't have too much trouble, and if you do, they'll come around, you'll see." He wiggled his fingers in farewell.

Trouble? What kind of trouble?

Clark scrunched his nose. "Do you think Klink realized he just compared Harshberger to dog food? Small but mighty?"

"Naw. He probably thought he made that up," Miller said. He held up his hand, and Clark gave him a high five.

I broke into their gab session. "How small is Harshberger?"

"We have around seven hundred students," Clark said.

"That's tiny."

"You didn't research the college before moving here?" Clark asked.

"Well, I was interviewed last Wednesday. Dean Klink offered me the job over the phone and asked me to start as soon as possible. I didn't have enough time to research the college as much as I normally would have." I didn't tell them how desperate I was for a job—any job—and that this one seemed tailor-made for me. At least it did over the phone. Maybe I should have asked more questions before accepting.

Miller turned a wireless mouse over and over again in his hands. "Joel was right."

Clark widened his eyes at Miller.

Miller shrugged and said it again. "Joel was right about what?" I asked.

Clark laughed. "Just ignore Miller. Sometimes what he says doesn't make sense. Programmer talk. If you hear him muttering to himself throughout the day, don't be alarmed."

Yeah, right. I reminded myself to breathe. "What are your positions here?"

Clark spoke for both of them. "I'm the media guy. Video, audio, stuff like that. I set up for campus events. Miller is a programmer, as if you couldn't tell from his mole-like squint."

Miller ignored the comment.

I hid a smile. "Do either of you want to show me around?"

Miller and Clark shared another look. "Joel will want to do that."

I raised my eyebrows. "Okay."

I skirted around the enormous desk and sat in my captain's chair. Although small, the office had a nice window that overlooked a pond. Charlie had called the pond Archer Lake, but it wasn't large enough to hold a rowboat, and the dozen or so mallards wading in it jostled for space. Compared to Lake Erie where I grew up, Archer was a puddle.

I opened my briefcase and pulled out the two frames that held my master's degrees, and a third, a photo of Tanisha and me. I set all three on the desk for the time being and logged onto my new work e-mail account. Nothing of any importance there yet—mostly generic campus announcements and a few welcome e-mails. One welcome e-mail was from Clark, which made me feel a little better. I wasn't sure what was going on in the computer services department, but I was surprised by how nervous the dean became when we stepped into the office. What could possibly make the man so nervous? And what was Joel right about?

I shook away my thoughts, making way for new ones. I typed "rumspringa Amish" into Google and thousands of hits came back. I leaned toward the screen. *Rumspringa* was loosely translated as "running around." It was a time of freedom for Amish youth, a time for them to consider whether or not to join the church. The website said that after joining the church, the young men and women were expected to get married and raise families.

I typed "Amish Ohio" into my search engine and received even more hits. Holmes County was the largest concentration of Amish in the state and country with a population more than twenty thousand. Although a smaller population than Holmes, Amish have lived in Knox County for generations.

A male voice spoke up behind me. "Researching the locals, I see."

I jumped and closed the browser, then spun my chair to find a man in about his early fifties standing over me. His pale complexion looked nearly translucent against his neatly parted brown hair. A roll of fat hung over his waistband.

I stood. "I'm Chloe Humphrey."

"I know who you are. I'm Joel Shrock." He held out his hand, and I shook it, his palm damp. I fought the urge to wipe my hand on my pant leg.

"It's nice to meet you. You're the assistant director of our department, correct?"

His lip curled when I said "assistant," and he didn't respond.

"I know we will be working closely together. I'm sure we will get along just great." I found myself babbling, and the more I did, the more Joel scowled.

He glared at the two master's degrees on my desk, one in computer programming, the other in information technology. "I know those fancy degrees from those lofty schools are the reason you got this job." He examined me. "But by the looks of you, you won't be here long."

I recoiled. True, it wasn't my plan to be in Appleseed Creek long, but that was my choice, not some employee's. I laughed as if he'd told a joke. "It's only my first day, but I'm excited to get to work."

He scowled. "I thought you'd like to see the server room."

I set my jaw. "I would."

I waved to Clark and Miller as we passed through the workroom, but both stayed hunched over their computers with their heads down. Something was going on, and I made a mental note to ask Dean Klink about it at the first opportunity. What had I gotten myself into?

I followed Joel down the employee stairs and through a labyrinth of dark hallways to reach a far corner of the building with a locked door. Since summer classes were over and the faculty wasn't on campus, the classrooms, offices, and hallways sat empty.

Joel unlocked the door, and inside loomed a seven-foot tall rack of ten servers. The hum of them at work soothed my nerves. This was my strength. This is what I knew. Here, I was the expert.

I stepped closer to the rack and examined the machines, black rectangles, one stacked on top of the other. My shoulders tensed. "These models are at least nine years old." Usually a server was replaced every five years, max. Keeping one any longer than that was gambling with your network. I zeroed my sights on Joel. "What's the server replacement plan?"

He smirked. "I suppose that's your decision as director."

I blew out a breath and slipped out of the room, the closed space far too tight. Especially with Joel snarling over my shoulder.

Joel closed and locked the door behind us. "I guess you have your work cut out for you, Miss Director." He turned and stomped away, leaving me alone to find my own way back to my office.

Chapter Six

I returned from my new employee orientation by midafternoon. My mind had wandered to Joel during most of the meeting. What was his problem with me? I couldn't expect all of my employees to like me, but I hadn't expected them to be antagonistic toward me either.

Lord, help me to understand Joel and get this department on the right track. If that doesn't work, You might have to shorten my time here from two years. I couldn't imagine working with Joel and his awful attitude for long.

I pulled the sack lunch of a ham sandwich, pickles, crackers, and chocolate chip cookies from my tote bag. If Becky kept feeding me like this, it would be hard to ask her to leave my house. It would also be hard to avoid gaining fifteen pounds like Harshberger's freshmen. Becky's food was delicious, but it packed more calories into one meal than I usually ate in three days.

As I ate lunch, I read the employee manual. A *tap, tap* on my doorframe caught my attention. Timothy smiled at me. "I see Becky's made good use of the groceries I brought you."

I gathered up the remnants of my lunch, tucked the sack under my desk, and stood. "Yes, she has. Thank you so much for the food. It was very kind of you." As I sat on the corner of my desk, I knocked over the metal cup filled with pens and pencils. The cup rolled off the desk, its contents flying every direction. I stifled a groan. Between this and the bed frame incident, Timothy was bound to consider me a complete klutz.

Timothy started to pick up the writing utensils from the floor.

"You don't have to do that," I said. "I can get it."

He ignored me and finished gathering up all the fallen pieces.

I peeked out the door, happy to see the computer guys had left for lunch. At least my clumsiness was limited to Timothy's inspection . . . again.

He placed the last pencil in the cup. "Becky tells me she's living with you."

I swallowed. "I said she could stay with me for a few days. We haven't discussed anything permanent. She's a nice girl and has been a big help as I get settled here." I cracked a smile. "And my cat likes her. That's no small feat."

He didn't smile back. "My sister needs to go back home. My parents are worried."

"I can understand their worry. Maybe it would help if Becky explains how she's feeling to your parents."

Timothy shook his head. "It's time for her go home, join the church, and marry a nice man."

"You mean Bishop Glick's son."

"She told you, then?"

I nodded. The ham sandwich felt like a rock in my stomach.

His blue eyes narrowed. "This is none of your concern. It's a private business. The church is important."

"I agree. The church is very important. Becky told you I was a Christian."

Timothy's brows shot up and he took a tiny step back. "That's what she said." He spoke slowly, as if unconvinced.

His doubt stung. "You decided not to join the church, isn't that right?"

He paused, as if weighing my question. "It is a decision you could never understand." Then he turned on the heel of his boots and marched from the room.

He was right. I couldn't understand. Not at all.

I was exhausted by the time I left Harshberger that afternoon to meet Becky downtown. When I pulled the RAV4 into a parking space in front of the bakery, it was after five, and many of the shops along the square were closed for the day. Buggies waited by the curbs ready to take shopkeepers home. I kept an eye out for any who may come along and roll up the sidewalks. Within two minutes Becky stumbled out of the bakery.

She jumped into my car, tears rolling down her cheeks.

"Are you okay?"

"Just go."

"Becky—"

"Please!"

"All right." I shifted the car into reverse. Through the display window, a girl in a bright white apron and dark blonde hair watched us drive away.

When we reached the house, I pulled into the driveway, but Becky ran into the house before the car came to a complete stop.

Upstairs, I stood in her doorway. "Do you want to talk about it?" She was lying across her bed.

Becky mumbled into her pillow.

"I can't understand you when you talk into your pillow like that."

She flipped over. "No one will give me a job."

I sat on the edge of her bed. "No one?

"I went to every shop in Appleseed Creek and no one would hire me." She rolled over and clutched the pillow to her chest. "They wouldn't even talk to me," Becky added in a whisper.

"Maybe they didn't have any openings."

"It wasn't that." Tears threatened to fall again. "They wouldn't talk to me because I left home, because I'm no longer Amish."

"I'm sorry, Becky." I didn't know what else to say.

"And now you are going to kick me out. Where am I going to go? I can't go home. I can't." Her huge blue eyes swam with tears.

Ten years earlier, when I was fourteen, I'd lain across Tanisha's bed in tears, begging Mr. and Mrs. Green to take me in. They had. How could I turn her away now? Becky was five years older than I was at the time, but in many ways I had been older than she. I certainly knew the kind of pain that the outside world could cause.

"Listen," I said, smoothing the wrinkles away from the comforter, "you can stay here as long as you need to."

Her face lit up, and she sat up and wrapped me in a hug. "Thank you, Chloe! You're like a big sister to me now."

My cell phone rang, and I jumped off the bed to answer it. I fished through my purse, checked the readout, and grimaced.

Becky clutched that pillow to her chest again. "Who is it?"

My shoulders drooped. "My evil stepmother." I took the phone into my bedroom. "Hello, Sabrina."

My stepmother sniffed into the phone. "Chloe, your father's sorry he couldn't speak to you himself, but you know how busy he is."

"I do." I stood by my bedroom window.

"I'm glad," Sabrina replied. "He's pleased you found gainful employment. We were worried that all the money spent on your education would go to waste."

I gripped the cell phone. "Please tell him thank you."

Gigabyte jumped on the windowsill and bumped his head on my hip. The sound of a truck backfiring tore through the quiet, and I shivered. The green pickup rolled by on the street below.

Sabrina continued. "I'm glad I have you on the line. I wanted to talk to you about Thanksgiving."

"That's four months away."

The truck's taillights disappeared around the corner.

Sabrina sniffed. "Yes, I know, but you can't know how difficult it is to coordinate everyone's schedules. Your father and I have decided to go on a cruise Thanksgiving week, so we won't be having our usual get-together. It will be good for him to get away. He works far too hard. I told him you'd understand."

"Are you taking the kids?" I barely knew my eight-year-old half sister Brin and six-year-old half brother Blake. I only saw them when my father flew me out to California for Thanksgiving once a year. I flew in on Wednesday night and out on Friday morning. That's how it had always been since he'd met Sabrina.

"Of course, they are too young to leave behind." She said this as if I should have known better. "This must come as a relief for you. I know you'd much rather visit with your friend Tamara than come see us."

"It's Tanisha," I said. "She's in Italy."

"Oh, well, Thanksgiving in the country will be nice for you." Her voice trilled. "It will be a learning experience."

I inhaled a deep breath, listening to her chatter on about all that Brin and Blake had accomplished since we'd last talked. Then she hung up. As I set down the phone, the green pickup cruised down the street for the second time that evening.

Chapter Seven

For the next week, I watched for signs of the green pickup. The nights I didn't see it cruise up and down Grover were the worst, because I lay awake half the night waiting to hear the familiar backfire. When it would finally split the night air, it almost came as a relief.

On Friday morning, I tried to put the green pickup out of my head as I walked to Harshberger. As I stepped onto campus, a silver sedan turned onto the college's private road and sped past me, dangerously close. I stumbled onto the grass, my heel sinking into the damp earth. I stood there until my heart slowed, then slipped my foot out of the shoe and headed to work.

That morning I had scheduled a meeting with my staff, knowing I would need to be alert. In the week I'd known him, Joel had been, at best, passive-aggressive toward me; at worst, openly hostile. I was pleased to see all were there when I entered the workroom. Maybe there was hope for our little department yet.

Clark smiled at me when I took my seat at the head of the table; Miller fidgeted with his laptop cord, wrapping it around and around his index finger; and Joel glared at me. I repressed a sigh.

"Good morning, everyone," I said. "I—"

"How's your shoe, boss." Joel smirked.

My chest constricted. "My shoe?"

"I saw you almost take a tumble. You should be more careful."

"Seriously, dude," Clark mumbled.

I gritted my teeth. "I want to begin this meeting today by saying I'm so glad to be here at Harshberger. I'm looking forward to offering new services to our students. For one, we need to investigate a course management system so that professors can more easily communicate with their students online, and—"

My cell phone played the "Star Spangled Banner." The Fourth of July was long over, but I'd yet to change my ringtone.

Joel glowered at me. "Most of us don't carry our personal phones while on campus. It interferes with college business."

I ignored Joel's comment and fumbled to reach the phone in my pocket. I didn't recognize the number, but it was an Appleseed Creek area code. I silenced the phone and placed it on the table next to my laptop computer. "I'm excited about working with all of you. Together, we can bring Harshberger up to speed in the twenty-first century."

Joel scowled. "Are you saying we aren't in the twenty-first century?"

"No, no, of course, I'm not saying that at all. However, there are things we can do to improve."

"I'm sure the college thinks having you here is a big improvement." Joel muttered just loud enough for me to overhear.

Clark leaned back in his chair. "Joel, give it a rest, man."

I shot him a grateful smile, but he didn't meet my gaze.

Joel glared at Clark but shut his mouth.

I straightened the stack of files on the table. "As I was saying—"

My phone played the "Star Spangled Banner" again. I checked the readout. It was the same number as before.

"How patriotic of you," Joel quipped.

I stood up. "I think I better take this. It's a local number. It could be related to the college."

Joel rolled his eyes. "If it was college related, whoever it was would call your office phone."

"I'll be right back." I stepped inside my office and shut the door. "Hello?"

From the other end of the line came a muffled sob. "Chloe?"

"Becky? I can't understand you."

Another sob came over the phone.

"Becky? What's wrong? Are you okay? Do you need me to come get you?" I peered through the small window in my office door. Joel said something to Clark and Miller. They both laughed. Whatever he said, I knew it was at my expense.

"Chloe?" Becky whispered.

"Yes, I'm here."

"Bishop Glick is dead." She took a shuddered breath. "And I killed him."

Chapter Eight

My throat clenched. "What do you mean you killed Bishop Glick?" *Please God, no.*

An incoherent sob came from the other end of the call.

"Becky! Listen to me! Tell me what happened." The computer guys watched me. They must have heard me yell at Becky. I lowered my voice. "I can't help if you don't tell me."

Her voice shook. "I borrowed your car, and—"

"You borrowed my car?" Disbelief filled me.

"I'm sorry!" She was wailing now.

"No, no, it's fine." It was nothing close to fine, but I couldn't let Becky get sidetracked. "Keep talking."

"I took your car because I had a job interview."

"An interview?"

"Close to Mount Vernon."

Mount Vernon was twice the size of Appleseed Creek, and only seven miles away from our little town.

Her voice shook. "I know it was wrong. I know I shouldn't have done it, but I knew you'd be proud of me if I had a job by the time you got home today."

"What happened?"

"I—I don't know. I was driving up the big hill on Butler Road, and everything was fine. Then when I came over the crest of the hill the brakes stopped working. I flew down the hill." She took a deep breath. "A buggy was at the bottom. I couldn't slow down. I tried to move the car away from the buggy, but the road was too narrow. The impact pushed the buggy into the trees."

Dear God, not again! The prayer flew through my mind. Images from my mother's accident started to play in my head: the police photos I wasn't supposed to have seen, her lying in a hospital bed under a sheet, my father shutting down. *Don't think about it. Focus on Becky.*

"Are you okay?" My tone sounded sharper than I'd wanted.

"I'm not hurt—not really. The officer said the car's airbag and seatbelt saved me."

A loud voice reverberated on the other end. "Miss, time's up."

"I have to go," Becky said. "Please come."

"I will. Where are you now?"

"I'm still at the bottom of the hill on Butler Road. I'm in the back of an ambulance."

"Miss." The loud voice warned again.

I pulled my purse out of my desk drawer. "I'll be there as soon as I can."

Before she hung up, she whispered, "Thank you, Chloe. You are a *gut* friend."

I don't remember what I said to the computer guys when I cancelled our meeting. Whatever it was, I'm sure Joel hadn't believed it anyway. I stumbled into the staff parking lot looking for my car. *My car, my car. I need to get to her.* What was I doing? My car wasn't here.

Lord, help me. Tell me what to do.

Find Timothy.

The familiar sound of hammering came from the barn area. I

ran around the building and found Timothy alone, mending the barn doors.

"Timothy!"

His whole face lit up when he saw me running toward him. Just as suddenly, his expression fell. "What's wrong?"

I tried to catch my breath. "It's Becky. There's been an accident. We need to go to her." My sentences came in short spurts.

"My truck is right over here." He pointed at his pickup parked on the grass behind the barn. "You can tell me the rest on the way."

On the drive over to Butler Road, I related to Timothy everything Becky had told me over the phone. He wrung his hands over and over on top of the steering wheel. Did he think this was my fault? That if I'd made Becky go home to her family and Isaac Glick this would never have happened? Did I think that?

I leaned out of the passenger side window. *Please Lord, let Becky be okay. Let us all be okay.*

Timothy drove the pickup to the top of the big hill on Butler Road. As we crested the top, I saw a bird's-eye view of the accident. Bishop Glick's buggy was wrapped around a large sycamore tree. The RAV4 lay on its right side wedged behind the buggy, the hood crunched into an accordion shape. No question the car was totaled. Miraculously, the bishop's horse stood on the side of the road and didn't appear hurt. My mind wandered back to my first day at Harshberger when I met the bishop with his fluffy gray beard and welcoming smile.

I felt light-headed, images from my mother's accident in my mind.

Slowly, Timothy drove down the hill, where four county police cars and two ambulances were parked along the road. A little further away, four Amish buggies had also pulled to the side. Somehow the Amish district already knew about the accident. Timothy parked behind the last buggy. He reached across the front seat and squeezed my elbow. "I'm glad you came."

I started to say that I was glad he was there too when he added, "My sister will be happy to see you." He climbed out of the car.

With a heavy heart, I got out of the pickup. The sight before me was too much—the buggy wrapped around the tree, the RAV4 on its side. I pulled my gaze away and focused on the tops of my heels instead, the worst possible footwear choice for visiting the scene of an accident. I'd never wear them again.

Timothy took my elbow and guided me around the cop cars and Amish buggies. "Are you all right?"

I nodded, unable to speak.

Timothy stopped, and I lifted my gaze to see the coroner wheeling a gurney with a body bag on it toward a waiting van. Beyond a bevy of paramedics, a line of Amish men stood along the road, glaring at us. Timothy dropped his hand from my elbow.

A wave of nausea washed over me. It was my mother all over again. *Focus, Chloe, focus. Where is Becky? Find Becky.*

I hurried over to a young police officer, not much older than Becky. He wore a sober expression, as if he'd seen many accidents like this before. Maybe he had.

"We're here for Becky Troyer," I said. "Can we see her?"

"Are you family?"

Timothy joined me. "I'm her brother."

"You'll need to talk to the sheriff." The young deputy pointed to a tall, lean man, probably in his sixties, with gray hair growing in tufts on top of his head. He looked more like someone's grandfather than a seasoned lawman.

He squinted up at us from his clipboard. "Can I help you?"

"We'd like to see my sister, Becky Troyer. I'm Timothy Troyer."

The sheriff eyed me. "Who's this?"

"I'm Chloe Humphrey. Becky called me after the accident."

"Ah, yes, Chloe. Becky has been asking for you. I'm glad you came. Please, follow me." He stepped around an officer collecting shards of glass and other evidence.

"How is she?" I asked the sheriff while maneuvering around the officer.

"She's in a whole mess of trouble."

I shivered.

Becky stood outside the ambulance's bay with a silver insulation blanket wrapped around her. Seeing us, she dropped the blanket and ran into her brother's arms. I glanced back at the Amish men lined up along the road, their bodies rigid, their faces radiating anger.

Timothy walked Becky back to the ambulance's bay, and together they sat on the edge. Powerlessness overwhelmed me. My thoughts flashed back to Isaac Glick's friendly eyes. Did he know? How would he deal with this? More than anyone, I knew how an accident like this tore lives apart. I said a silent prayer for him and the entire Glick family.

I prayed for Becky, Timothy, and their family, too. Then I whispered one for myself. I moved to the country for a professional experience and the chance to live the simple life. Right from the beginning, however, my life in Appleseed Creek had been anything but simple.

Timothy said something to his sister. The sheriff's eyes narrowed. "You're going to have to speak English, or I'm not going to let you talk to her at all."

Timothy met the sheriff's eyes with a steady blue gaze. "I told her everything would be all right and that God would protect her."

Becky gazed at me with tearful eyes. A bandage bisected her right eyebrow and her left arm hung in a sling.

Timothy glared at me. "She's hurt. You said she was fine."

I took a step back. "She told me she wasn't hurt."

"Considering what could have happened, she's in good shape." The sheriff's voice was calm. "She's lucky to be alive."

"It was not luck." Timothy studied me. "You bought an unsafe car."

My face grew hot. He had no idea how his words cut me. I had been obsessed with car safety ever since my mother's accident. "No, I had the car checked before I bought it." I clenched my hand. "I drove it all the way to Appleseed Creek from Cleveland. There was nothing wrong with the car."

Timothy frowned.

"The county forensic mechanic will inspect it in his lab, and he will determine how safe the car was before the accident," the sheriff said.

Did Timothy blame me for what happened? Would this be like my father all over again? My father blamed me for my mother's accident. I couldn't bear to have another life on my conscience.

Becky. Focus on Becky. She needs you.

I bit the inside of my lip. "Sheriff, what's going to happen to Becky?"

"She drove without a license. She will be charged with that. There will be a fine and community service, and her chances of earning a driver's license in the foreseeable future are slim."

"What about the crash?" I asked.

He sighed and ran a hand along the side of his face. "If it's proven that she was at fault, she'll be charged with vehicular homicide, which is a first degree felony. If she's lucky, vehicular manslaughter, which is a first degree misdemeanor. There would be a trial, and she could do prison time."

Dizziness threatened to overtake me. "Even if it was an accident?"

"Accident or no accident. A human life was taken and that's a crime." The sheriff scrutinized the Amish men along the road.

Becky buried her head in her brother's chest and cried deep, body-wracking sobs. Despite the humid summer air, my body shivered.

"Miss Troyer, it's time to go," the sheriff said. He put his hand on her arm.

Timothy eyed him. "Where are you taking her?"

"The paramedics checked her out here, but we'll take her to the hospital for a more thorough exam."

"Then what?" I asked.

"I'll have to take her to the station to be booked."

"You mean arrest her?" Timothy's mouth fell open and he pulled Becky closer to him.

Becky clung to her brother.

The sheriff nodded, his face grim. "I suggest you get your sister a good lawyer."

Chapter Nine

After advising Timothy to find Becky a lawyer, the sheriff left us to return to the accident scene. So many unanswered questions. Did the bishop die immediately? Did his family know? Did Becky's parents know? Would they send an Amish girl to prison? The line of accusatory Amish men remained on the side of the road, their dour expressions and scowls focused on us.

My hand brushed against Timothy, making me hyper-aware of his presence. I sidestepped, placing a foot of black pavement between us.

An EMT approached Becky, but looked at Timothy. "Your sister's not in any danger, but we need to take her to the hospital to set that arm."

Becky winced.

A van pulled up behind Timothy's truck, and Isaac Glick jumped out of the passenger seat. I glanced at Timothy. Isaac wove through the police to the line of Amish men.

Timothy cracked the knuckles in his left hand, the same hand that had touched mine. "I need to talk to Isaac."

"That's probably not the best idea right now. He's not going to want to see anyone from your family." I kept my voice a whisper, hoping Becky didn't overhear. I needn't have bothered. Becky's face paled when she spotted Isaac.

Despite the heavy shade from an enormous oak tree, Timothy squinted, holding back tears. "He's my friend."

My heart sank. "I know."

Isaac reached the line of Amish men, and they huddled around him like a black wool blanket. He stumbled out of their protective circle, but a man placed his hand on Isaac's shoulder and spoke. He jerked away from the man and shook his head, his gaze darting around. Then the man at Isaac's side pointed at Becky.

My stomach clenched. I forced my gaze to the EMT. "Shouldn't you be going? She needs to get to the hospital."

He looked up from his clipboard. "Just as soon as I finish my paperwork. I'm almost done."

I stole a glance over my shoulder to find Isaac marching toward us. I turned back to the EMT. "Can't you do that when you get to the hospital?"

Too late.

"Becky?" Isaac's voice shook.

Tears ran down her cheeks.

Isaac's jaw twitched. "Look what you did. Is this what you wanted?"

Becky opened her mouth, then snapped it shut.

I tilted my head and stared at the EMT.

He nodded. "Come on, Miss Troyer. It's time to go." He reached for Becky, and she allowed him to help her climb into the ambulance's bay.

"Run away!" Isaac cried. "It's what you're good at." He added something else in Pennsylvania Dutch.

The paramedic closed the ambulance's bay doors. Through the square rear window, Becky's red-rimmed eyes stared at Timothy and me. She cradled her arm, and tears fell onto her cheeks. I prayed I was wrong, but I knew this nightmare could only get worse.

Timothy squeezed my hand. The driver turned on his flashing lights and whooped the siren as he drove up the hill in the direction of Mount Vernon, the largest town in Knox County and the only one with a hospital.

Isaac's chest heaved.

Timothy reached out to touch his friend, but Isaac jerked away.

"It was an accident," I said.

Timothy scowled, and Isaac gaped at me as if he'd never seen me before. I couldn't blame him for not remembering me. "Who are you?"

"Chloe. I met you at Harshberger last week." My throat constricted under his intense glare.

"I remember. You are the computer person, and you're the reason she left the district."

"No, no," I stammered. "That's not it at all."

He frowned, his eyes boring into me. "This is what leaving the Amish has done. My father is dead. This never would have happened if Becky had known her place. Never."

The older Amish man Isaac had been talking to earlier strode up to us, his presence formidable. Thin and more than six feet tall, he had a long dark beard and eyes narrowed into slits. He placed his hand on Isaac's shoulder again. "Son, you are angry now, but you must forgive."

Good advice, although was he able to follow it himself?

Isaac's eyes welled with tears. "What about my mother? My brothers and sisters? What will they do without my father?"

"Son." The man's voice grew stern. "You are the eldest. You must be strong for them. You are the man of the house now."

Isaac bowed his head and staggered back to the waiting van. The driver backed it up until it had a clear place to turn around. And then he was gone.

"Timothy," the Honest Abe doppelganger said, "you should think of your family now too."

Timothy's jaw twitched.

The man brushed the bottom of his beard with the back of his hand. "You can't always expect someone else to carry your burden."

What did that mean? Carry your burden?

"Deacon." Timothy's tone sounded sharper than I'd ever heard it. He added something in Pennsylvania Dutch.

The deacon's beard twitched, and the corners of his mouth turned up in a tiny smile. "The district must find a new bishop. A position your father would have wanted. I know some were hoping to put him up for the lot of preacher. Many will change their minds."

"My father is not ambitious."

"That's where you differ?"

Timothy clenched his jaw and again spoke in Pennsylvania Dutch. The deacon glanced at me but gave me no acknowledgment.

The sheriff stood off to the side, fiddling with a cell phone. This could be my only opportunity to ask him my unanswered questions, so I left Timothy speaking to the deacon. He didn't appear to notice that I had gone.

As I approached the sheriff, a female officer jogged up to his side. "Got here as soon as I could, sheriff. Deputy Gertz briefed me." Petite with short curly brown hair, she wore a dark blue uniform, which stood out against the sea of tan uniforms at the scene. Aviator sunglasses gave her a tough cop image despite her small frame.

He poked at his phone. "Stupid gadget."

"Sheriff."

"Oh, Greta. Nice of you to finally make it."

She adjusted the sunglasses on her nose. "I was on another case."

"Good to know. I've got another one for you."

Her eyes sparkled. "This is my case?"

"Yup. If you want it."

"I want it."

He tucked the cell phone into the breast pocket of his uniform. "You can start by questioning Miss Humphrey." He pointed a thumb at me. "I have another call-out." He ambled away.

She peered at me and held out her hand. "Miss Humphrey?"

I nodded and shook her hand.

"I'm Appleseed Creek's Chief of Police, Greta Rose. You can call me Chief Rose. Can I ask you a few questions?"

I glanced back at Timothy and the deacon, still deep in conversation. "Will it take long? Timothy, Becky's brother, and I need to get to the hospital to see her. Becky was the driver of the car."

"I know who the driver was, and I know Timothy is her brother too. My questions will only take a few minutes. Let's walk over here." With a manicured nail, she pointed at a huge briar bush on the side of the road, far from where the Amish men stood.

"You are Chloe Humphrey, correct?"

"Yes."

She pulled a printout from her pocket and scanned it. "The vehicle in the accident is registered to you."

I nodded.

"And the car is insured."

"Yes, of course."

"I'm going to need to see proof of that."

I bristled. "Is my insurance responsible for the accident?"

Her eyebrows peeked out over those huge glasses. "Someone will have to pay for the damage and injuries."

My throat tightened.

"Amish don't take out insurance policies on their buggies, and Miss Troyer was an uninsured motorist. Since it was your vehicle involved . . ."

My chest constricted. "I'm not responsible for the accident."

"It's your vehicle. I'd advise you to contact your insurance company."

"I wasn't driving the car," I insisted. "Becky was."

"Are you saying she stole your car?" She removed her sunglasses, revealing peridot-colored eyes highlighted by black eye liner and heavy mascara. She trained her gaze on me like a green laser beam.

I jerked back. "No . . . she borrowed it."

Chief Rose ran her hand through her brown curls, her tone all business. "An unlicensed driver doesn't borrow a car. Did you allow her to take it?"

"No! I had no idea. I wouldn't let her drive my car without a license."

She folded the printout and stuck it back in the pocket of her navy uniform. "If she drove it without your permission, that's stealing. There may be an additional charge against Becky."

"If I say she stole the car, which I don't."

Chief Rose shrugged as if it made no difference to her. "I need to see that insurance card now."

"It's in my purse inside Timothy's truck."

"I'll wait for you to get it."

I nodded.

"I'd like to see your registration too," she called out.

My back stiffened as I wove through the crowd to Timothy's truck. Many of the Amish men had left. Three stood around the bishop's horse, trying to convince the frightened animal to step into the back of a trailer. At first I thought the horse unharmed, but now that I had a clear view of the animal, I saw a long gash on her left shoulder. I knew nothing about caring for farm animals, but I prayed the animal would make it. One tragic loss was more than enough.

"Miss Humphrey! The insurance card, please."

I glanced back at Chief Rose, who stood in the middle of the road, tapping her foot.

The truck was unlocked, and my purse lay on the passenger side. I grabbed it.

Chief Rose took the registration and insurance card from my hand. "I'll give them back to you in a minute, then you will be free to go. Do you plan to go to the hospital to see your friend?"

"Yes."

She ambled to her cruiser parked on the side of the road.

Leaving the cruiser door open, Chief Rose logged onto the computer between the driver and passenger seats. Fear trickled through me. How would I pay for the accident if I was held financially responsible? Would Bishop Glick's family sue me? Do the Amish sue? My stomach roiled. Would I have to ask my father and Sabrina for help? They had the money, although Sabrina would deny it. My stepmother would let me go to jail first.

Becky, the nineteen-year-old would-be artist, was in much more trouble than I. Nearby, Timothy and the deacon continued to argue in their own language. What did the deacon mean about Timothy's father being a preacher?

Chief Rose returned and handed me my insurance card and registration. "You know, Miss Humphrey, you might want to rethink the company you keep."

"What does that mean?"

She cocked her head at Timothy before slipping her sunglasses back on. "Your insurance company will know what to do about the accident. Sadly, this is not the first time we've had a buggy and auto collision in Appleseed Creek—and it won't be the last."

Timothy jogged toward them. "Chloe, are you ready to go to the hospital now?" It was the first time I'd heard Timothy say my name, and despite the tragic circumstances, I liked the sound of it.

"Yes, I'm ready." I adjusted my purse strap on my shoulder.

"Hello, Timothy," Chief Rose said. "Staying out of trouble?"

Timothy's jaw twitched. "Nice to see you, Greta."

"You can call me Chief Rose."

"Do you two know each other?" I don't know why I was surprised. Knox County was so small.

Greta nodded. "We have mutual friends."

Timothy winced.

My stomach tightened again. *What did I walk into when I moved to Appleseed Creek?*

Chapter Ten

A stoplight greeted us at each intersection along the way to the hospital in Mount Vernon, and each time we stopped, Timothy's grip on the steering wheel became a little bit tighter.

"How do you know the police chief?" The question popped out of my mouth, and I wished I could take it back.

Timothy kept his eyes on the road as we were held up by yet another stoplight. "Appleseed Creek is a small town."

I suspected there was more to it than that. "You called the man you were talking with Deacon. Is that his name?"

"No. Deacon is his position in the church. We call him Deacon Sutter."

Timothy made a left turn and we drove up a small hill that led to the hospital parking lot. The ambulance idled by the entrance to the emergency room. Timothy found a parking place quickly.

The waiting room was white with dark blue linoleum floor. Padded wooden chairs sat back-to-back in three rows. A flat-screen television in the corner played ESPN to an empty room. A sheriff's deputy stood by the nurses' station, drinking coffee from a paper cup and flirting with the pretty receptionist.

Although a different hospital, I remembered the horrible night my mother died and how my father dragged me to the emergency room.

Timothy spoke to the receptionist. "My sister, Becky Troyer, just arrived in an ambulance. How is she?"

The receptionist smiled at him. Her even, white teeth stood out against thick magenta-colored lipstick. The young deputy scowled. Obviously, he would have preferred she keep her smile aimed at him.

"She's getting a cast for her arm," the receptionist said. "It's broken."

I stepped up next to Timothy. "Can we see her?"

She scrutinized me. "Who are you?"

"Chloe Humphrey. I'm Becky's roommate."

The woman shook her head. "Only immediate family in the back. Her brother can see her."

"How long will she be here?" I asked.

"They are with her now. It should only be a few minutes."

The deputy shifted at the desk. "But then I have to take her to the sheriff's office for questioning."

Timothy winced. "Can we go with her?"

The deputy shrugged. "You can wait for her at the station if you like."

The phone on the receptionist's desk rang and the woman picked up the receiver, listening for a moment. "All right." She hung up. "Mr. Troyer, you can go back and see your sister now."

"I'll show you where she is," the deputy said.

Timothy's brow wrinkled.

"Go on." I shooed him. "I'll be here."

He nodded and followed the deputy down the hallway.

I removed my cell phone from purse, and the receptionist pointed at the NO CELL PHONE sign.

Outside the emergency room's automatic doors, the humid air hit me like a wall. I checked my cell phone for the temperature. Ninety degrees. With nowhere to sit outside, I decided to make my phone call in Timothy's truck, which he'd left unlocked.

I dialed Dean Klink's office number.

"Hello." His jovial voice contrasted with my emotions.

"Hello, Dean Klink? It's Chloe Humphrey." I rested my hand on the steering wheel, only to yank it away from the hot surface.

"Chloe, hello? How are you doing? We're keeping you busy I suspect. By the way, I love your proposal for a learning management system. An absolute must! I'm making it a top priority the next time I meet with the president's cabinet. I knew you were the right one to hire."

"Thank you, sir."

He barked a laugh. "Sir? I thought we told you we weren't much for formality here."

"You did. I'm sorry."

"No need to apologize for that! What can I do for you?" A *rap-rap-rap* echoed through the line. I imagined the dean tapping the end of his pen on his desk.

"I'm off campus and will be for the rest of the day. My roommate was in a car accident." I didn't mention my roommate was a runaway Amish or that the bishop was dead. Details of the accident would travel through Appleseed Creek soon enough.

He took a sharp breath. "Oh dear, that's awful. Is she all right?"

Was she all right? An excellent question. "She has a broken arm."

"She's lucky to be alive. Take all the time you need."

"Thank you, Dean."

"Now, I told you to call me Charlie." His upbeat tone had returned.

"I'll try."

A vehicle backfired behind me, and a truck roared into the

parking place next to mine. A green pickup. My stomach turned. The two men who had harassed Becky on the highway were inside.

"Well, well, well, looky who's here," the scrawny one said.

"It's Red." Babyface climbed out of the pickup. "We haven't seen her since her little friend made me skin my knee."

"Go away," I said as he sauntered up to my door. The power windows were down, and I didn't have the truck's keys to raise them. I hit the locks, but knew that Babyface could reach inside the cabin and open the door if he wanted.

"Do you want to see the scar I have from falling down?" The faint hint of alcohol sullied the air between us.

The driver snorted a laugh.

"Leave me alone."

The driver spat. "We're just visiting with you. That's not very neighborly of you to turn us away like this—and we are neighbors of yours. Grover is a real nice street, real nice."

A shiver traveled down my spine. The green pickup *had* been driving up and down my street, watching the house. "There are police inside the hospital. If I scream, they will hear me."

He snickered. "We wouldn't want that."

"What are you doing here anyway?" Babyface leered. "Are you visiting your little friend?"

"'Course she is, Brock. Red loves to save little Amish girls in trouble. This one is in a heap of trouble too." He tsked. "Mowing down an Amish big shot is never a good idea. I wonder what made her do it."

Brock let loose a laugh. "Maybe the big shot had it coming."

The other one nodded, like this was all making sense. "Could be. I always suspected there was something off about those buggy riders." His grin widened. "Hate to see a pretty girl end up in prison."

Brock smirked and fingered the door lock. "She'll be very popular on the cellblock, I'm sure."

Nausea washed over me.

I scanned the cabin for something I could use as a weapon. Timothy's tool belt lay on the floor, a screwdriver sticking out of one of the pockets. I would have preferred a hammer, but the screwdriver would work.

"Why don't you get out of the truck and we can talk about this?" Brock taunted. "We have some experience with the police. Maybe we can help you and your friend." He doubled over in laughter, his hand still on the door.

I grabbed the screwdriver by the blade and whacked the handle on Brock's fingers. He yelped and let go.

The thinner man convulsed with laughter until the hospital door opened and the deputy stepped outside. He spoke into a cell phone with his back to us.

The driver cocked his head at Brock. "Let's go."

Brock climbed back into the truck, cradling his hand. "See you around, Red." Somehow I knew he meant that.

Chapter Eleven

Becky stepped out of the hospital, hugging her right arm to her chest. The doctors had set the arm in a hot pink cast. My breath caught as the deputy led her away from Timothy's side to his cruiser, her eyes wide.

I slipped the screwdriver back into Timothy's tool belt and slid to the passenger's side as he opened the driver's door. "How is she?"

He shook his head.

The cruiser pulled out of the parking lot.

"Shouldn't we follow him?"

Timothy started the truck. "I know where the sheriff's department is."

My brow knit together. First a confrontation with Becky's harassers, and now Timothy's surly demeanor. I was relieved that the sheriff's department was a short drive away.

At the station, the deputy and Becky waited in a hallway before they entered the department. Tears rolled down Becky's cheeks. I wanted to reach over and give her a hug, but I wasn't sure that was allowed.

"What's going to happen now?" Timothy asked.

"We're waiting for the desk sergeant to be ready for us. Another case came in just before we got here. When he's ready, Becky will be fingerprinted."

Becky started to shiver.

"It won't hurt, Becky," I said. "They are just going to put ink on your fingertips and make a copy on a card."

Becky looked at the fingertips on her left hand like she'd never seen them before.

The deputy smiled. "That's basically it, but now it's all electronic. Takes half the time and no mess."

A crash followed by scuffling sounds and a string of swear words bellowed from a nearby room. I suspected Becky had never heard words like that before.

The deputy peeked into the room but appeared unconcerned. "This may be a while."

Becky stared at her shoes and continued to shiver. Timothy reached into his jeans pocket and pulled out his truck keys. "Chloe, why don't you go home?"

I cocked my head. "How will you get home? Will you call me to pick you up?"

He shook his head. "I'll have my housemate Danny pick us up. He knows where the sheriff's office is. I don't want you to get lost trying to find your way back here."

"But Becky—"

"I'll take care of Becky," he said. "She's my sister."

I glanced at Becky, her head leaning against Timothy's shoulder. Although his dismissal stung, I took the keys from Timothy's hand. "Okay."

While exiting the parking lot, I took a wrong turn and found myself on a road behind the hospital. How would I find Appleseed Creek? Timothy's truck wasn't equipped with GPS—not that Pepper would be much help to me on the tiny roads in Mount Vernon. I winced. The last time I saw Pepper had been in my car, which was now totaled.

I checked the rearview mirror, keeping an eye out for the green pickup, then shook my head. Rapping Brock on the knuckles with a screwdriver might not have been the best idea I'd ever had. I hoped I wouldn't come to regret it.

I continued down a narrow county road, hoping my sense of direction would kick in soon. The oak trees lining the edge reached across the road like an overhead bridge to the opposing trees. Hot air blew through the truck's open window, and the back of my bare legs stuck to the leather seats.

I approached a street sign that read Butler Road, and slowed down. How did I end up back here? I continued forward. Men in white jumpsuits picked up debris from the road. A tow truck driver hitched chains onto my car and rolled it back onto its tires. *This must have been the same corner that Bishop Glick had rounded.*

The Amish men were gone, as was the horse. The mangled buggy lay on its side in the back of a flatbed truck. One of its tail-lights hung over the side of the flatbed. Sunlight broke through the trees and reflected a red circle onto the spot where the buggy had once been. It was easy to see why the bishop had not survived. That the horse could still stand upright was a miracle.

One of the white-suited men approached me. "Sorry, Miss, this road is closed. You're going to have to turn around."

I swallowed. "Can you direct me to Appleseed Creek?"

"Sure thing." He rattled off the directions.

As I turned the truck around, I spotted Chief Rose leaning against the hood of her cruiser, arms crossed in front of her chest. She waved, her expression somewhere between a grin and a grimace.

GIGABYTE YOWLED A GREETING when I entered the house. His dark brown tail swished back and forth on the hardwood floor. I bent to pick him up, but he slipped out of my hands and jumped onto the back of the only chair in the house. I'd give him a few minutes. Eventually, he'd forgive me for the audacity of leaving him.

The tap of my heels on the hardwood echoed through the unfurnished home. The large house didn't feel safe to me. Becky had left the front window open, and the curtains rolled in and out with the breeze. I kicked off my shoes and hurried over, shutting and locking the window in one movement.

Gig paced the arm of the lone chair. I picked him up and carried him around as I checked the rest of the house. When I was satisfied that I was truly alone, I pulled out my cell phone and called my insurance company.

"You ran into a horse trailer?" He asked the same question three times. Apparently the insurance agent could not wrap his mind around an auto and buggy collision.

A half hour later, I hung up with no firm answers to my questions, then debated calling my father for help. Chances were he wouldn't answer the phone, and I'd end up more upset than I already was. Usually I would turn to Mr. and Mrs. Green for advice, but since they were in Italy, there was no point in worrying them or Tanisha until I had all the facts.

There was a knock on my front door. Gig jumped straight up in the air and fled up the stairs, his claws scratching the wooden steps. Would my landlord notice? Since he rented me a house without a working front door, we'd call it a draw.

Through the peephole I saw a young Amish girl, so I opened the door. "Hi." The girl wore a navy dress with pleated skirt, and a full-body black apron. Dirt marred the bottom of her skirt. Over her white-blonde hair she wore a black bonnet, its ribbons untied. I recognized her as the girl from Becky's painting.

She blinked at me with huge blue eyes the same color as her siblings'.

"Are you Ruth?" I asked.

She dropped her gaze to her black sneakers. "Is my sister here?"

I stalled. "You're looking for Becky?" *Does she know about the accident?* "I'm Chloe," I said. "Becky's friend."

"I know. Timothy told *Daed* about you. He said you were a

good *Englisch* girl and Becky lived with you. *Daed* was upset. He wants Becky to come home. We all do. We miss her."

My cheeks warmed. *A good* English *girl? What does that mean?* I stopped myself from asking Becky what else her brother had said.

"I want to see my sister." She stamped her foot.

"She's not here."

Ruth peered up at me, fighting tears. "Because she is in jail?"

I swallowed, avoiding her questions. "How did you know to come here? Did Timothy tell you where Becky lived?"

"Timothy wouldn't tell me, but I know he told *Mamm* and *Daed*. Becky sent me a letter from this address, and I found it on my own." She put her hands on her hips. "Now, where is my sister?"

"She's with Timothy. Do you want to come inside?"

"No, I want to get my sister and go home." She pointed at her brother's blue truck. "Isn't Timothy here?"

I shook my head. The door's hinges creaked as I pushed against it.

"Is Becky in jail?" She tugged at her bonnet's black ribbon.

I glanced up and down the street. No buggy. No Amish in sight. No one at all. "Are you here alone?"

"Our *Englisch* driver drove me in from the farm to take eggs to Amish Bread Bakery in town. That nosy Esther Yoder told me about the buggy accident. I didn't believe her at first, but when her mother came out and didn't say hello to me, I knew something was wrong." Her eyes welled up with tears. "Is it true? Is Bishop Glick dead?" She took a shaky breath. "Did Becky kill him?"

I steeled myself. "There was an accident, and the bishop was killed."

Ruth's small white hand flew to her mouth. "Is Becky safe?"

I nodded. "She has a broken arm and a few cuts and bruises. She was lucky."

"*Daed* say there is no such thing as luck, just providence." She put the end of her ribbon in her mouth and bit on it. "Where's my sister? I want to see her."

"As I said, she's with Timothy."

"Where are they? Are they coming here?" The wet end of the ribbon clung to her cheek, and she flicked it away with her hand.

"I don't know." I hadn't asked Timothy where he would take his sister after the police station—if he was allowed to leave with her. Part of me had expected them to come back here, but why would they? I let out a sigh. "I left them at the sheriff's department in Mount Vernon."

"I want to go there."

"That's not a good idea. Your parents wouldn't like it." I peered over her shoulder again. "Is your driver waiting for you at the bakery?"

"He's not." She shook her head. "I told him I had another ride home."

I looked at her, brow furrowed. "And do you?"

"No." Her face flushed. "I know I shouldn't lie, but he wouldn't leave unless I told him that. He would never bring me here. He knew *Daed* would be angry."

"I don't know if Becky's coming here, and if she does how long it will be. Your parents will be worried." I stepped back into the house. "Let me grab the truck keys. I'll take you home."

This time she didn't argue.

Chapter Twelve

Ruth directed me onto an unnamed gravel road. The old truck jostled over every pebble, shaking loose my vertebrae. When was the last time Timothy had the shocks checked? How much worse the ride must feel in an Amish buggy. *Are the buggies' ceilings padded? For that matter, are the seats?*

Out of the corner of my eye, I saw Ruth's hands folded neatly in her lap. Her knuckles were milk white, the black ribbon back in her mouth.

"Do you start school soon?" I asked.

The ribbon fell out of her mouth. "What?"

"School? Are you starting soon? I work at the college, and we're getting ready for a new school year there. It starts in a few weeks."

"In her letter, Becky told me you worked at the college. She said you are in charge of the computers."

I smiled. "Among other things, but yes, that's basically my job."

"I used a computer once," she whispered, as if confessing.

"Where?"

"At the library. My friend Alex took me there. Alex is a girl," she added quickly. "Her father is a dairy farmer too. Their farm is a few miles from ours. She doesn't have any brothers or sisters."

I suppressed a smile at her serious tone.

"It's my last year," Ruth said.

"Your last year of school?" I knew the Amish didn't go to high school, but Ruth looked to be no more than eleven.

Ruth wiggled in her seat. "I'm almost thirteen," she said as if she read my mind. "About the computer, we didn't do anything really. I was just looking at Alex's pictures from her family's vacation. They went to the Grand Canyon. Have you ever been there?"

"I have." As a teen, I drove across the country with the Greens on their family vacation, stopping at the St. Louis Arch, the Rocky Mountains, the Grand Canyon, and California. We'd hoped Sabrina and my father would meet us in San Diego when we arrived, but according to Sabrina, "It was a bad time."

"Is my sister going to prison?"

As she asked the question, a white utility truck barreled around the curve in front of me. I pulled to the side to let the driver pass, and as I did, Timothy's truck rolled through a crater-sized pothole. "Uff," I said, wincing from the impact. Ruth's bonnet bounced off of the truck's ceiling.

"Becky will be fine," I assured her. In the rearview mirror, I caught a glimpse of the words MATHEWS REAL ESTATE DEVELOPMENT stamped on the back door of the speeding truck.

A tear rolled down Ruth's cheek, her voice a whisper. "She should never have left me."

"Ruth, Becky did—"

"There's the farm." Gruffly, she brushed away the tear and turned to her window.

The farmhouse sat on the property about a quarter mile from the asphalt road. A screened-in porch dominated the front of the house, and chest-high teddy bear sunflowers grew in a cheerful line. Beyond the house stood several wooden outbuildings and a large barn. All the whitewashed wood buildings sat on a tan brick foundation. Black and white dairy cows congregated in the fenced area around the barn. North of the barn, soybeans grew low to the ground. Plain clothes hung from a double clothesline in the sweltering afternoon heat. There was no breeze.

"It's suppertime," Ruth said. "*Daed* will be home."

I glanced at her. *Is that a bad thing?*

As the truck bounced along the gravel driveway, the screen door to the house snapped open and two tow-headed Amish children ran toward the truck. The little boy squealed. "Timothy!"

A little girl of about three years old cheered. She wore a light purple dress and a white apron. Her hair was tied back in a bun but was otherwise uncovered. She held a faceless doll by the leg, its clothes similar: a dark blue plain dress, black apron and bonnet.

Ruth's face broke into a grin. "That is my *bruder*, Thomas, and, *schweschder*, Naomi."

I shifted the truck into park. Thomas and Naomi ran full tilt for the driver's side door. They pulled up short when they saw my face sticking out of the window, their smiles dissolving as if I stole the last piece of apple cake. "It's okay," I assured them.

Ruth hopped out of the car and said something to her siblings in Pennsylvania Dutch. Their faces brightened, but they observed me with curiosity. I slipped out of the truck, then held out my hand. "I'm Chloe."

Thomas, who was no more than seven, squeezed my fingers. Naomi watched her brother closely and did the same thing.

Thomas asked Ruth something in their language, but I heard Becky's name.

Ruth shook her head.

The screen door swung open again, and an Amish man stepped outside, his blond hair and beard streaked with gray. Behind him a much younger woman followed. She twisted the edge of her black apron in her hands.

"Ruth." The man's voice cracked with anger.

Ruth ran to her father. He spoke to her, making no attempt to lower his voice. He knew I didn't understand a word. He glared in my direction, said something else to her, then walked toward me. My shoulders tensed.

"I'm Rebecca's father." He spoke in English, with no trace of an accent.

"It's nice to meet you . . ." *What do I call him? Mr. Troyer? Brother Troyer? How do Amish greet each other?* I decided to avoid saying his name at all.

"You're the *Englisch* girl. Rebecca's friend?"

I nodded.

The woman inched across the lawn. She gripped the end of her apron in her hands. "Do you know where my children, Becky and Timothy, are? Is it true what Deacon Sutter says? Is Bishop Glick dead?"

Becky's father's eyes flicked to his wife. "Martha." He added something in Pennsylvania Dutch.

I swallowed. "I'm so sorry. It's true."

Mrs. Troyer gasped, and Naomi ran to her mother. She buried her face in her mother's apron, crushing the doll to her as if it too needed comforting.

A white pickup's tires crunched on the gravel drive, then shuttered to a stop. The passenger door opened, and Timothy climbed out, followed by Becky cradling her arm in its hot pink cast. The driver waved and backed down the driveway.

The woman's eyes fixed on her eldest daughter's broken arm. "My *boppli*."

Thomas ran to them. "Timothy!"

Naomi squealed and raced after him, too, her tears forgotten. The doll thumped against her leg as she sprinted. Timothy knelt and grabbed a child in each arm, hugging them until the youngest Troyers shrieked.

Thomas and Naomi pounced on Becky next, and her drawn face broke into the tiniest of smiles. Ruth joined her siblings and grabbed her older sister around the waist. "Becky, are you home for gut?"

Becky's tiny smile disappeared.

"Ruth, you're squishing me." Thomas had become caught between the sisters' hug.

Ruth let go long enough to let Thomas and Naomi slip away. Mr. Troyer spoke in their language.

Timothy strode over to him. "I'm sorry, *Daed*. Yes, it's true."

Mrs. Troyer pulled a white handkerchief from her apron pocket. "She's hurt."

"The doctor said it was a clean break." Becky inched closer to her mother, dragging Ruth, who didn't look like she planned to let go any time soon, with her. "I will be fine in a few weeks."

Mr. Troyer examined Becky's arm. "It is your right arm."

Becky nodded.

"Your painting arm."

Tears gathered in the corners of Becky's eyes.

"Rebecca, go into the house," Mr. Troyer said.

Becky stepped out of her mother's embrace and shook her head. "No."

Her father's eyes doubled in size, warning her. "Rebecca."

Becky raised her chin. "I'm going home with Chloe."

Her father's brows knitted together, and he said something I couldn't understand.

She replied in English. "No. I can't stay here. It's better for the family if I go. I need to protect you. You can tell everyone you wouldn't let me come home. The district will be mad." She turned to me. "Chloe, are you ready to go?"

"Umm . . ." I looked from Becky to her family.

Mr. Troyer spoke to Timothy, who replied in their language.

Did Harshberger offer Pennsylvania Dutch classes? I needed one if I spent much more time with the Troyer family.

Becky glared at them. "What happened has nothing to do with my art. It was an accident. I'm so sorry." Her voice broke.

Her mother rushed over and wrapped her eldest daughter in a hug. In her mother's arms again, Becky began to sob.

Despite all of Becky's troubles, a twinge of jealousy nicked my heart. What I wouldn't give for my mother to hug me like that one more time.

Mr. Troyer's jaw relaxed. "It is time for supper. We will eat first, then talk."

Becky sniffled as her mother guided her to the house. Thomas bounded after them, and I wondered if the youngest Troyer son ever walked anywhere.

Naomi pulled on the hem of my T-shirt.

To my surprise, Mr. Troyer waved me in, his expression resigned. "Yes, Chloe, please join us."

Timothy watched me, hands stuffed into his pockets and expectation in his eyes. Would it be better for me to bow out gracefully? Or accept the dinner invitation?

My stomach growled, making the decision for me.

Chapter Thirteen

I followed the Troyer family inside. The kitchen looked typical with its refrigerator and oven. My forehead wrinkled. Nothing about it said "Amish" to me.

"They are powered by propane." Timothy smiled. "There is a propane tank behind the house."

"That's okay?" I whispered.

"For our order, yes. For other orders, no."

My forehead wrinkled again, but Timothy only smiled.

I took in the rest of the kitchen, its white walls with maple crown molding around the ceiling. The kitchen was at least twice the size of the Greens' and four times the size of the one in my rental.

The inside of the home was spotless. Rows of home-canned pickles, jams, jellies, and peppers lined the shelves of a gorgeous wooden hutch. In front of the hutch, a long kitchen table with enough room for the entire family was set and ready for supper to be served, including places for Timothy, Becky, and me.

An elderly man with a fluffy white beard and round wire-rimmed glasses stood in the doorway between the living room and kitchen. He held himself upright with metal braces on each arm. "About time you all came in," he said. "I'm hungry. I even set the table for the young people to move this along. I knew they'd be coming in. No one can pass up one of my daughter's home-cooked meals." He rubbed his stomach.

Naomi giggled.

"I'm hungry, too, *Grossdaddi*," Thomas declared.

Becky's grandfather stuck out his cheek as the children passed. Each grandchild gave him a kiss, even Timothy. I just smiled, but the man angled his cheek in my direction, awaiting another kiss.

I gave him a peck on the cheek.

He stood a little taller. "I like her."

Mr. Troyer said something I didn't understand.

"*Daed*," Becky's mother said. "I'm sorry, Chloe. My father thinks because he is old he can behave as he likes."

The old man settled into a padded chair at the table. "Chloe." He let the name roll around on his tongue. "I like the name. You can call me Grandfather Zook. All the *Englischers* do."

I nodded. "It's nice to meet you."

Thomas and Naomi washed their hands in the sink, which looked just like the one in my home, and fought over who got to sit next to their grandfather. Timothy and his father also washed their hands while Becky, Ruth, and their mother started serving food.

In the Green house, Tanisha's father was the cook. If Mrs. Green was cooking, our choices were Chinese or Mediterranean takeout or pizza. Mrs. Green did an excellent job teaching both Tanisha and me how to dial a phone. That's where our culinary training ended.

"Can I help?" I asked, unsure of what I could do other than carry platters to the table.

"No," Mrs. Troyer said. "You're our guest. Please sit." She pointed to a spot on the wooden bench next to Naomi. The little girl scooted over so that we touched, and she grinned up at me. My heart melted a little.

Mrs. Troyer hummed to herself as she pulled a roast out of the oven. She moved with assurance, and in her kitchen, she was transformed from the anxious woman I met a few minutes ago. She set the roast in the center of the table in front of her husband. As their mother sat down, Ruth and Becky, using only her left arm, placed the last few side dishes on the table: green beans with ham, red-skinned potatoes with parsley, sliced white bread, pickled beet slices, and roasted vegetables.

Becky slid onto the bench on my other side, and Ruth sat by Timothy, who was directly across from me.

"Let's give thanks," Mr. Troyer said. Even though I couldn't understand a word, I felt the sentiment and received the same comfort the Greens' blessing over the meal would always give me. In the middle of the prayer, Mr. Troyer said Becky's name. Next to me, Naomi tensed up until her father pronounced, "Amen."

Mrs. Troyer asked for my plate and piled it high with more food than I could eat in a week, let alone at one sitting.

"My daughter makes the best canned beets in the county," Grandfather Zook said proudly.

I forced a smile as Mrs. Troyer set the plate in front of me, eight huge beet slices on the side of the plate between the red potatoes and green beans. I hated beets. Somehow, I knew, I would choke them down.

"*Daed*," Mrs. Troyer said. "How could you know that? Have you tried every pickled beet in the county?"

His eyes twinkled. "I don't have to taste them all to recognize the best."

Mrs. Troyer gave him a shy smile.

Mr. Troyer peered up from his dish at his father-in-law. "We should not be prideful."

His wife's smile faded.

Grandfather Zook appeared unconcerned by his son-in-law's comment and diced the roast beef on his plate into small, uniform pieces. "Someone opened the door to the chicken pen again last night. Ruth and Thomas had an exciting morning chasing the chickens around the yard."

"We got them all," Thomas said.

Timothy frowned. "What do you mean *again*?"

"It's the third time this week. I suppose we are lucky. The Sutters found tire marks driven right through their soybean field. It destroyed the crop."

Timothy stopped eating. "How long has this been going on?"

Grandfather Zook opened his mouth, but his son-in-law snapped at him in Pennsylvania Dutch.

Timothy looked at his father, then lowered his gaze to the table.

Grandfather Zook changed the subject. "Thomas helped Mary Fisher take strawberries to the Fisher fruit stand again today." Another twinkle appeared in his eyes. "This is the third time," he said. "Mary Fisher lives on the next farm. Gut family."

"*Grossdaddi*!" Thomas's cheeks grew red.

His mother gave him a warning glance. "Thomas, don't raise your voice."

"*Ya, Mamm.*" Thomas scrunched up his nose at his grandfather.

Grandfather Zook sipped his water. "She is too old for you, *grandkinner*."

Thomas scrunched his nose again. "She's ten."

"And you are seven."

The meal reminded me of Christmas dinner with the Green family. Lots of food piled high on plates, lively discussion, and the whole family gathered together. There were differences of course. Tanisha's little brother would have been playing a handheld videogame under the table, and her grandmother would have fallen asleep. However, the same love and warmth I had experienced with the Green clan was in this room.

Except for the proverbial elephant in the room—the accident—it must be like Christmas dinner every day for the Troyer family. No one spoke of the accident. Instead, Grandfather Zook entertained the family with stories about his three younger grandchildren.

They pretended that it upset them, but the children clearly loved the attention. He also asked about Becky and my house, and laughed when I described how rundown it was and that we had no furniture to speak of.

Mr. Troyer didn't seem to find my description nearly as funny.

Through it all, Becky barely touched her food, her eyes ever-fixed on her plate. Timothy also stayed quiet.

Figaro! Figaro! Figaro!

I swallowed a groan. Tanisha had programmed that ringtone into my cell before she moved to Milan.

The Troyer family stared at me.

"I'm so sorry." I reached under the bench seat for my purse.

Mr. Troyer frowned, as if I'd just fallen a few pegs in his opinion.

"What was that?" Thomas asked.

"Someone is singing under the table," Grandfather Zook said. "We must have a musical mouse."

Mrs. Troyer straightened. "There are no mice in my home."

"A spider then." Grandfather Zook tugged his beard. "He is very talented."

Thomas's eyes grew wide. "Spiders sing?"

"*Grossdaddi* is teasing," Ruth said.

Thomas squinted. "I knew that."

My face burned like I had stepped under a heat lamp. "It's my cell phone. That's my friend Tanisha calling from Italy."

Thomas stared at me. "She called you all the way from Italy?"

I nodded.

Figaro! Figaro! Figaro!

I knew my face had turned the same color as my hair. "I'm so sorry. Will you excuse me for a minute? It must be important for her to call me back like that." Clumsily, I climbed out of the bench seat and hurried from the table, but not before noticing the scowl on Mr. Troyer's face.

Outside, I answered the phone. "Tee?"

"Did you hang up on me?" Tanisha asked by way of greeting.

I stepped under the shade of a large elm tree about ten yards from the house. "No. I silenced your first call."

"Nope. I think you hung up." She sounded strange.

"Why didn't you leave a message? Is something wrong?"

"Of course something is wrong. You didn't answer your phone and I *needed* to talk to you."

I sighed. "Tee, this really isn't a good time." I glanced back at the house. "I'm—"

"Cole dumped me."

"What?"

She sobbed.

"Tanisha, honey, tell me what happened."

"He said he thought about it." She gasped for air. "He said being apart for two years was too long to wait to get married. He said I either come home and marry him now or not marry him at all."

"That's ridiculous." My jaw tightened. Cole was lucky he was hundreds of miles away in Florida. Had he been in front of me, I would have given him a piece of my mind—or kicked him. Kicking him probably would have felt better.

The screen door opened, and Timothy stepped outside.

"I found out right after Mom and Dad left for the airport." Tanisha continued to whimper. "They are on the plane by now. I can't even talk to them. Cole knew when my parents were leaving. Why did he wait until then to tell me?"

"Because he's a jerk," I wanted to say. My best friend defenses were up right now, and Cole was the enemy. "I'm so sorry, Tee. I know you're upset." I glanced at Timothy standing on the porch, waiting for me.

"Do you think I should call him and tell him what a huge mistake he is making?"

"No! He should be calling you. He's probably realizing what a colossal error this is right now."

She sniffled. "I doubt that."

"Well, if you do break down and call him, make sure it's in the middle of the night Florida time." My anger rose at Cole. "You might as well wake the idiot up from a dead sleep. You can blame it on the time difference."

She laughed in my ear.

Timothy continued to watch me from the front of his parents' house. "I hate to do this, Tee, but can I call you later to talk more?" I pulled the phone away from my ear to check the time before continuing. "It must be evening over there. I can call you tomorrow."

"But I want to talk to you now."

"I know you do, but I'm at a friend's house and can't talk."

She paused. "A *friend's* house. What friend?"

"Becky."

"The Amish girl?" Her voice had lost some of its sadness. "You are at an Amish house?"

"Yes."

"What's it like?"

"Just like a normal house, I guess, without the TV or hairdryer."

"Who cares about that? Is her brother, the hot buggy boy, there too?"

I turned my back to Timothy. "Don't call him that," I half whispered. "Yes, he's here."

She whooped a little. "You must tell me everything when you get home. Thinking about your love life will cheer me up."

"I don't have one."

"You will." Some of her typical Tanisha spunk had returned.

I ended the call and returned to the house. "I'm so sorry to interrupt the meal like that, Timothy."

"Don't worry. We were almost finished anyway. My mother is cleaning up now." Timothy stood by the steps. "Is something wrong?"

"My best friend's fiancé broke up with her. She needed someone to talk to."

He frowned. "Your friend is in Italy."

I nodded. "And her fiancé—ex-fiancé—is in Florida. That's the problem, or at least the problem Cole—that's his name—sees."

"It must be hard for him with her being so far away."

My face tightened again. He wasn't supposed to defend Cole. No one should. In my mind, my best friend's fiancé was public enemy number one . . . well, maybe number two. Those two rednecks in the green pickup were number one.

Timothy's brow creased. "Did I say something wrong?"

I almost told Timothy what I really thought of Cole and men in general at that moment, but I thought better of it. Maybe Timothy was different. I hoped so. "No, you didn't say anything wrong."

"I'll pray for them," Timothy said.

"Thank you," I whispered.

The screen door opened and the rest of the Troyer family filed out. Mrs. Troyer approached us. "Is everything all right, Chloe?"

"My friend received some bad news."

"I'm sorry. We will pray for her. What is her name again?"

I smiled. "Tanisha. She'll appreciate the prayers."

Timothy turned to his parents. "I'll take Chloe home."

Mrs. Troyer's expression fell. "Stay for dessert. I made peach pie. The peaches are from our tree. You love when I make peach pie, Timothy."

"I'm going too," said Becky, who had been quiet up to this point.

"No, you're not," her father said.

"I can't stay here. The district will talk. It's better for the family if I am away"—she paused—"until this is all over."

"I am your *daed*." Mr. Troyer's voice was thunderous. "You must listen to what I say."

"Rebecca is right." Grandfather Zook spoke out from the doorway. He leaned heavily on his braces. "You should let her go."

Becky's father rounded on his father-in-law and snapped at him in their own language.

Grandfather Zook carefully made his way down the porch steps, using his braces for support. He replied in his native language.

Mr. Troyer shook his head.

"You know what the deacon will say," Grandfather Zook replied.

Mr. Troyer glowered at him, but finally, he lowered his head. When he looked up, tears had gathered in the corners of his eyes. "You may go."

"Danki, Daed," Becky whispered.

Chapter Fourteen

On the way back to Appleseed Creek, the truck bounced along the gravel road, and Becky, who sat between Timothy and me, wrapped her good arm around her cast to protect it.

"Does it hurt?" I asked.

"Not much." She considered her cast. "Do you like it? The doctor said I could pick any color I wanted. I want you to be the first one to sign it."

"What happened after I left the sheriff's department?"

"They fingerprinted me using a computer and asked lots of questions. Timothy got me out." She beamed when mentioning her brother.

"The police didn't charge you?"

Timothy cleared his throat. "She was charged with driving without a license. They haven't made any decision about the accident yet."

My heart sank. Was it too much to hope Becky would get off scot-free? "What happens now?"

"The police will examine the car and determine what caused the accident." He switched on the air-conditioning inside the cabin.

I didn't say it, but since Becky was driving, the accident appeared to be her fault. "Becky needs a lawyer."

"A lawyer won't help," Timothy said. "Even if he could, we can't afford one."

"Maybe I can help." I said this even though I trembled to think of what my car insurance premiums would be after the accident.

"No." Timothy spoke firmly, as if this wasn't up for discussion.

I exhaled a sigh. "If she doesn't hire someone, then a public defender will be assigned to her case. Whoever that is might not do what's best for Becky."

"Chief Rose told us that."

"She was the person who interviewed you even though it was at the sheriff's station?"

Timothy nodded. "She showed up not long after you left."

Again I wondered how the small town police chief and Timothy knew each other. I wasn't buying the "everybody knows everybody in a small town" speech. Chief Rose clearly wanted me to believe there was something more to it, but was there?

I shifted on the hot leather seat, then pointed the A/C vent at my face. "She needs a better defense." My hair grazed my cheeks as the cool air blew. What a welcome relief.

"Defense?" Timothy asked. "She doesn't have a defense. She admitted she was driving the car."

Tears rolled down Becky's cheeks. "Timothy is right. It's my fault. I must accept the blame."

I thought about Brock's threat, his leering face, and my stomach churned. *She'll be very popular in prison.* I hoped never to see him or his friend again, but knew that wasn't likely. *Should I tell Timothy about them?*

I aimed the cool air at Becky. "Maybe they will be lenient."

We rode in silence for the rest of the drive. Timothy turned into my driveway on Grover Lane, and Becky slipped out of the truck. "I'm not feeling well."

"What's wrong?" Timothy asked.

"I'm a little dizzy." She rubbed her temple with her uninjured hand. "I think it is the pain medicine. I'm going to lie down in my room."

The front door banged shut as she stumbled inside.

Timothy walked me to the door, and as I climbed the uneven porch steps, I turned to him. "What are we going to do?"

"What do you mean?" He grabbed hold of the porch post, and it moved with little force. "This isn't stable. I will come by tomorrow and fix it."

"We need to help Becky."

"Actually, the whole porch should be replaced."

"Timothy, I'm talking about Becky."

He removed his hand from the post. "I know, but I won't let you be hurt one day by this."

"Thank you," I said. "I appreciate anything you can do to help the house."

His lips pressed into a thin line. "This was why I wanted my sister to return home."

"Because of the condition of my house?"

He sighed. "No. I was afraid something like this would happen."

"The accident?"

He nodded.

"There was no way you could know this would happen." I watched Gigabyte stalking back and forth in front of the living room's large picture window. He meowed and batted at the glass.

Timothy pursed his lips. "Becky shouldn't have left home. She should have joined the church and married Isaac."

I put my hands on my hips. "Why is it okay for you to leave the Amish, and not for her?"

His blue eyes fixed on mine. “I can’t answer that.”

“Why not?”

His expression softened. “I’m glad that you met the rest of my family. They liked you.”

“I liked them,” I replied. “At dinner your grandfather mentioned someone let the chickens out on the farm. You seemed surprised.”

“I was.” Timothy flexed his jaw. “I knew there have been problems in the district.”

“What kind of problems?”

“Animals let out of pens, rowdy *Englischers* driving through the district at night firing shotguns into the air.”

“What have the police done?”

“Not much. The district won’t talk to them. That’s not the Amish way.”

“But—”

“Chloe, I know it’s hard for you to understand why the district hasn’t complained to the police. It’s even hard for me sometimes, and I grew up Amish.”

“You would go to the police.”

“Yes.” His tone left no doubt.

I had another question. “If you didn’t know about your own family, how did you know about these other incidents?”

He wiggled the post. “A friend told me.”

“Could the attacks on the Amish be related to the accident?”

Timothy looked taken aback. “How?”

“I . . . I don’t know, but doesn’t it seem odd that some unknown person is pestering the Amish, and then the bishop dies in an accident? How can that be a coincidence?”

“It’s odd, but what I think is even odder is that you haven’t even considered it could have been you in that accident. *You* could have been seriously hurt or even killed.”

I shivered.

"If your car had been in working order, this could have all been avoided."

"I told you the car was fine." I sounded defensive, but I couldn't help it. The car had been fine.

Timothy blew out a sigh. "I'll fix the porch tomorrow," he said, and left.

Later that night, I sat beside my bedroom window unable to sleep. I tortured myself by waiting for the green pickup and wondering what Timothy meant by *I can't answer that*. Did that mean he really couldn't, or he *wouldn't* answer my question?

The white gauzy curtains blew in with the breeze. The weatherman had promised a cold front was coming in and tomorrow would be a beautiful eighty-degree day. I stared at the curtains. Part of me wanted to close the window so I wouldn't hear the green truck when it roared up my street, but it was too hot. The cold front hadn't reached us yet, and my house wasn't air-conditioned. A white floor fan circulated the humid air around the room.

Tap, tap sounded on my bedroom door. Becky slipped into the room. "Chloe? Are you awake?"

I sat up against the headboard. "What's wrong?" As if I needed to ask.

Gig ran into the room and jumped on my bed. He seemed to know that Becky needed him that night and had chosen to sleep with her. He climbed on my pillows and bumped his head on my shoulder. I knew Becky needed what comfort he could offer, but I was glad to have the cat in my room again. I missed his weight on my pillow.

"I can't sleep," Becky whispered. She looked like a ghost as she moved across the room in her white nightgown. The gown reflected the yellow streetlamp light coming in through my window.

I pulled my knees up to my chest, shivering against the unknown. "That's understandable."

She sat on the end of my bed. "What about Cookie?"

"You want a cookie? Do we have any? I can get you one."

"Not cookies. I mean Cookie, the person."

I racked my sleep-deprived brain. *Was there a Cookie I was supposed to remember? It didn't sound like an Amish name.* "Becky, I don't know what you're talking about. Who is Cookie?"

"That's right, I didn't tell you why I was driving the car."

"You said you had an interview."

"The interview was with Cookie and her husband, Scotch. They own a greenhouse outside of town."

I held up my hand. "Are you making these names up?"

She giggled, but then her voice faded. "She must think I'm horrible for missing the interview. She will never give me a job now." The draft from my standup fan caught her white-blonde hair, moving it back and forth.

"Becky, that's the least of your worries. You can call Cookie tomorrow and explain. I'm sure she will understand. Anyone would."

She started to cry. "I'm so sorry, Chloe. No one will ever know how sorry I am." Her cries turned to sobs, her body shuddering with each breath. She collapsed face down on the bed, and I reached for her good arm, holding it. Gigabyte curled up beside her and purred with the ferocity of a motorboat. I prayed as hard for Becky as I did the day of my mother's accident.

Soon, Becky fell into slumber. Just before I drifted off, a truck backfired outside my window.

Chapter Fifteen

Boom! Boom! Boom!

My eyes popped open. Gig jumped off my pillow and hid. Becky, curled up like a cat, slept soundly at the foot of my bed.

In the early morning, I slipped out of bed quietly, zipped a hoodie over my pajamas, and went downstairs. Through the peephole Chief Rose smiled at me. I opened the door. Already dressed in her uniform, she carried a small tote bag in her hand that I recognized as Becky's.

"Good morning, Miss Humphrey. Is Miss Troyer here? I'd like to talk to both of you."

"Come in. Becky's upstairs. I'll go get her. Please make yourself comfortable." I pointed at the one armchair in the living room. "I'm sorry I don't have more furniture."

"I can stand."

I hurried upstairs and into my bedroom. Becky wasn't there. I found her in her own room on the bed. "The police are here."

Her eyes grew wide. "Are they taking me away?"

"I don't know." I picked up a long canvas skirt from the milk crate, which served as her dresser, and handed it to her. "Get dressed."

I dashed into my bedroom and threw on a pair of jeans, a clean T-shirt, and zipped up the hoodie again. Becky met me in the hall wearing the skirt and a bright blue T-shirt. Her long blonde hair was secured at the nape of her neck in a tight bun.

When Becky and I entered the living room, Chief Rose was examining the photographs on the mantel over the fireplace. She set down the photograph of my mother, and I gritted my teeth. "Let me grab some more chairs." I escaped to the kitchen where I took a few deep breaths, and returned with two wooden chairs, placing them across from the chief who now sat in the armchair. I sat in one, and Becky perched on the edge of the other.

Chief Rose reached into Becky's tote bag and pulled out my GPS, Pepper. Still in her protective black case, she didn't appear any worse for wear. The chief leaned over and handed it to me. "I thought you might need this seeing as how you got lost on the way home from the hospital yesterday."

I tensed and opened the case. The GPS was fine. "Thank you for returning it."

"I took the liberty to change the mode to 'on foot' since you don't have a car to use anymore."

My brow wrinkled, and I cocked my head in her direction.

She handed the tote bag to Becky. "We found this in the RAV4 too."

Becky grabbed the tote and opened it. "My sketchbook," she cried. "Thank you so much."

The chief nodded. "You're welcome."

"You don't need these things for"—I paused—"evidence?"

Chief Rose shook her head. "I'm sure you are wondering why I'm here this early." She placed a hand on each knee and leaned forward. "It's not to return your things."

Gigabyte peeked his head out from around the kitchen wall, then disappeared.

The police chief cleared her throat. "We examined the car and discovered something."

I straightened. "What?"

"Prior to the accident, your car's brake line had been cut three quarters of the way through."

My stomach dropped. Good thing Becky hadn't made breakfast yet. I doubted it would have stayed in my stomach after the police chief made that announcement.

Becky's brow puckered. "What does that mean?"

Chief Rose stood and picked up a vase from the mantel, spinning it in her hand. "It means sabotage. It means a premeditated crime."

I inhaled a deep breath. "It also means the accident wasn't Becky's fault."

She set the vase back on the mantel. "Yes."

"Praise God," I said.

Becky's mouth hung open.

Chief Rose glowered at Becky. "You are still in trouble, Becky. Driving without a license is a serious offense. I don't take that lightly."

Becky bowed her head. "I'm so sorry."

The chief returned to the armchair and sat on the edge of it. "Do you know anyone who might want to hurt you?" She directed her question at me.

I blinked at her. "Me?"

"The severed brake line was inside *your* car. It's safe to assume whoever cut it thought you would be behind the wheel. In fact, if Becky hadn't *borrowed* it," she made quote signs with her fingers, "you'd have been the one in the accident."

A chill ran down my spine. *The green pickup. It had to be them.* My stomach rumbled. Yes, it was definitely good that I hadn't eaten anything yet.

Becky's eyes watered. "Chloe, you could have been killed."

And Bishop Glick would still be alive.

Becky shook her head and played with the end of her braid. "Chloe just moved here. No one would want to hurt her."

I thought back to my encounter with Brock and his sidekick in the hospital parking lot. "There might be someone."

Becky looked up, one eyebrow raised.

A grin formed on Chief Rose's mouth. She leaned forward again and placed her elbows on her knees. I scooted my chair back an inch.

"Tell me who you suspect," she said.

"It goes back to my first day in Knox County." I told Chief Rose how Becky and I met and about my run-in with the two thugs in the hospital parking lot.

"Describe the men." The chief removed a small notebook from her breast pocket and jotted down notes.

"One is thin, kind of wiry. They both had dark hair, but the wiry guy had a dirty blond goatee. The other one was clean shaven. He had the face of a twelve-year-old, but he was enormous. He looked like he could wrestle a bear to the ground if he ever had the need."

Chief Rose smiled a little at the description.

"I know his name. The thin one called him Brock."

"It must be Brock Buckley." The police chief stopped just short of rubbing her hands together. "Your description fits him to a T. If it is Brock, dollars to donuts the other man is Curt Fanning."

"Do you know them?" Becky asked.

"I've picked them up for disorderly conduct more times than I can count. Murder is new for them."

I cocked my chin. "You think they meant to kill the bishop?"

"Not the bishop. *You*."

My body began to shake the way it did whenever I had to speak in front a large group of people—a constant, full body shiver. I tensed my muscles in an effort to make the shaking stop, but it didn't help. I prayed, too, needing to be in control. Disorderly conduct and harassing Becky was one thing . . . but murder?

Chief Rose leaned back in the armchair. "They have a well-earned reputation in the county, but let's not jump to conclusions. We need a positive ID before we move forward."

She stared at me until I broke eye contact.

"I need you to come to my station and view some photos."

"Is it very far?" I held up Pepper as evidence. "I don't have a car anymore, remember?"

She shook her head. "The police station is in the city hall building right on the square."

Easy walking distance. "Sure," I said.

"Great." A smug smile played on Chief Rose's lips. "I can take you there."

I bit the inside of my lip. "Okay."

"Can I go with her?" Becky asked.

The chief shook her head. "No. I might need you to ID these men later, but I'd like Chloe to make a positive ID all by herself first." She stood. "Are you ready, Chloe?"

"Right now?"

"Yes, right now. The sooner you make the ID, the sooner I can bring them in."

I took another breath and let it go. "Okay. I'm ready." The shivering stopped, but the fear lingered.

Chapter Sixteen

It was Saturday, market day in Appleseed Creek. Buggies surrounded the town square, and Amish women sold homemade bread, canned jams and jellies, and fresh produce to their English neighbors and visitors. Chief Rose's police car idled as a tour bus unloaded thirty elderly tourists in the middle of the street.

"I hate market day," the police chief said.

Finally, the bus was emptied of passengers, and Chief Rose whooped her siren as she cut around it. She turned off the square and made an immediate left into an alley behind the town hall, a two-story, tan brick building with a rooster weathervane on top. There was a small patch of grass, maybe three feet wide, between the building and the road with a flagpole sticking out of it. Red geraniums decorated white boxes below first-floor windows. The American and Ohio flags flapped in the light breeze. A handful of cotton-like clouds bounced across an otherwise clear, blue sky. The weatherman had been right—it was cooler than the day before.

Chief Rose parked in the spot labeled "Chief." From the parking lot, two doors led into the building, each labeled with forest green lettering. One read, CITY OFFICES, and the other, VILLAGE POLICE. *So is Appleseed Creek a city or a village?*

The chief unlocked the village police door and flicked on the lights. A scarred-up metal desk sat in the corner of the waiting room with a ten-year-old CPU monitor and computer on it next to a solid black telephone, circa 1980. A door in the middle of the back wall was flanked by windows on either side, their vertical blinds drawn. Wooden folding chairs lined the walls. Not much of an office. *Where are the other officers?*

"We share a 911 system with the city of Mount Vernon." Chief Rose spoke as if reading my mind. "If it's minor enough, we respond; if not, we call on Mount Vernon or the Knox County sheriff's department for support. If it has something to do with Harshberger College, which most of our calls do, we work in conjunction with campus security."

She used the royal "we" even though she was the only one here.

She stopped and regarded me. "I have two officers, in case you're wondering, but they are both busy today keeping an eye on the farmers' market. It's always good to have a police presence there. You never know when city folk are going to put up a fight over the price of watermelon." She kept a straight face when she said that.

The chief sorted through her key ring, found what she needed, and unlocked the second door, which opened into a meeting room. A long cafeteria-type table sat in the middle of the room surrounded by more wooden folding chairs. "Have a seat. I'll grab the photos."

I sat, careful not to pinch myself on the chair. The chief unlocked a third door and slipped through, closing it behind her before I could see inside. Seconds later she returned, carrying a three-inch black binder.

She sat catty-corner from me at the table and placed the binder on the table. "How's Becky doing?"

"She's upset." I stopped myself from telling her what a stupid question that was. *How does the chief think Becky is?*

"She seemed better this morning than I expected her to."

My brow wrinkled.

"I assumed she would be more upset, considering her relationship with Isaac Glick."

"I thought I came here to check photos, not to talk about how Becky is doing. If you wanted to do that, why didn't you ask her when you were at my house?" I frowned. "How would you know about Becky and Bishop Glick's son anyway?" I moved my seat a few inches back from the table.

"The Amish aren't as closemouthed as some would think." She tapped the cover of the binder with blunt, clear-polished nails. "There are other complications too, of course. Becky's father could lose his chance to be a preacher. His grasp was already tentative with his two oldest children leaving the Amish life behind. Now, the Troyer family will always be associated with the death of a beloved bishop."

"What about the recent harassment of the Amish?" I asked. "The shotgun fire? The destruction of crops?"

She raised one eyebrow. "How do you know about that?"

"I heard the Troyer family discussing it, and I asked Timothy about it."

"For being here less than two weeks, you've gotten a lot closer to them than I ever have."

I remained steadfast. "What are you doing about the problems?"

She scowled and blew out a long breath. "Everything I can. It's hard to investigate the case when none of the witnesses will tell you what they saw. They are too busy 'turning the other cheek' to talk to me."

"But it could be related, right?"

"Look at you. You're like the Pippi Longstocking version of Nancy Drew."

I slapped both hands on the table. "Chief Rose, you came to my house this morning and basically told me that someone tried to kill me. Is it any surprise that I would have questions?"

Her brows arched over her peridot-colored eyes. "Maybe I've

been dealing with the Amish too long to know how a big-city girl like you would react."

"May I see the photographs, please?" I reached out my hand.

She shrugged and slid the binder in front of me. "This is a book of thirty eight-by-ten mug shots. Look at each photo carefully. If you recognize one or both of the men who threatened you and Becky, let me know."

I opened the binder. The first photograph was a man with a blunt nose and a horizontal scar across his right cheek. I wondered if he moonlighted as a pirate. The next photo held the likeness of a glaring man with huge ears. Each picture was scarier than the last. I glanced up at Chief Rose. "Do all these guys live in Appleseed Creek?"

She didn't answer my question, so I flipped to the next page. Brock's dark eyes stared at me. I knew him right away. Even in the mug shot he looked like a giant teddy bear, which he was not. "This one," I said. "This is the one called Brock."

She made a note in the spiral notebook in front of her. "Keep going."

I was a bit disappointed with her reaction but moved on. Three ugly mugs later, I reached the end of the notebook and viewed the last photograph—Brock's friend. I'd know that dirty goatee anywhere. "This is the other one."

"Are you sure?"

"Yes."

"You are positive on IDs?"

"Yes."

She studied me with her disquieting green eyes for a long moment. Finally, she sat back. "You ID'd Brock Buckley and Curt Fanning, just as I thought." She tapped her index finger on the dirty goatee guy's nose. "Curt Fanning." She flipped back through the binder and came to Brock's photograph. "Brock Buckley."

For some reason, knowing their names gave me courage. As unknown men in the green pickup, they were terrifying, but now that they were Brock Buckley and Curt Fanning—real people however unsavory—they were just scary.

The chief closed the binder. "We'll pick them up and bring them in for questioning." She slipped her hand into the breast pocket of her uniform, removed a business card, and placed it on the table in front of me. "If you see them again, or if they approach you, or even if you see their truck on your street, call me."

I examined the card, embossed with the Appleseed Creek seal. It listed Chief Rose's name, phone numbers, and address. "Shouldn't I just call 911?" I tapped the card on the table before dropping it into my purse.

"If you feel you are or someone else is in danger, by all means dial 911, but in any other case, call me." She stood. "I'll give you a ride back home."

I shook my head. "I'd rather walk." The Pippi Longstocking comment still annoyed me.

She shrugged.

Before I left the room, the chief said, "I forgot to tell you, welcome to Appleseed Creek."

I glanced back at her, and she smiled. Only it didn't reach her eyes.

Chapter Seventeen

Instead of walking around the Amish farmers' market, I decided to go through it. The more people around, the safer I would feel. Besides, if I brought home some fresh fruit, it might cheer up Becky. I kept my eye out for Curt and Brock. Part of me expected them to jump out from behind one of the buggies parked around the square.

I meandered near three young women sitting at a table of pies and staring at me. As I passed, I heard whispering but tried to think nothing of it. The acknowledgment that someone had deliberately tried to cause me harm—a.k.a. *kill* me—left a burning in my stomach and a trembling in my body that I couldn't completely control.

The fruit stand sat in the middle of the square by the town's fountain, which had a bronze replica of Johnny Appleseed leaning against an apple tree in it. A mischievous grin marked the statue's face. Dozens of donor names were chiseled into the cement wall encircling the fountain.

I picked up a green quart container of strawberries. Becky would be able to make a pie with them. "How much for the strawberries?" I asked the fruit seller, an Amish girl who was no more than fifteen.

The Amish girl scowled. "Two dollars."

"I'll take them."

Gruffly, she took the strawberries from my hand and dumped them into a plastic shopping bag. I handed her the money.

A middle-aged Amish woman marched to the girl's side and said something in their language. The girl hung her head and put the strawberries back into the green carton while the older woman removed my two dollars from the money pouch sitting on the table. "Here is your money."

I didn't take the bills. "Is something wrong?"

She tried to force the money back into my hands.

"What about the strawberries?"

Her eyes narrowed. "We cannot sell to you."

When I wouldn't take the money, she placed it on the table in front of me. "What do you mean?"

The younger Amish woman replied in their language, but the only word I understood was "Glick." My stomach dropped. This was about Bishop Glick and Becky. I stepped away from them and left the money on the table. Part of me wanted to scream for this injustice against Becky, and reveal that my brake line had been cut, but my saner, calmer side prevailed. I bit back the retorts that would only spread more gossip through the district.

I felt the eyes of the Amish watching me as I wove around the booths and card tables. Not until I turned the corner on Grover Lane did I let out a sigh of relief. *If the Amish treat me this way, how will they treat Becky?*

At the house, Becky sat on a brown folding chair on our rickety front porch. Gig was in her lap, purring. Since the house faced east, the morning light leaked though holes in the porch's roof and reflected off of her white-blonde hair, giving her an otherworldly halo.

When she saw me, she jumped up from the chair. Gigabyte

hung from her unbroken arm and yowled, so Becky opened the front door and placed the cat inside. "Chloe, I have great news!"

I blinked. "You do?"

She hopped from foot to foot. "Remember, I told you about Cookie and Scotch last night?"

I climbed the last step to the porch. "Yes."

"They own Little Owl Greenhouse, and I called Cookie this morning. She offered me a job!"

I leaned against the post. It shifted under my weight, and I shuffled away. Probably a good thing Timothy planned to mend it. "She gave you a job over the phone?"

"Yes. I start Monday!"

"Without an interview?"

"Cookie said she didn't need to interview me because I was so responsible for calling her right away. She knew I would be perfect for the greenhouse."

My forehead wrinkled. "Do you know anything about plants?"

"Of course. My family has a huge garden."

I paused. "Are the plants the greenhouse sells different from those in an Amish garden?"

Her face fell. "I thought you'd be happy."

"Becky, I am happy, but I'm surprised too. Where is the greenhouse?"

"Just off"—she paused—"Butler Road."

I inhaled and glanced at the sky before bringing my gaze back to Becky. "How are you going to get there? We don't have a car."

Becky shifted from one foot to another. "I told Cookie that, and she and Scotch will drive me until you have a car again."

I mulled that one over. "That's awfully nice of them."

"They live near the square too, so they don't have to go out of their way or anything."

I pointed at her cast. "Did you tell them about your arm?"

"Yes, but Cookie said there was plenty of other work for me to do." She peered at me. "Isn't this great?"

I nodded, still unsure. And yet, I too was hired over the phone.

Becky sat back down in her chair. "What happened at the police station?"

I relayed my visit to the police station, but decided not to mention the incident at the farmers' market.

"Why didn't you tell me about those men in the pickup?"

"I didn't want to worry you." Tentatively, until I knew it could hold my weight, I leaned on the crooked railing surrounding the porch. Sunshine warmed my back.

She frowned. "Why does everyone treat me like a child? Even you, Chloe."

"We want to protect you."

She took a deep breath and looked away. "What's going to happen to me?"

"I don't know." I shifted to allow more sun onto my shoulders. "Can you tell me about the accident? I haven't heard about it from you yet, at least not all of it."

"I turned onto Butler Road and drove to the top of the hill. Everything was fine. I thought I would make it to the greenhouse and back before you got home from work." Becky faced me again. "I wanted to surprise you with my new job."

"How do you know how to drive a car?"

"Isaac has a license. He got it during his *rumspringa*. He's always been fascinated with mechanical contraptions, so he took me out several times in his truck and taught me. I know we shouldn't have been doing that. It was a secret we shared."

I winced. Having been the one who taught Becky how to drive could only make the young Amish man feel worse. "Isaac is no longer in *rumspringa*?"

"No, he was baptized last spring."

"What happened when you reached the top of the hill?"

"I wasn't going fast, maybe thirty-five miles per hour. It's steep there and the truck's speed picked up fast. I tapped the brake to slow down and the pedal went all the way to the floor. By this time, the car was coasting at over fifty. I saw it on the numbers behind the steering wheel."

"The speedometer?"

She shrugged. "If that's what you call it." She closed her eyes and her voice shook. "I couldn't stop. There were brambles along the road at the bottom where the road curves. I pointed the car at those, thinking they'd stop me." She was silent, her eyes closed for a full minute. If I didn't know better I would have thought she had dozed off.

I prodded her. "So you hit the brambles . . ."

She took a shuddering breath and opened her eyes. "No. As I got there, Bishop Glick's buggy came around the bend in the road. I couldn't do anything. There was no time to turn the car in another direction."

Despite the warm sun on my back, a chill ran down my spine.

"I saw the horse first. I turned the steering wheel hard to the right to miss the animal, but by doing that I hit the buggy full on instead." She rubbed her hands up and down her bare arms. Tears sprang to her eyes. "Bishop Glick recognized me. He saw it was me who hit him before he died."

I walked over to her, knelt by the chair, and wrapped her in a hug.

"It's my fault," she whispered between sobs.

Her tears soaked through the shoulder of my yellow T-shirt. "You shouldn't have been driving the car. You know that, but remember what the police chief said. Someone cut the brake line. You had nothing to do with that."

She sat up and used the end of her long braid to dry her eyes. "Do you really think it was those men?"

I shook my head. "I don't know."

A hiccup escaped her. "What if it's not? Who else could have done this?"

"I don't know."

"What's going to happen to me?" She asked the question again, her voice an octave higher.

Again, I told her all that I really could at this point. "I don't know."

Chapter Eighteen

An hour later, Becky lay on the floor flipping through her sketchbook while I sat in the armchair and researched on my iPad how someone could cut a car's brake line. It was frighteningly easy. Through a simple search, I obtained step-by-step instructions with pictures.

The article I read claimed that a brake warning light would be illuminated on the car's dash. "Becky, did you see any strange lights glowing on the front of the car near the place you watch your speed?"

She looked up from her sketchbook. "I don't think so."

"It would have said 'brake.'"

She shook her head and I repressed a sigh. *Would I have noticed the brake light either? Probably.* I doubted Becky was familiar enough with a car's dashboard to notice something was wrong. She didn't even know the word "speedometer."

A *clack, clack, clack* came from outside. I closed the cover to my iPad and looked toward the door.

"It sounds like a buggy." Becky hurried to the window. "*Grossdaddi* and the *kinner* are here!" Some of the music had returned to her voice. She threw open the door and disappeared outside.

I followed her.

"*Gude mariye!*" Grandfather Zook grinned from his perch at the front of his glossy black six-seater buggy. The three younger Troyer children waved from the back. "Get in!" he said. "We're going to Young's Flea Market!"

Becky shook her head so hard I was afraid she'd give herself a crick in her neck. "*Grossdaddi*, I can't go to Young's."

Grandfather Zook cocked his head. "Why not?"

Becky looked up, and tears welled in her eyes.

"Come here," her grandfather said.

Becky moped around the side of the buggy. Grandfather Zook placed his hand on her head and leaned down, whispering to her.

His horse nudged me in the shoulder and snorted. He was a beautiful, dark brown, lean animal with a white star in the middle of his forehead. Thomas climbed over his sisters and hopped out of the buggy. "That's Sparky."

I scratched the horse's star. "Sparky? That doesn't seem like an Amish name."

"That's the name he came with. He's a racehorse," he said proudly. "He's the fastest horse in Knox County. We can get places in half the time it takes most folks."

Grandfather Zook squeezed Becky's shoulder. "Sparky's a retired racehorse and not as fast as he used to be. His full name is Sir Sparkalot Lightning March."

"That's quite a name."

"Sparky sounds better," Thomas declared.

Sparky's ear flicked back and forth as if he listened to the conversation.

"Old Spark doesn't like it when I say he's slowed up," Grandfather Zook said. "He's plenty fast for us. Any faster and we'd be breaking the speed limit. I'd hate to be pulled over by the coppers."

My jaw dropped. "The police pull over Amish buggies?"

Grandfather Zook laughed. I liked the sound of it. It was a rumble that came up from deep inside and shook his whole body, making his long white beard wave back and forth like a flag. What would my life have been like if I'd had a grandfather? My mother's parents both died long before I was born, and my father was estranged from his mother and father. His mother is gone now, and if I tried to find my grandfather, my father would be furious. Sabrina wouldn't be too happy about it either, but then again, nothing I did made Sabrina happy.

"I bought him from a thoroughbred breeder two years ago." Grandfather Zook moved the reins from hand to hand. "Lots of Amish carriage horses are retired thoroughbreds. We can give them a quiet retirement, and what horse wouldn't want to be trotting around the countryside pulling a sharp-looking buggy like mine?"

"Can we go now?" Ruth asked. "Anna Lambright is waiting for me at the market."

"You girls run back into the house and grab the things you need for the day," Grandfather Zook shooed us on, not taking no for an answer.

Despite the humid air, Becky wrapped her good arm around her shoulder as if she felt a chill. "Why do you want to take us to the flea market, *Grossdaddi*?"

"We need to find you *kinner* some furniture. You said at supper yesterday that you have one chair between you." He tsked. "The flea market is the best place to find everything you need, especially if I'm at your side."

Cheer returned to Becky's face. "*Grossdaddi* can talk a fat man out of his fry pie."

Thomas giggled.

Ruth jumped from foot to foot. "Can we go now, please?"

Becky looked up at her grandfather. "*Grossdaddi*, I don't want to go there. Not after what I did . . ."

"*Ya*, you made a mistake, but you cannot hide. That will just make folks talk more. If you look them in the eye, they might think twice before they say something."

Or, I thought, if you're dealing with someone like Sabrina, she'll just insult you to your face. It was difficult for me to imagine anyone like my stepmother among the Amish.

Becky considered me. "What do you think, Chloe?"

I observed the sky, bright blue and clear. A sky I wasn't used to. Rarely was there a clear sky like this one in Cleveland on the banks of Lake Erie. Instead, huge clouds rolled off the great lake and hung overtop the city. Today was a perfect day for a buggy ride. "We could use another chair or two." I scratched Sparky behind the ear. *And I could get out of the house and stop obsessing over the accident.*

Becky smiled just a little. "I am tired of sitting on the floor."

Grandfather Zook grinned. "No more talk, then. Into the buggy with the both of you."

Ten minutes later, Becky sat in the back of the buggy in between Thomas and Ruth, and I sat in the front next to Grandfather Zook with Naomi on my lap clutching her doll.

Grandfather made a clicking sound with his tongue. "Head 'em up, Sparky."

I grinned. "Head 'em up?" *Amish meets Old West?*

He winked at me.

The black paint inside the buggy was polished to such a high sheen that I saw my reflection in the ceiling. Everything was spotless, even the high-gloss floorboards. "Your buggy's beautiful," I told Grandfather Zook.

"It better be," Thomas said from the back row. "*Grossdaddi* has me polish it once a week."

"I pay you in candy." Grandfather Zook pretended to be offended.

The girls laughed, even Becky. Maybe Grandfather Zook was right and the trip to the flea market would lift her spirits.

Naomi held up her doll for me to see.

"She's beautiful," I said. "But where is her face?"

"No, thanks, I have a job over in Fredericktown this afternoon." He smiled at me. "You must be Chloe. I've heard a *lot* about you."

I felt myself blush. Did Timothy talk about me? "Nice to meet you."

Timothy stepped out the front door and jumped down the steps. "*Gude mariye.* Ready to go furniture shopping?" he asked me with twinkling eyes.

"Yes." My voice still squeaked.

Danny and Grandfather Zook shared a grin.

Timothy didn't seem to notice. "If we buy anything, there won't be any room in the buggy to bring it home. I'll take my truck. Anyone want to ride with me?"

"I do!" Ruth and Thomas both clamored at the same time to ride with Timothy.

Grandfather Zook waited for Timothy to start his pickup before he flicked the reins on his buggy. "I think it's only fair to give Timothy a head start." He chuckled.

Sparky wove through the narrow one-way brick streets surrounding the square as the Amish selling their wares were packing up for the day. Behind me, Becky put her head down. The two Amish women who refused to sell me the strawberries stared at us as we trotted past.

Soon the houses and gas stations gave way to open farmland. In the distance, half a dozen Amish children ran around a yard as their mother sat on a stool shucking corn. If it had not been for the electric posts taking power back to the small town of Appleseed Creek, I would have thought I had wandered into the nineteenth century. *Does it look like the nineteenth century to Becky and her family? Or is this normal?*

Sparky rocked his head back and forth.

"Stop preening, Sparky." Grandfather Zook glanced at me. "He's such a showboat. Thinks he's the most attractive horse in the county."

"Naomi doesn't speak *Englisch*," Thomas said. "She hasn't started school yet."

"Oh."

"Her doll doesn't have a face because *Daed* says it's wrong."

I glanced at Grandfather Zook. "Wrong?"

"It makes a craven image," Thomas said.

Ruth snorted. "Graven image, you goof."

Thomas made a face at his sister.

"That's why *Daed* and Becky fight. Becky draws people with faces," Ruth said.

I glanced back at Becky, and a grim line crossed her delicate face. She wouldn't meet my gaze.

Naomi looked up at me with huge blue eyes, her forehead creased.

"She's a lovely doll with or without a face."

She smiled and snuggled into my lap.

Grandfather Zook flicked the reins, and Sparky stepped away from the curb. "Enough talk about dolls. Off to the flea market, but first we must swing by Timothy's."

I told the butterflies in my stomach to be quiet. "Timothy?" My voice squeaked.

A wide smile spread across Grandfather Zook's face, and I felt my own turn red. Was I that obvious? Thankfully, the children didn't seem to notice.

"Oh, yes, I want *all* my *grandkinner* on this trip," Grandfather Zook said.

"Yea, Timothy!" Thomas shouted from the back row.

"Yea, Timothy!" Naomi agreed on my lap.

Yea, Timothy, my heart whispered.

Chapter Nineteen

As Grandfather Zook drove the buggy through the neighborhood, neighbors peeked out of their windows to catch a glimpse. Yet no one seemed surprised to see an Amish buggy rolling down their street. This was an everyday event in Appleseed Creek. I tried to imagine what would happen if a buggy turned into the Greens' cul-de-sac in Shaker Heights. I smiled at the image. *Hopefully, Grandfather Zook didn't think I was smiling because of Timothy.*

"Do you have other grandchildren?" I asked.

"Oh yes, I have." He thought for a minute. "Thirty-two back in Lancaster."

My mouth fell open. "Thirty-two!"

His beard waved with a chuckle. "And eight, almost nine, great-grandchildren."

"Wow."

"Do you have any brothers and sisters, Chloe?" Ruth asked. She leaned forward and folded her thin arms over the front seat.

"I have a younger brother and sister. They live in California."

"California!" Ruth cried. "I'd love to go there. I want to see the ocean."

"Don't let your *daed* hear you say that," Grandfather Zook teased. "He'd have a heart attack."

"Anna Lambright saw the ocean. Her whole family did. They took the bus to Florida two years ago. She said it was the best place in the world and what heaven must be like."

Becky barked a laugh. "Until she stepped on the jellyfish. She wasn't too keen on the ocean after that."

Ruth fell back into her seat and crossed her arms over her chest. "I still want to see it."

"If you want to see it someday, Ruthie, I'm sure you will." Grandfather Zook spoke in a soothing voice.

Sparky turned a corner, and the low limbs of a buckeye tree grazed the top of the buggy.

"Sparky," Grandfather Zook reprimanded. "Watch the paint job."

I laughed.

"There's Timothy's house," Thomas cried. He pointed at a large Victorian home three driveways down, its exterior walls lavender with dark purple shutters. It seemed like a strange place for guys to live, especially former Amish guys.

A young man in a brown plaid short-sleeve shirt and cargo shorts dribbled a basketball on the asphalt driveway. When the buggy parked in front of the purple Victorian, he stopped playing and tucked the basketball under his arm. "Yo, Tim! Your family is here."

Ruth leaned forward in her seat again. "That's Danny Lapp."

"Ruthie has a crush on Danny," Becky said.

"I do not," Ruth hissed.

Danny sauntered over to the buggy with the basketball still under his arm.

"Want to come to the flea market with us today, Danny?" Grandfather Zook asked.

"He *is* the most handsome horse in the county," Becky said, coming to Sparky's defense.

Sparky wiggled his ears, and Naomi, now curled up on Becky's lap in the backseat, laughed.

I moved my foot and knocked Grandfather Zook's crutches that were tucked under the front bench seat. "I'm sorry."

He glanced down. "Don't worry about those old things. They are built to last. You wouldn't believe how many times I've dropped them off the buggy."

"Why do you need them?" As soon as it came out of my mouth, I regretted my question.

Grandfather Zook smiled. "I had polio when I was a child."

"Oh. You weren't vaccinated?" I squirmed. "I'm sorry. That's a personal question."

He laughed. "I'm glad you think I'm that young, but I had polio long before the vaccine was out. I made sure my daughter had all my *grandkinner* vaccinated. It took some convincing for my son-in-law to agree."

"The Amish usually don't vaccinate their children?"

"There are no rules against it, but many times they don't because they don't know any better. I do, so I insisted."

I thought about that as we fell into a peaceful silence. For the next thirty minutes, the only sounds were the *clomp, clomp* of Sparky's hooves on the pavement and the rattle of the buggy.

I shifted as my back began to ache from leaning against the hard wooden seat. No one else seemed to be uncomfortable, not even Grandfather Zook.

"Almost there." Becky pointed to a line of buggies and cars that appeared on the side of the road. "They are all here for the flea market. People, *Englisch* and Amish, come from all over."

"Best sales in the county," Grandfather Zook declared. "Parking lot must be full. Not to worry, though, I always have a place to park."

"Ellie Young lets *Grossdaddi* park the buggy behind the restaurant. She won't let anyone else park there." Becky laughed. "Ellie Young's a widow and has eyes for *Grossdaddi*."

Grandfather Zook snorted. "Your *grossmammi* and Ellie were *freinden*. *Grossmammi* asked Ellie to look after me after she was gone. That's the end of that."

"Ellie takes her job seriously," Becky said in a mock somber tone.

Grandfather Zook's grinning face reflected in the buggy's glossy dash.

We passed buggies of all shapes and sizes. Some had orange triangles on the back, others had headlights and taillights, and still others had simple white strips of reflective tape. I'd never noticed the variation before. "The buggies aren't identical," I said. "I thought they would be. Some have headlights."

"Mine has headlights too." He pointed to the switch on the dash. "The bishop permitted battery-operated headlights in our district."

"That's allowed?"

"It's for safety," he said. "You can tell by the buggy what type of Amish it is. Most of the folks around here are Old Order, like us, but there are a few Swartentruber Amish. They are the strictest. Those are the buggies without the SMV, or slow moving vehicle, triangles. They are also the ones you see selling baskets on the side of the road. They rarely work outside of the farm. For instance, they wouldn't run any of the shops in town," Grandfather Zook explained.

"Why not?"

"It is the rules of their order." He spoke as if that was answer enough.

Becky peeked over the front seat. "The kids aren't even allowed to ride bicycles."

"I never knew there were different types of Amish," I said. "Most English people think all Amish are the same."

Grandfather Zook nodded. "One size doesn't fit all." He laughed.

I frowned.

"Don't feel bad. Some Amish think all *Englisch* are the same."

Finally, Young's Flea Market and Restaurant came into view. "Wow." The parking lot could easily hold three hundred cars. It was packed with Amish buggies, cars, trucks, tractor trailers, and motorcycles.

Grandfather Zook grinned.

A huge sign welcomed us to the market. Beyond the enormous parking lot stood a large white building that resembled a farmhouse, the words YOUNG'S FAMILY KITCHEN emblazoned on the front. Oak rockers lined the restaurants wide front porch, and diners rocked back and forth while waiting for an early lunch table.

As the buggy rounded the corner of the restaurant, the first pavilion came into view. Amish and English visitors moved in and out of the pavilion weighed down with fresh produce and wrapped packages.

I had never seen so many happy customers. "This is amazing."

Becky nodded at me. "You should see it on auction day." Some of the old cheerfulness was back in her voice.

Grandfather Zook didn't even have to tell Sparky what to do. The old racehorse trotted the perimeter of the parking lot and looped around the back of the restaurant. He stopped beside Timothy's truck parked near the restaurant's "Deliveries only" door. Apparently, Ellie extended parking rights to the entire family. The children waved, and as Grandfather Zook parked the buggy, Timothy grabbed the reins and tied Sparky to a hitching post.

Becky and Naomi jumped from the buggy.

"You guys are too slow." Thomas balanced Naomi on his hip. She took up half his body length and her feet almost touched the gravel on the ground. "We've been here for ages."

I grinned at them. "You had a little more horsepower than we did."

Thomas laughed and set his sister on her feet.

The back screen door to the restaurant opened and a plump Amish woman with steel gray hair and a white prayer cap stepped outside. Her plain dress was light blue and she wore a white apron with "Young's Family Kitchen" stitched on the pocket. "I thought I heard you and Sparky coming. Glad to see you out and about, Joseph. You brought the whole brood with you. Coming in for a bite?" She picked up a large wooden crate that was leaning against the back wall of the restaurant. Timothy took it from her and placed it on the ground beside Grandfather Zook's side of the buggy.

"My daughter wouldn't like it if we filled up on all your good food and weren't able to eat her home cooking." Grandfather Zook smiled.

She snorted. "I'm certain you have a hollow leg, Joseph Zook. You can eat my meal *and* hers."

I climbed out of the buggy, my exit not as graceful as Becky's.

Grandfather Zook handed Timothy his titanium crutches and stepped out of the buggy. Timothy held the crutches in one hand and steadied his grandfather with the other. Safely on the ground, Grandfather Zook slipped his crutches onto his forearms.

Ellie looked me over "Who's this?"

"This is Chloe," Thomas announced. "She's an *Englischer*."

Her chin bounced and she grinned at Thomas. "Her blue jeans were my first tip."

"You must be new to the county. I thought I knew everyone. This wouldn't be another relative of yours from Lancaster now would it, Joseph?"

I stepped forward. "I'm from Cleveland. I moved here to take a job at Harshberger College."

She nodded. "That's probably why I haven't seen you yet. Can't say I have much use for the college. I'm Ellie Young. Don't believe a word any of these children say about me." She gave them a mock scowl, then directed her attention back to Grandfather Zook. "If you're not here to eat my good cooking, what brings you out this way?"

"Chloe does," he replied. "She needs furniture for her new home, and your flea market is the best place in the county."

A smile spread across Ellie's wide mouth. "That's a fact. When they see a naïve *Englisch* girl like you coming, some of the old timers might try to pull one over you on their prices. Stay close to Joseph. He'll keep them in check." She wiped her hand on her apron. "I'd better get back into the kitchen. We have a new baker on hand. You'd think she's never seen a pie before by her crust crimping." She gave Grandfather Zook a beady look. "You'd better promise to stop in the restaurant for a piece of pie before you go."

"Since you badgered me into it, I guess I will." He returned her look with a grin.

She harrumphed and went back inside the kitchen.

Ruth pulled on his arm. "Can I go find Anna now, please? She's been waiting forever."

He tugged at his beard. "Ya, you can go. Take Thomas and Naomi with you."

Her expression fell.

"They might as well have some fun too." He tweaked the ear of his youngest grandson. "Do you want to go with Ruthie or help us shop?"

"Ruthie," he said immediately.

"See?" Grandfather Zook said. "Now, go before I change my mind and make all of you shop with us."

Ruth grabbed Naomi and Thomas's hands and ran off.

Becky gave Sparky a parting pat, and then we followed Grandfather Zook toward the flea market. Despite his crutches, he moved confidently.

Three long shelter houses, standing in three straight lines behind the restaurant, comprised the flea market. Crowded with English and Amish alike, they sold everything from fresh strawberries to sneakers. As we strolled down the first aisle, I took in the colors and smells. An Amish man stirred popcorn kernels with a long-handled spatula in a black cast iron pot that hung from a cooking tripod over a fire. The smell of fresh kettle corn and campfire hung heavy in air.

Next to him, an English woman with three-inch-long red fingernails sold Beanie Babies. Had she collected them at the height of the fad? There were hundreds. An Amish girl about Becky's age held a rainbow bear in her hand. Her father said something in their language; reluctantly, she dropped the bear back onto the table.

Across from the kettle corn, crudely drawn cardboard signs advertised vegetables for sale, such as *Ohio-grown heirloom tomatoes.* Amish women sold eggplants, zucchinis, carrots, and every other vegetable imaginable.

An Amish boy ran by me with a box of potatoes and bumped into a teenager texting on her cell phone. She glared at him.

Beyond the vegetables, another group of Amish women sold fruit-filled fry pies and cobblers. The baked goods all sat in clear plastic boxes so shoppers could see the contents. Next to the baked goods, an English man in a black leather vest sold hunting knives and fishing poles from the back of his tractor-trailer.

I threw my hands into the air. "I don't know where to start."

"Don't worry." Timothy watched me, his gaze assuring. "*Grossdaddi* knows where all the deals are."

Becky stepped closer to her brother, her voice a harsh whisper. "*Grossdaddi*," she said. "Everyone is staring at us."

I followed her line of sight and realized—she was right.

Chapter Twenty

"Let 'em stare." Grandfather Zook adjusted the braces on his arms.

Becky shook her head tightly. "I knew this was a bad idea."

Timothy put a hand on his sister's shoulder. "Let's not stand around and give them something to gawk at. The furniture is in the next pavilion."

We wove through the crowd. I tried to ignore the whispers in both English and Pennsylvania Dutch as we passed booths selling sweet corn, fresh bread, purses, tennis shoes, and antique buttons.

The second pavilion was identical to the first—a cement slap with thick white-washed posts holding up an asphalt roof. Where the first pavilion was a hodgepodge of wares, the second pavilion had a theme: furniture. It was easy to tell the Amish from the English furniture. Nearly everything in the Amish section was made of light-colored wood varnished to a high sheen. The scent of vinegar polish hung heavy in the pavilion. The English furniture was secondhand and contained everything from an old beauty shop hair dryer chair to an Art Deco glass end table.

Grandfather Zook stopped and looked around. "Where should we start?"

Timothy and Becky watched me for direction.

I rubbed my lips together, glancing about. "We could use a couch."

Within twenty minutes we had reclined on half a dozen different sofas. As I stood up from a particularly ugly orange leather couch, I noticed the color of Grandfather Zook's face had paled to white-gray.

"Maybe we should head home," I said. "Now that I know the flea market is here, I can come back another time and shop for furniture."

Grandfather Zook shook his head. "Don't worry about me." He coughed. "I could use a cup of water."

"I'll find you one," Becky volunteered and ran back toward the restaurant.

Grandfather Zook stood on his crutches. Timothy stood close by, ready to catch his grandfather if necessary. Grandfather Zook coughed again and cleared his throat. "I told you I'm fine." He started down the line of furniture again and pulled up short, pointing to a blue plush sofa jammed between a television cabinet and a bookshelf. "What about that one?"

I squeezed behind the television cabinet and sat on the couch. "I like it." I flipped over the price tag pinned to the arm. "Eighty bucks! I like it even more now."

Grandfather Zook snorted. "That's too much."

A large man with a gray beard and mustache approached us. "May I help you?" The mustache gave him away as English. Well, that and his Beatles T-shirt.

"I'd like to buy this couch," I said.

Grandfather Zook tapped his right crutch on the cement. "Eighty dollars is high. What else will you throw in with it?"

The man ran a finger along his mustache and sized up

Grandfather Zook. Then he turned toward me. "Is there anything else you'd like?"

"I could use some tables for the living room." I spied a dark wood set that included two end tables and a coffee table. "I like these."

"We'll take all four pieces for eighty dollars." Grandfather Zook's eyes sparkled, his complexion no longer gray.

The salesman's eyes narrowed. "I'll give you all four pieces for one thirty."

Grandfather Zook tugged on his beard. "Ninety."

"No way," the man said.

Grandfather Zook waved me over. "Come on, Chloe, we will go somewhere else."

Reluctantly, I stood.

"Fine," the man grumbled. "One hundred dollars."

Grandfather Zook grinned. "Sold!"

The man reached into his pocket for his receipt tablet, his mouth twisted as if annoyed.

I couldn't wait to tell Tanisha about my finds. She was the real bargain hunter between us. If she and Grandfather Zook ever joined forces, they would be dangerous.

Becky approached us carrying a paper cup of water, and Grandfather Zook took notice of her. "I'll let you finish up here, and go wait with Becky." He pointed at a blue velvet sofa two booths away. "I'll be waiting over there."

Timothy and I agreed.

Timothy smiled after his grandfather, then moved his gaze to me. "I've never seen anyone so excited about furniture before."

I blushed. "Are you sure everything will fit in your truck?"

"No problem. I've hauled twice that before."

Ten minutes later, Timothy and I found Grandfather Zook on the velvet sofa. Becky was no where to be seen. However, Grandfather Zook was not alone. Deacon Sutter stood in front of him with his arms crossed in front of his chest. The deacon stood up straight, as if a yard stick ran the length of his spine. His black plain jacket was spotless and without wrinkles, and his hat sat atop the center of his head.

The deacon glared at us. "Joseph, you have all your grandchildren with you today. I'm surprised by this."

"Ya, even my *grandkinner.*" Grandfather Zook winked at me. "Here are two of them now."

I smiled back. Grandfather Zook considered me one of his grandchildren.

The deacon nodded at Timothy, then turned his dark stare to me. "You were at the accident. Who are you?"

I bit my tongue to hold back a smart remark. "I'm Chloe Humphrey."

"Humphrey is not an Amish name."

"I'm not Amish." As if I could be mistaken for Amish considering I wore jeans, a T-shirt, and sandals.

Deacon Sutter scowled at Grandfather Zook. "I thought you said she was one of your *grandkinner.* From Pennsylvania? Maybe a Beachy? They are loose like you are."

My brow wrinkled. *What's a Beachy?*

"My grandfather was making a joke," Timothy said.

The deacon's jaw twitched, and his eyes narrowed further as he scrutinized me. "You're the owner of the car."

"I am."

He turned his back to me. "Joseph, Preacher Hooley and I visited your son-in-law and daughter this morning."

Grandfather Zook struggled to his feet. Timothy helped his grandfather up. "Why?"

"For the sake of the rest of the family, it would be best if you distanced yourself from Rebecca and the *Englischer.* It is not good for the younger children to be around them."

Grandfather Zook didn't answer right away. Instead he took his time slipping his crutches onto his thin arms with Timothy by his side. "What did my daughter and son-in-law say?"

"They will follow the advice of the church." He smirked. "They always do."

"You may be able to intimidate my son-in-law, but you can't do that to me." He stamped a crutch on the cement ground.

"You shouldn't be talking to my grandfather alone, Deacon," Timothy said. "You don't have a witness to this conversation." With Grandfather Zook's weight supported on the crutches, Timothy let go of his grandfather's arm.

"You're not Amish anymore, Timothy. I don't see why you have a right to comment on our ways. You made your choice. In your case it was the right decision for the district."

Timothy recoiled as if the deacon had just slapped him across the mouth. "At least I can choose what rules to follow."

Deacon Sutter bared his teeth. "You may have decided to leave our district, but the rest of your family has not. You should think of how your behavior and your sister Rebecca's will affect them."

I stepped around the deacon and stood on the other side of Grandfather Zook. Deacon Sutter's stormy expression sent a shiver down my spine. He glared back at me before stomping away.

"*Grossdaddi*," Timothy began. "You shouldn't speak to the deacon that way."

Grandfather Zook snorted. "And what were you doing?"

Timothy frowned. "The deacon is right. It is different for me." He didn't sound happy about that.

"Deacon Sutter has no use for our family. Timothy, you know that better than anyone."

I watched Timothy's face, his mouth twisted in sadness.

"Why does the deacon feel that way?" I asked.

He didn't answer.

I was beginning to realize the Amish world was much more complicated and less tranquil than I ever thought. *If the deacon disliked the Troyers, would he cut the brake line of my car to hurt Becky, their daughter? Maybe Curt and Brock aren't my only enemies in Knox County.*

Grandfather Zook shook his head. "Let's not talk about that man."

"Where's Becky?" I asked.

"When the deacon showed up, I told her to go find her brother and sisters. They are going to meet us at the restaurant for a piece of pie. We'd better get going. You don't want Ellie to come after me, do you?"

Timothy and I followed Grandfather Zook through the maze of furniture. Before we reached the first pavilion, Becky walked up to us. Ruth hugged her around the waist, her thin shoulders bobbing up and down. Thomas held Naomi close. All four children looked stricken.

Grandfather Zook increased his pace. "What happened? Is someone hurt?"

Ruth mumbled something into her sister's dress.

Becky tucked a stray blonde hair under her sister's bonnet. "Anna's father won't let her see Ruth." Tears pooled in her blue eyes. "It's because of me."

Chapter Twenty-One

Grandfather Zook ushered the family into Young's Family Kitchen, insisting a piece of pie would make everyone feel better. I had my doubts. Ruth couldn't stop crying. I imagined how I would feel if Tanisha's parents forbade her to see me.

We entered the restaurant at the height of the lunch rush. Senior citizens in wheelchairs and walkers complained as they waited for tables, and families with young children perused the gift shop and bakery to distract their toddlers until it was time to sit down and eat.

Ellie spotted us as soon as we stepped through the door. She sidestepped her hostess, a young Amish woman, and grabbed a handful of menus. "I was afraid you left without pie." She tsked. "I have your table right over here." She made a beeline for an open table by a large picture window overlooking a cornfield east of Young's property. A red barn sat just beyond the field, making the scene look like an oil painting.

As soon as we sat down, Ellie removed a notepad and pen from her white apron pocket. "What would you all like?"

Without opening the menu, the Troyer family ordered. They came to Young's often and knew the offerings.

Ruth had downcast eyes. "I'm not hungry."

Ellie shook her pen at Ruth. "You need chocolate pie. I can always tell when a girl needs a big piece of my chocolate silk pie."

The corners of Ruth's mouth turned up ever so slightly, and she gave her choice.

Ellie scribbled down the order. "What kind of pie would you like, Chloe?"

I flipped through the tabletop menu. Each page had a photograph of a delicious-looking piece of pie. "It's too hard to decide."

"The mixed berry is good," Ruth said.

"With ice cream," Thomas replied.

Ruth nodded in agreement. "With ice cream."

I decided my diet started tomorrow. "I'll have the mixed berries with ice cream then." The smile my choice brought to Ruth's face was worth the calories.

After Ellie left the table, I excused myself in search of the restroom. As I moved through the gift shop, a little boy in a Cleveland Indians T-shirt tried to convince his mother to buy him a stuffed tiger. A small waiting area with rocking chairs outside the restroom was empty. When I exited the restroom, two Amish women sat in those white rocking chairs, flour on their aprons and their feet swollen from working in the restaurant's bakery. They didn't appear to notice me.

I was about to slip by them when the older of the two women spoke. "Deacon Sutter finally has his chance to be a preacher."

"And maybe bishop too," the younger added.

"No, that won't happen."

I took a step back into the alcove.

The younger one frowned. "It could."

The older one leaned her head to one side. "Ya, maybe now that the bishop is gone. Bishop Glick would have never allowed it."

Did the deacon cut the brake line on my car to get the bishop out of the way? I pushed the wayward thought from my head, yet I knew I would feel safer if Becky or I weren't the intended targets for the sabotage.

"The bishop will be missed. We need him now more than ever." The younger of the pair sighed. "Did you hear about Deacon Sutter's soybean field?"

"No. What happened?"

"*Englischer* drove through it and destroyed almost every plant. I heard it from his son. He was there at the time. Of course, he couldn't do anything considering . . ."

The older woman shook her head. "The deacon wouldn't let his son do anything if he'd been able to."

In the restroom doorway, I shivered. The attacks on the Amish farms had to be related to Becky's accident, didn't they? Why was Chief Rose so reluctant to consider that? *And why would they cut the brake line on my car?* I took a deep breath and considered that maybe I was forcing the connection between the two incidents. Yet the prospect that they weren't connected was too terrifying to consider, because that would mean that two different people were causing trouble in Knox County. *Who knew Cleveland would be the safer place to live?*

"You're right, but people are scared. I heard the Fishers may move. They have family in the district in Colorado."

"Colorado." The older one snorted, then rubbed her knee and sighed. "It's a shame about the Troyer girl."

"She is a pretty one, but too flighty. No one was surprised when she decided she'd rather live with the *Englisch.* My daughter said she draws portraits." She spoke in a conspiratorial whisper. "The deacon spoke to her father about it several times."

The older woman murmured something I couldn't make out.

I knew I should make my exit, but found no way to do so gracefully. So I continued to hover in the ladies' room doorway.

The younger one continued, apparently rested. "Her older brother was a surprise though."

"He was." The older woman nodded. "He broke hearts when he left."

"But the deacon was happy."

"Of course he was—after what happened."

"We shouldn't speak of that. I saw the deacon here earlier," the younger woman added in a whisper.

Her friend agreed.

My breath caught. Had Timothy left someone he cared about behind when he left the Amish community? What could have happened to make the deacon happy that a member of his district left the Amish?

The older woman tucked a stray hair into her white cap. "The family still sees Timothy often."

"That's Joseph Zook's influence. He's from Lancaster."

"Ah." The second one nodded as if that explained Grandfather Zook's behavior.

Stranded, I wondered if I should go back into the bathroom until they left when one of the women said, "Hello, Becky, how are you doing?"

I peeked out to see Becky give the pair a tentative smile. "*Gut, danki.*"

The older one spoke. "We were so sorry to hear the news."

The younger woman nodded. "Very sorry."

"*Danki.*"

The pair seemed to have gained steam. The woman leaned forward in their rockers, listening.

"Can you tell us what happened?" the older woman asked.

I stepped out of the bathroom doorway.

Becky noticed me and let out a breath. "Chloe, there you are. Our pie is on the table. Timothy asked me to find you. He was afraid you might have gotten lost."

I smiled. "I'm fine."

The two women had the good sense to blush.

As we left, Becky smiled back at the women. "It was nice to see you." We made our way to the table, and Becky turned to me. "Is something wrong, Chloe? You look upset."

"I'm fine." I forced a bright smile onto my face. "I can't wait for that piece of pie." *At least that much is true.*

Chapter Twenty-Two

We left Young's after three. My furniture was then loaded into the back of Timothy's pickup and tied down with neon green bungee cords. Timothy helped Grandfather Zook into the buggy, and the three younger Troyer children climbed into the back.

Grandfather Zook winked. "I must get the *grandkinner* back to the farm to their *mamm*. She's going to be mad at me already for having them home late for supper."

Ruth, who seemed to have perked up while eating her chocolate silk pie, frowned.

Becky squeezed her little sister's hand and whispered in her ear. But Ruth shook her head, and Becky stepped back from the buggy with tears in her eyes.

Grandfather Zook flicked the reins, and Sparky pulled the buggy away from the hitching post. Timothy, Becky, and I waited until the buggy rounded the corner before climbing into the truck.

Becky rode in silence, wedged between Timothy and me. The ride, which had taken thirty minutes by buggy, took only ten by car.

At the house, Becky and I each carried in an end table, while Timothy set the coffee table in the middle of the room. Then with Becky holding open the door, Timothy and I carried in the couch and set it in the middle of the room. Becky flopped onto it. "I might sleep here tonight."

I leaned my head to one side. "You can if you want to."

Gig jumped onto the back of the sofa, walking its length until he found a comfortable place to curl up.

Timothy laughed. "I think your cat likes it."

I nodded. "I think so."

Timothy moved toward the door. "I'd better get going. I have a job I promised to finish today." He glanced at his sister. "Are you coming to church tomorrow, Becky?"

Becky's nose wrinkled. "I can't, Timothy. Everyone will be talking about me. You saw what happened between Anna and Ruth. I can't take more of that. I hope Ruth will speak to me again."

He furrowed his brow. "Who said she wasn't speaking to you?"

Becky eyed him. "She didn't say good-bye at Young's."

"She was upset."

Becky flung her good arm over her face. "For good reason."

"So are you coming to church tomorrow? People are more likely to talk if you aren't there. Maybe if they see you, they will think twice."

Becky sat up. "I'll go if Chloe goes."

"I . . ." Since I'd moved to Appleseed Creek, I had every intention of finding a new church to attend, but the previous Sunday I'd found an excuse to avoid it. I would never admit it to anyone but myself, but I was afraid. Entering a new church where everyone already knew each other and had a history was a terrifying prospect. In Cleveland, I'd attended the same church with the Green family since Tanisha invited me to Sunday school in the second grade.

Timothy was probably right. If Becky didn't go to church tomorrow, tongues would be wagging. I knew how gossip spread through a church. I remembered how people had talked after my mother's accident. Not all the talk had been malicious, but even well-intentioned gossip hurt.

I shrugged as if it were no big deal. "Sure, I can go."

Becky gave me one of her dazzling smiles and flopped back down on the couch.

I followed Timothy to his truck. "Can I talk to you a minute?"

He slammed the tailgate of his pickup, and I jumped.

"Are you nervous?" Timothy asked.

"Me? Nervous? No."

"You seem to be jumpy every time I see you."

I shrugged. He was the one who made me nervous, but should I tell him that? "I'm worried about Becky."

Timothy followed me, his brows knitted in concern. "How is my sister?"

I turned to face him. "Much better than I would be, but I have a feeling it might get worse for her before it gets better." I told him about my encounter with the women at the farmers' market and outside the restroom at Young's.

Timothy let out a long, slow sigh. "That's what I was afraid of. Bishop Glick was a favorite. Many are devastated at the news. Not just for him and his family, but for themselves. The district will have to choose a new bishop, and he might not be as popular as Bishop Glick."

"Does the district elect the new bishop?"

He shook his head. "It's not like running for president, if that's what you think. The preachers from the area churches will be held up as possible bishops, and God chooses the leader from them. I've never actually seen a bishop being chosen since I didn't join the church."

It sounded like an odd way to choose a leader to me. "Did everyone like the bishop?"

"No one is universally liked."

"I'm worried about this thing with Anna, too." I hugged myself about the waist. "This doesn't just affect Becky. Your whole family is involved."

"I know that." His blue eyes scanned my face. "How are you?"

"Afraid. I thought a lot about what you said last night"—I gazed into his concerned eyes—"that I could have been killed."

"Because your car was in disrepair." He shook the tailgate as if to make sure it was latched properly.

"No, it's worse than that. Chief Rose was here this morning."

His forehead wrinkled. "She was? Why didn't you or Becky say anything?"

"I didn't want to talk about it in front of the kids."

"What did she say?"

I took a deep breath. "That my car was fine. Someone cut the brake line."

Timothy's eyes grew wide, and he pounded his fist on the gate of his truck. "What?"

I took a step back, and then told him what the police chief said about the condition of the car.

He wagged his head back and forth. Slowly. "She thinks someone tried to kill you and Becky?"

"Or hurt us. Yes."

"Who?"

"I don't know, but it could be two men in town named Curt and Brock. They were harassing Becky when I met her. "

His eyes flashed angrily. "Greta thinks these men cut the brake line?"

"They are one possibility. She was going to question them. I imagine she already has by now."

His eyes bored into me, his jaw set. "Both of you need to be careful."

"I know." The nauseous feeling from that morning washed over me again. I needed to think about something other than my fear. *Becky. Think about Becky.* "Becky's still in trouble too. Even though the brake line was cut and the accident wasn't completely her fault, she will always be blamed for what happened." I paused, allowing my eyes to meet his. "Unless we do something."

"Like what?" He folded up the neon green bungee cords and dropped them in a white bucket in the bed of his truck.

"Maybe the police are wrong. Maybe the bishop was the intended victim all along."

Timothy frowned. "What are you saying?"

"We need to find out what really happened."

"We?"

"I need your help, Timothy. I could never find out everything I need from the Amish. You can."

He shook his head, his lips pressed into a grim line. "Chloe, you don't understand. I grew up Amish, but I'm not Amish anymore. There's a difference. A big difference. Deacon Sutter made that clear today."

"You are still closer than I could ever be." I placed my hand on the edge of the tailgate.

He sighed.

I held my gaze on him. "Will you help me?"

"I will do whatever I can to protect my sister"—he paused—"and you." He covered my hand with his own and squeezed it for a fraction of a second. His motion was so quick, I wondered if it really happened.

My stomach did a flip, but not from fear.

Timothy walked toward the driver's side of his truck and stopped, his gaze fixed on me again. "Do you need a ride to church tomorrow?"

I shook my head. "It's not far. We can walk."

He nodded, hopped into his truck, and drove away.

Chapter Twenty-Three

Timothy and Becky attended a Mennonite church two blocks from Appleseed Creek's square. It was another beautiful day, and I was happy we could walk to enjoy the weather. It also gave me a chance to burn off another of Becky's colossal breakfasts. I knew she missed her family, but my cholesterol levels shouldn't be put into jeopardy because of it.

I wore a knee-length skirt and a white blouse, and Becky wore an ankle-length skirt and blue T-shirt she'd worn the day before. Note to self: take her clothes shopping soon. It might be a fun outing and get our minds off the accident.

The church was a simple white building with a steeple, but I didn't see a cross outside. "Is this church much different from your parents'?"

Becky scrunched her brows. "My family doesn't go to a church building for Sunday meeting. Old Order Amish don't have church buildings. The Amish have services in homes in the district." She glanced at the simple structure. "This is the first church building I've ever been inside."

"Oh." I cocked my chin. "But Mennonites build churches? Why?"

She shrugged. "They're just different." She said this as if it were explanation enough, but I suspected something deeper than that.

Although Becky had insisted my outfit was fine for church, I felt self-conscious when we started up the walkway. All the women and girls wore long skirts similar to Becky's. I tugged at the hem of mine, willing it to grow another twelve inches.

Despite the long skirts, the women wore colors and patterns. Many sported flowered blouses similar to the one Becky wore when I met her on the side of the road.

Becky took a deep breath. Three young women about Becky's age stood at the base of the church's cement steps.

"You okay?" I asked.

She straightened her shoulders. "I can do this."

I squeezed her hand. "Of course you can."

She walked up to them, and I followed. A pretty brunette held out her hand to me. "Welcome to our church. I'm Hannah Hilty. You must be Chloe."

I blinked at her use of my name. Then again, I imagined the buggy accident had been a big topic of conversation in the Amish and Mennonite communities in Knox County.

I shook her hand. "Nice to meet you, Hannah."

She pointed to her friend with bright red cheeks. Was she embarrassed or recovering from a sunburn? "This is Emily," Hannah said. She pointed to a second friend, this one rail thin and at least six feet tall. I wondered how she found skirts long enough for her frame. "And that's Kim."

I waved a hello.

Hannah examined Becky's cast, now covered with the signatures of her siblings, grandfather, and me. "Becky, I'm glad to see you're not more seriously injured. Does it hurt?"

Becky wrapped her left hand protectively around the cast. "Not much."

"Have you spoken to Isaac?" Kim asked.

Becky tilted up her chin to look at the much taller girl.

"Do you know Isaac?" I asked. "Are you former Amish too?"

Emily snorted. "She thinks we're Amish."

Hannah looked annoyed. "No, we are all Mennonites. The church has a few former Amish members like Timothy, but most of us have never been Amish."

Definitely the wrong question to ask. My first day at a new church and I was already inserting my foot in my mouth.

"Is Timothy here?" I asked.

Hannah's eyes narrowed. "Are you looking for him?"

What's her problem?

The church bell rang, cutting our conversation short. We headed inside to find wooden pews, white walls, and not a shard of stained glass in the place. Across the sanctuary, Timothy laughed at something his roommate Danny said. He looked handsome in dress pants, a blue button-down shirt, and a solid blue tie. It was the first time I'd seen him in anything other than work clothes.

He looked across the pews in my direction, and his eyes lit up, making my heart skip a beat. But his gaze didn't meet mine. I turned and saw Hannah's eyes locked on his, a full-mouthed smile greeting him.

I looked away and bit the inside of my lip.

Becky gave her brother a big hug as he approached us. "Chloe came just like she said she would."

He smiled at me. "I never doubted that she would."

My cheeks grew hot.

Hannah sidestepped me. "Timothy, we missed you at the social yesterday." She pouted.

"Sorry I couldn't make it," he said.

Hannah glanced at Becky. "I hope it wasn't because of the accident. I'm glad to see Becky is okay. We were so worried." She turned to her friends. "Weren't we, girls?"

"Terrified," red-cheeked Emily said.

Hannah's eyes darted to Becky's cast. "The poor Glick family. I don't know how they will ever recover, and Isaac must be devastated."

Becky gave a small gasp when Hannah mentioned Isaac by name. Tears welled in her eyes, and she blinked them away.

Timothy took a step back from the Mennonite girl. "They are in our prayers."

"Becky, this must be so hard for you, considering how close you were to the Glick family." Hannah wrapped her arm around Becky's shoulder and whispered something to her.

Becky gasped and pulled away. "Excuse me," she whispered and left the church.

Timothy glared at Hannah. "What did you say to her?"

Hannah's eyes grew wide as a doe's. "I said I was praying for her. Why do you think that would upset her?"

The praise band at the front of the church began playing the prelude to the service.

Hannah linked her arm through Timothy's and threw her minions a look. "Let's find our seats." They followed her as she walked with Timothy down the aisle.

Instead of trailing in their wake, I went in search of Becky and found her under a maple tree, cradling her right arm.

"Are you okay?"

She nodded, but tears brimmed her eyes.

"Gee, that Hannah seems like a real sweetheart."

Becky chuckled, but the sound of her laughter died away.

"No wonder you didn't want to come today. What did she say to you?"

She shook her head. "It doesn't matter."

"What's going on between her and Timothy?" I hoped my question sounded casual.

Her brows shot up. "Timothy and Hannah?" She sounded genuinely surprised. "Nothing. Why?"

I shrugged. "No reason. " I doubted Hannah would give me the same answer, but I was happy to hear it from Becky. I changed the subject. "When I get a new car, we need to go shopping. You need some new things to wear to your new job."

"I don't have any money."

"You can pay me back when you get paid."

She grinned. "Okay. Can I buy a pair of jeans?"

I laughed. "You can buy whatever you want." I glanced at the doors to the church. "Are you ready to go inside?"

She inhaled a deep breath. "Yes."

I helped her up, then looped my arm through her good one, and together we strolled back into the church.

Chapter Twenty-Four

As we exited the church an hour later, I spotted Chief Rose across the street leaning against her police cruiser. Church members whispered as they traversed the lawn to their cars. The police chief, with her unwavering gaze and arms crossed at the chest, seemed to revel in the attention.

Becky scowled. "What is she doing here?"

"I have no idea." I scanned the crowd for Timothy. He and Danny stood with Hannah and her pals. I wasn't going to interrupt *that* conversation.

"I can't talk to her here," Becky said. "People will see."

I nodded, licking my lips. "Why don't you start walking home, and I'll talk to her. If she needs you, she knows where to find you."

Becky gave me a grateful smile and hurried down the sidewalk.

I ignored the stares from the people leaving the church as I approached the police chief. "Can I help you with something, Chief Rose?"

"I need to talk to you."

"You know where I live. Why did you have to show up here at church? Becky is already the main topic of conversation in town.

You glowering at us from across the street doesn't help." I paused. "How did you know we would be here anyway?"

She adjusted the aviator sunglasses on her nose. Did she think she looked like a TV cop? "This is the church Becky's been attending, isn't it?"

"How would you know that?"

She shrugged. "It's called police work. This is my town. It's my business to know everything."

I clenched my jaw to stop a smart retort. Sarcasm wasn't going to help Becky.

"I was hoping to talk to both you and Becky, but I guess just you will do."

"What is it?"

"Curt and Brock have an airtight alibi. They were in lockup in the county jail for drunk and disorderly conduct on Friday. They weren't released until eight on Friday morning. According to Becky, she left your house around eight that morning, so the timetable rules them out."

My heart sank. "Maybe they cut the brake line before they were arrested."

Chief Rose shook her head. "The crime scene investigator doesn't think so. He said the line was cut so deeply that he estimates it would have given way your first drive with it."

"So what."

The chief folded her arms across her chest. "So *what*?"

"The last time I drove the car was Wednesday afternoon. There was a lot of time between Wednesday afternoon and Thursday night. They still could have done it."

Chief Rose sighed. "I know that. Wednesday and Thursday they were on a job in Columbus. I have a reliable witness for that one, too."

"Oh." I hadn't realized how much I wanted it to be Curt and Brock, how much I wanted this to all be over. Unfortunately, it was turning out to be a lot harder than I expected.

"Any other possibilities?" the police chief asked.

My shoulders slumped. "I have no idea who else could have done it."

She stared at me intently. "Is there anyone else who doesn't like you?"

Sabrina came to mind, but the thought of my stepmother making the effort was laughable. "No, I can't think of anyone."

She removed her sunglasses, revealing blue eye liner. Did she go through a pencil a week? "They must have been after Becky, then. Do you know if she has any enemies?"

"No."

"She left the Amish, correct? Maybe her family was upset about it." She tapped her sunglasses on her cheek.

I barked a laugh. "Upset enough to cut the brake line in my car? No way."

Her mouth formed a hard line.

I debated telling her my theory that the bishop was the intended victim, but I held my tongue. Truth be told, there were a lot of holes in my idea. First of all, how would the person who cut the brake line know that Becky would come across the bishop on Butler Road? The more I thought about my idea, the more ridiculous it seemed.

"Have you thought about the accident in relation to the problems on the Amish farms?" I asked.

"If Curt and Brock had nothing to do with your car, then the incidents can't be related. I'm almost certain those two are behind damage in the Amish district. I just can't get any Amish witnesses to help me prove it." She opened the door to her cruiser. "I'd be careful, Chloe. Curt and Brock know they were questioned about the accident. They aren't the sharpest tools in the shed, but they'll figure out who turned them in. You see them, you call me."

I shivered. "What about their threats against me? Or driving by my house at night?"

She shrugged as if it didn't matter to her. "You can always open a restraining order on them if you want to."

I didn't like that idea. Maybe telling the police chief my suspicions was enough to encourage them to leave Becky and me alone.

Chief Rose slapped the hood of her car. "I'll be in touch."

I don't doubt it.

She hopped into her cruiser and drove away. When I could no longer see Chief Rose's car, I started down the sidewalk in the direction that Becky went.

Footsteps running behind me on the sidewalk made my heart nearly jump out of my chest. Was it Curt or Brock? I spun around to see Timothy jogging toward me. "Chloe, wait!"

I stopped and tried not to think about Hannah and him together.

"What did Greta say?"

I blinked at him. "Greta?"

His face flushed. "Chief Rose, I mean."

I ignored the knot in my stomach and instead relayed my conversation with the police chief. Despite doubts about my own theory, I added, "We need to make sure it was just a coincidence Bishop Glick was on that road when Becky was."

He nodded.

"What can we do?"

"Nothing today. It's Sunday. The Amish will be at church meetings that will last most of the day."

I was itching to do something, but knew he was right.

He stood close, his head leaning to one side, as if considering our plight. "What time do you get off work tomorrow?"

"I can go in early and leave at four."

"Okay, I'll pick you up at your office then."

"To do what?"

"You'll see." He lightly punched me on the arm before jogging back to the church.

If anyone had heard that conversation, he or she might think Timothy and I had set a date. Sadly, we had not. Guys over eight years old don't punch girls they like on the arm. *At least none of the guys I'd known before moving to Appleseed Creek.*

I glanced back at the church. Timothy and Hannah were talking. Alone. Her two delightful buddies nowhere in view. My meeting with Timothy tomorrow was definitely *not* a date.

As I walked the rest of the way back to the house, my mind drifted away from thoughts of Timothy. Instead, I found myself watching for the green pickup around every corner. Thankfully, I never saw it.

Back at the house, I found Becky curled up on the couch, her legs tucked under her skirt. She held Gigabyte in her lap, and tears rolled down her pale cheeks.

"Becky, are you okay? Did something else happen?"

She nodded but couldn't speak.

I sat across from her on the edge of my new coffee table. "What is it?"

When she didn't answer, I stood and grabbed a box of tissues from the tiny half bath on the first floor. I handed her the box.

Finally, she calmed down enough to speak. "Hannah told me she heard my family wasn't allowed to see me because of the accident."

Wow, that Hannah is a real gem. I perched on the edge of the armchair. "How would she know that?"

"She's friends with Esther Yoder."

"Who is Esther Yoder?"

"An Amish girl. It doesn't matter how she found out. I know it's true. You saw what happened between Ruth and Anna yesterday. It must be bad. The Lambrights and my family are close friends."

"That's ridiculous." I sat back on the coffee table. "We had dinner with your family that night and spent most of yesterday with your grandfather and the children."

Gigabyte wiggled from her grasp and jumped to the top of the couch. He bumped his head against her shoulder.

"That was before. She said Deacon Sutter visited the farm and warned them not to talk to me."

At least this much was true. Its truth made Hannah's story

plausible. "Why would she tell you that anyway?" I was beginning to dislike Hannah more by the second, and my feelings had nothing to do with Timothy's possible affection for her.

She shook her head.

"Let's call Timothy, and he can take us out to the farm to visit your family."

She shook her head. "It's Sunday. They'll be at church. If I show up there, it will be even worse."

"Your family loves you. I saw it, Becky. They are worried about you. Even if what Hannah says is true, they won't let that come between you and your family, especially your younger siblings."

"You don't know what it's like. They won't let me be who I want to be." Her blue eyes were watery pools. "I want to paint portraits. They don't understand that. They say it's wrong, that I'm breaking God's law when I do it. I'm not. I'm trying to capture a little piece of the beauty He made. How can that be wrong?" She dissolved into tears again.

"Becky, look at me."

She lifted her head.

"It's not wrong. It's not. Do you believe me?"

"I'll try," she whispered.

"Let's call Timothy." I hopped off the chair. "I have an idea of how to cheer you up."

She wiped at her eyes. "What?"

"You'll see." I grinned. "You will love it."

And seeing it for myself will put my mind at ease, too.

Chapter Twenty-Five

Timothy turned into our driveway two hours later with Mabel asleep in the tiny backseat. Becky and I climbed in the truck as Timothy waited. "Becky, why didn't you tell me yesterday about the job?"

She shrugged. "I haven't started yet."

"Well, I'm glad Chloe called because I want to see this place. *Daed* would be furious with me if I didn't check it out. Are they open on Sundays?"

"One to seven," I said. "I found their business Web site."

Timothy's brow furrowed as he backed the truck onto Grove Lane. "Will you have to work on Sunday, Becky?"

She shook her head. "Cookie said I didn't have to."

Woof. Mabel was up.

"Who's Cookie?"

Woof.

Timothy pushed his dog's nose into the backseat. "She thinks cookie—"

Woof!

"—means dog biscuit." Timothy sighed. "I suggest we use another name in Mabel's presence."

"Coo—she is my boss. Well, one of them. The other is Scotch."

He peered around Becky at me. "Is she making up these names?"

I wagged my head. "Nope."

He laughed, and I liked the sound of it. "So where is this place?"

"Sand River Road. It's off of Butler." Becky spoke quietly.

Timothy shrugged. "That may be one way to get there, but I know another. It might take a little longer in travel time, but it's a nice day for a drive."

Becky let out the breath she held.

I sat back, happy to avoid the scene of the accident. "Absolutely."

Twenty minutes later, we turned into the parking lot in front of Little Owl Greenhouse. Half a dozen cars dotted the small lot. Every cement statue possible congregated on the right side of the building, from a replica of *David*, to frogs, to dozens of garden gnomes of all shapes and sizes. Overflowing hanging baskets dangled from hooks in the greenhouse's porch eaves, and a rack of garden spades sat by the front door.

Timothy got out of the truck and pushed his seat forward so Mabel could jump out. Becky didn't move. I nudged her. "Don't you want to get out?"

"I'm scared. What if I can't do it? I've never had a job before."

"Never?"

She shook her head. "I helped on the farm. I helped *Mamm* with the younger children."

"That's why we came here today. Timothy and I are with you. We'll make sure it's okay. You won't have to be afraid tomorrow."

"I wasn't afraid until we got here."

"I knew you would be."

"How?"

"Because I was afraid before I started my new job."

She stared at me. "At Harshberger?"

I nodded.

"You seemed fine your first day."

"I'm good at hiding it," I said. "Now, get out."

She opened the cabin door. "What about Mabel?" Becky asked.

Timothy pointed at a hand-painted sign next to the front door: WELL-BEHAVED DOGS WELCOME. He bent down until eye to eye with his dog. "That means you need to show your best manners, Miss."

She barked softly, as if she understood exactly what he said.

The inside of Little Owl Greenhouse smelled like fertilizer and dirt. The front showroom held more lawn ornaments, garden tools, and dozens of birdfeeders. Beyond that an open garage door separated the shop from the main part of the greenhouse where plants were housed. Bright sunlight shone through the Plexiglas ceiling, warming the plants to their full potential. The shop's cash register sat on a no-frills plank wooden counter.

I watched Becky as she took it in.

A woman at the cash register, who looked like she bought stock in Cover Girl makeup, accepted a twenty-dollar bill from an elderly man buying a hanging basket of purple petunias. A pair of rainbow-framed reading glasses hung from a red ribbon around her neck. "Don't forget to pinch them after each flower fades," she advised. "That's how you will keep it blooming."

The man picked up his basket, promised to take good care of it, and shuffled out of the greenhouse.

The woman with the clown makeup smiled. "Can I help you find something?"

I poked Becky in the back, my voice a whisper. "Introduce yourself."

Becky's eyes had grown to twice their normal size. Had she ever met anyone with such an obvious love of makeup? The woman wore hot pink lipstick and eye shadow that covered her from eyelid to eyebrow in peacock blue.

The woman's gaze fell to Becky's cast, and for a second, she appeared suspended in time, just like Becky.

"You must be Becky!" The woman hurried around the counter. "So glad to meet you! I'm Cookie MacGruen." The foundation on her forehead creased. "Didn't I tell you to come in tomorrow? I hope we didn't get our wires crossed."

Becky stayed silent.

"Becky's not starting until tomorrow." I held out my hand. "Hi, I'm Chloe. We were in the neighborhood, so Timothy"—I pointed to Timothy—"her brother and I wanted to see where she would be working."

"You chose a good day to come. It's the end of summer, and our business is winding down for the growing season."

Her comment gave me pause. If their business was winding down, why did they hire Becky?

"You have to meet my husband." She turned her head. "Scotch, get out here!"

Nothing. Crickets.

"Scotch!"

Mabel, who sat at Timothy's feet, whimpered and covered one of her ears with her paw. I wished I could do the same. If Cookie yelled like that one more time, there was a chance we would all be deaf before the day ended.

A chubby man, about a foot shorter than Cookie and who wore denim overalls over a tie-dye T-shirt, limped through the open garage door. "What is all that yellin' about? Are you trying to give me a stroke?"

"Scotch, we have guests."

"I can see that," he grunted and held onto a sales rack of garden tools for support.

"Becky's here," his wife said.

One side of his forehead drooped down. "Becky?"

Cookie looked to us and shook her head. "You will have to forgive my husband. He spent too much time restocking fertilizer today, and the fumes have gone to his head." She put her hands on her hips. "Becky is the Amish girl. Remember?"

"The girl who was in the accident that killed the Amish monk?"

Cookie shook her head. "He was a bishop."

"Monk? Bishop? Aren't they all the same?"

Not exactly.

Becky tensed up beside me.

Cookie winced. "My husband's not one to beat around the bush."

No kidding.

"If you are Becky, who are these two?" He flicked his thumb toward Timothy and me. "Cookie, I hope you didn't hire all three of them."

Cookie scowled at her husband. "Don't pay any attention to him. He's only teasing."

Becky still seemed unable to speak. This time Timothy made introductions.

"Have you shown them around, Cook?" Scotch grasped the straps of his overalls, moving them like puppet strings.

"That's what I was calling you for, you dolt. I thought you'd want to."

"'Course, I would." He looked unfazed by the name-calling. He hobbled in the direction of the greenhouse, then stopped and looked behind him. "Y'all comin' or what?"

We hurried after him.

We stepped into the greenhouse, the first section under a green roof. Automatic misters spread water droplets that evaporated almost as soon as they hit the hot air. *Must be what steamed broccoli feels like.*

"This is where we keep all our tropical plants, as well as others that wouldn't make it three minutes through one of our frigid Ohio winters," Scotch explained. "Becky, you will be working in here a lot until your arm's healed. There's not too much heavy lifting."

Timothy tapped a finger on a bird-of-paradise, and the leaf bounced back in his face. I hid my smile. He caught me watching him and winked. I blushed and hoped he'd think I was flushed from the stifling humidity. I cleared my throat. "What type of work will Becky be doing, Scotch?"

His eyes darted back and forth. "We haven't—"

"This and that." Cookie, who had followed along behind, interrupted her husband. "We'll have her pitch in where we need help. There's always watering, pruning, and weeding to do. You've done all that before, haven't you, Becky?"

Becky nodded.

I elbowed her.

"Yes, I helped my mother care for our garden back home and helped my father in the fields too. We grew lots of different vegetables and flowers."

"See, she will have no trouble." Scotch waved us on. "Next up is ground covering." He winced as he started walking again.

"Are you okay?" I asked.

A strange expression crossed Scotch's face. "Yes."

"You seem to have some trouble walking."

Scotch opened his mouth, but Cookie chimed in. "It's old age. Arthritis."

Scotch rotated a small cactus pot on the table. "Right." He laughed. "I don't recommend getting old to anyone."

He went on to show us the rest of the greenhouse, including the outdoor plant area, surrounded by a ten-foot high chain-link fence. Dozens of potted trees, bushes of every shape and size, and fruit and vegetable plants filled the area. Scotch rattled off their names, both common and scientific.

Cookie sniffed. "Stop showing off with those fancy plant names." She pointed her index finger at her husband. "He fancies himself a botanist."

Scotch scrunched up his nose. "I almost was." He led us back into the hothouse.

"Until you dropped out of college to follow that rock band," Cookie said.

Scotch folded his arms over his wide chest. "Says the girl I met on tour!"

I buried a smile, slipped my cell phone out of my purse, and checked the clock. "Gee, look at the time; we should get going."

Timothy peered at me curiously, before his face split into a grin. "You're right. We need to head home."

Scotch held up a hand. "You can't leave without a plant!" He paced the greenhouse and selected an aloe. "Here. It's easy to take care of and can double as a first aid kit."

He set the plant in Becky's arms as if handing over a baby. Becky cradled the aloe plant to her chest between her cast and good arm. "Thank you. I start at ten tomorrow, right? Thank you so much for hiring me."

Cookie smiled. "Aren't you sweet? We'll pick you up at nine thirty."

"Do you need my address?" Becky asked.

"No," Scotch shook his head. "I know where you live."

I glanced at Timothy, but his face showed no reaction. Was I the only one who found Scotch's comment odd?

I turned to Cookie. "Are you sure you can drive Becky back and forth to work?"

"'Course we don't mind." Cookie sounded huffy, and I was sorry for questioning her. "We are in the neighborhood. Why should you waste the gas by driving her all the way out here?"

Why indeed?

"And we can keep an eye on her that way," Scotch said.

Why would they need to keep an eye on her?

With travel arrangements made, we said our good-byes. Back in the truck, Becky stared at her plant, her expression serene. "Didn't you think they were nice, Chloe? I think this job is just what I need."

I wasn't so sure. Something about the arrangement struck me as odd. Surely in the current economy they could find someone to work for them who could find her own transportation. I glanced again at Becky, who for the first time since the accident looked genuinely happy, carefree.

So I said nothing.

Chapter Twenty-Six

Monday morning arrived. Becky was already up, dressed, and perched on the sofa, watching for Cookie and Scotch's car—even though they wouldn't arrive for another hour and a half.

"If anything comes up at work, call me. I'm sure Cookie and Scotch will let you use their phone. You remember my cell number, don't you?" I felt like Mrs. Green. How many times had she asked Tanisha and me that same thing when we were teenagers? *I'm becoming my foster mother!*

"Yes, don't worry, Chloe, everything will be fine. I'm going to do a good job."

"I'm not worried about that." I moved toward the door. "As soon as I get a new car, we will buy you a cell phone. I don't like you not being able to call."

Becky's eyes sparkled. "Like yours?"

I laughed before heading out the door to work. "Not that fancy."

On the walk to Harshberger, I decided to put the accident and Becky out of my mind. I needed my wits about me to survive another day with Joel.

Even though I arrived early, Miller was already there. It was the first time I would be alone with the fidgety programmer.

I strode in. "Morning, Miller."

He jumped up from his seat, and in the same movement turned off his monitor. I pretended not to notice, but stood beside his desk, waiting for a return greeting. None came. "How are you today?"

He blinked at me from behind thick glasses. "Fine," he muttered.

I swallowed a sigh and walked to my office.

Thirty minutes later, I was engrossed in a report for Dean Klink when Clark and Joel arrived in the office. I could hear them greet Miller, and he in turn returned their hellos. I tried not to take it personally.

Laughter floated into my office.

I e-mailed the report to the dean and emerged from my office. Clark, Miller, and Joel sat around the conference table working on their respective laptops.

"Good morning," I said and stepped over to the coffee machine. When my mug was full, I turned. "I'll be sending you all an e-mail later to reschedule our Friday meeting."

Joel grinned. "Why was last Friday's meeting canceled? Car trouble?"

Clark shook his head. "Man . . ." He shared a glance with Miller, whose eyes looked the size of silver dollars behind those glasses.

I closed my eyes briefly. When I opened them, the assistant director smirked at me. "Gone on a buggy ride lately?"

I stepped up to him and put on my best Tanisha impersonation. I wouldn't tell a man Joel's size off, but my best friend would. "Do you have something to say to me, Joel?"

"No, boss, just making conversation." He winked at Miller.

Miller licked his lips, his eyes darting around.

"Come on, man," Clark said.

Joel snapped his fingers as if he just remembered something. "Know anything about Friday's auto-buggy accident?"

My cheeks heated, but I held my ground.

"The car they mentioned sounded an awful lot like yours." He wore an unnerving grin. "I didn't see your vehicle in the parking lot today."

I squinted up at him. *Is he for real?*

"Oh, so your car is safely in your driveway at home. No doubt."

"Seriously," Clark said.

I folded my arms across my chest. "I've lived here long enough to realize just how fast news travels through this town. Yes, it was my car."

Joel pushed his laptop forward and placed his elbows on the table. "This is the accident that killed the Amish bishop, right?"

Miller gasped.

A smile spread across Joel's face. "Miller, you didn't know."

Clark dropped his pen. "Were you driving, Chloe? Are you okay?"

I could have hugged him. "No, I wasn't driving. I wasn't in the car."

"Well, then, who was driving?" Joel asked.

I suspected Joel already knew the answer to that. In fact, I was beginning to learn he didn't ask any questions that he didn't already know the answer to. Every question was a mini-test set so I would fail. I refused to bring Becky into this argument.

I shook my head. "This conversation is over."

Joel smirked. "If you say so, boss."

I turned and walked back to my office.

An hour later, Dean Klink's voice rang through the office. "Hello, hello, hello! I see you are all hard at work. I hope Chloe isn't too hard of a taskmaster." He laughed.

A low murmur carried throughout the room, but I couldn't make out the computer services team's response.

I stepped out of my office.

Dean Klink smiled from ear to ear. "Chloe, there you are."

As if I would be anywhere else.

"Let's go for a stroll. I want to talk to you about your proposal."

"Great." I was surprised he read it so quickly. "Let me grab my files."

He waved that idea away. "No need, no need. It's all up here." He tapped the side of his temple with his index finger.

"Gentlemen, keep up the good work," he said as we exited the office.

Outside, I followed the dean across campus. He didn't speak for several minutes.

"Do you want me to go over the proposal? I should be able to do it without my notes."

He stuck his hands in his pockets. "I haven't read it yet, but I'm sure it's on point. Everything you've done so far has been. I'm impressed."

I stopped dead still. Dean Klink didn't seem to notice and kept on going. I caught up to him in three strides. "Thank you, sir, but if you didn't read the proposal, what's this about?"

"Let's walk over to the softball field. It's a great place to think."

To think? This doesn't sound good.

He sat on the lowest bleacher. It squeaked under his weight. "I played baseball when I was a kid. Catcher. I wasn't any good, but I remember how much fun it was."

"Dean Klink, what does softball have to do with my department?"

"Have a seat."

I sat on the same bleacher two feet away from him.

"I need you to cut your budget by twenty percent," he said.

My stomach dropped. "What? Why?"

His bottom lip stuck out slightly. "Times are tough for the college. We all have to tighten our belts."

"But Dean, the proposal I sent you was to request more money—a lot more money."

"I thought as much. That's why I didn't bother to read it. No point wishing for resources we can't afford." He gave me a weak smile.

"The resources we need are expensive."

He nodded. "You can blame it on the economy if it makes you feel better. It's not just your department. All departments will make cuts. Students can't afford to go to a small liberal arts college out in the country like ours when they can go to the state school down the street and live at home for free."

"The servers are outdated, and what about the wireless network?"

"I don't want you to make cuts there. Those improvements are vital so we can compete with other colleges and universities in the state."

A maintenance worker rode by on a golf cart, and Dean Klink waved at him.

"Where do you want me to make the cuts?" I asked the question even though I suspected I knew the answer. There was only one place cuts that size could be made.

"Personnel."

I inhaled a deep breath and let it out. "If that's the area you want to cut, why did you hire me?"

A security guard strolled by on the field and tipped his hat at us.

The dean perked up. "Hey, Norm!"

I gritted my teeth.

He grinned at me now. "Because we needed a qualified director of computer services, and no one here could fill that role."

"What about Joel? He's been the assistant director for more than ten years."

"I think you know by now why we didn't hire Joel." He smiled and bobbed his chin. "I want you to be the one to show us who is essential—and who is not."

I swallowed, pausing. "Does the department know I'm doing this?"

"They might not know for sure, but they may suspect something."

Terrific. That explained the department's cold reception and Joel's outright hostility.

"What do you want me to do?" I asked.

"You need to tell me where to make cuts, what to outsource, who on your staff is a keeper, and who is not."

"You want me to fire someone."

He slapped his knees with both hands. "Let's call it restructuring."

My stomach churned, and I felt as if I would be sick. "Why would the staff suspect anything?"

"Recently, we've done this to other departments, and it's worked out well for the college."

What about the people working in those departments who lost their jobs?

Dean Klink stood. "I know you're up to the task and will do what's best for the college. We're so excited to have you here at Harshberger."

He left me sitting on the bleachers.

Chapter Twenty-Seven

A buzzing motor shook me from my daze. The maintenance guy ran a gas-powered bush trimmer up and around an evergreen bush, shaping it into a perfect circle. As Dean Klink had told me on my first day at the college, everything had to be shipshape for the students.

"Dear Lord," I prayed. "Help me make the right decision."

Back in my department, Miller and Clark huddled over a laptop at the conference table, their expressions sober. Joel was absent. I can't say I missed him. "What's up, guys?"

Clark waved me over. "The college just sent an e-mail to all the staff." He elbowed Miller out of the way so I could read it.

I skimmed the e-mail, and my stomach tightened. If my staff didn't suspect something before, they certainly did now. The e-mail was from Dean Klink, with the subject line Tightening Our Belt. Part of it read:

> These are tough financial times, but Harshberger College will be leaner and stronger as the result. We will be able

> to give our students the education they need to be leaders who change the world.

"Wow." Sarcasm dripped from Clark's voice. "I feel like the last part should be on a billboard or something."

"Don't even say that," Miller said. "Klink would be all over it."

"Yeah, because a billboard is money well spent." Clark took a step back from the table and stretched. He was so tall his fingers brushed the dropped ceiling when he reached overhead. "There are going to be layoffs." Clark's voice turned sad.

Miller pulled at his blond spiky hair. "Don't say that!"

"Come on, man. Everyone knows that people are the most expensive piece of an organization."

I bit my lip. "I'm sure the college wouldn't be doing this unless they had no other choice."

Clark fell into a seat on the other side of the conference table. "That doesn't make it stink any less."

No it didn't.

"What if it's one of us?" Miller asked. "I don't know how to do anything else."

Clark cocked his head. "I don't know, man, I think you would fit right in with a bonnet and white apron selling cheese downtown."

Miller groaned. "Like that's my only option."

Clark shrugged. "Most of the Amish are better off than the rest of us in the county."

Time to change the subject. "Where's Joel?"

Miller closed the laptop. "He said he needed to check on something in the server room."

Clark rolled his eyes. "Code for coffee run."

My brow wrinkled. What did Joel do for the college other than manage the servers, which were too old and in poor condition? If the servers were his sole responsibility, then why didn't he give them more attention? I gave the men a reassuring smile. "I'll be in my office."

Clark nodded. "Sure thing."

By twelve o'clock my eyes were crossed. I'd gone over my budget three times searching for every possible way to cut twenty percent without laying off a member of my staff. Each time, the money saved wasn't enough—and that didn't include the proposal the dean had ignored in which I requested an additional seven thousand dollars.

Concerned my calculator might soon start to smoke, I decided to get out of the office and eat lunch by Archer Pond. I still couldn't bring myself to call it a lake.

As I walked the flagstone path to the pond, the mallards and Canadian geese waddled up Archer's muddy banks. A rotund goose led the pack. He had a white band stamped with the number 789 wrapped round his neck. Some wildlife organization must be tracking him.

"Don't worry," I told them. "Knowing Becky, there will be plenty for all of us."

I opened my lunchbox and found two sandwiches, crackers, fresh-baked cookies, an apple, and a carton of milk. My stomach turned. Any appetite I would normally have had was destroyed by the dean's announcement. I sighed. I should be happy he told me about it before sending the e-mail to the entire college.

I tore the top slice of sandwich bread into tiny bits and threw it to the birds piece by piece. A blue jay hopped onto a branch on the golden locust tree above me. I forced myself to take a bite from the rest of the sandwich. *How will I get my department on track?* I was all out of ideas.

A twig snapped behind me. I recoiled as a large hand clamped onto my shoulder. "Well, hello there, Red. Did you miss us?"

I turned around to find myself peering up at Brock's baby face, and the one bite of Becky's ham sandwich caught in my throat.

Curt sauntered out from behind his larger friend and sat on the bench next to me. He smelled like a cigarette that had been dipped into a gallon of cheap aftershave. "Is this the sweetest picture?

Pretty little city girl feeding the ducks. It almost makes me want to paint a picture. I'm not much of an artist though. All I can do is stick figures."

"Come on, Curt, your stick figures are some of the best I've seen." Brock dug his meaty fingers into my shoulder. I flinched and tried to wriggle out of his grasp. His fingertips dug in that much harder. There would be a bruise, I just knew it.

"Thank you, brother, but I'm no artist. Not like the Amish girl."

How would he know about Becky's art?

"Too bad she won't be painting much since she broke her arm and all."

I tried to stand up, but Brock pushed down on both of my shoulders. "Don't you want to stay and talk?" He sneered. "We're having a nice visit with friends."

The ducks and geese seemed to sense feeding time was over and waddled back into the pond.

I threw everything back into my lunchbox and snapped it shut. "We're not friends, and I need to get back to work."

Curt stood and picked up a flat stone off the ground. He held the stone between his thumb and index finger as if he were aiming to throw it at my forehead. Every muscle in my body tensed.

"I know we're not friends. A friend wouldn't send the police after a pal." He pasted a mock hurt expression on his face and grabbed my lunchbox. "What's the rush anyway? Isn't this your lunchtime?" He handed Brock my lunchbox. "Here you go, buddy. I know you're hungry."

"Always." Brock let go of my shoulders. I leaped up, but Brock reached out and shoved me back down. "Not so fast."

My spine rattled as I landed back on the hard, wooden bench. "What are you doing here?"

"We were in the neighborhood and saw you sitting here," Curt said.

Brock twisted to face me. "Yeah, can't we stop and say hello?"

Stay alert, Chloe, stay alert.

The rock whizzed by my ear as Curt threw it into the pond. It landed in the middle of the water with a *plunk,* and the birds flew away.

"Here's the thing," Curt began. "Brock and I got picked up by Chief Rose on Saturday morning."

"The chief sure is pretty." Brock leered at me. "Maybe not as pretty as your Amish friend though."

My stomach curdled.

Brock continued, turning to Curt. "She is kind on the eyes. Looks a lot like Cassie now that I think about it. It must be the blonde hair."

Curt glared at him. "Shut up about her."

"Who's Cassie?" *Maybe if the two start fighting, I can get away.*

"Curt's ex," Brock said. "She left him for a Menno."

The scrawny one's eyes narrowed. "I said shut up."

Brock circled me. His beefy hand found my shoulder again. "Okay, man. Jeez, you are way sensitive."

Curt took a step closer to me. "We aren't here to talk about my ex-girlfriend or even the Amish girl. We're here because someone told the police lady we had something to do with the high priest, or buggyman, or whatever he's called, meeting his maker."

I didn't say anything. My eyes searched the ground for something I could use to defend myself: a stick, a rock, anything. There was nothing. Just pebbles not much bigger than nickels. Harshberger's groundskeepers were too good at their job.

The stench of Curt's breath burned my nostrils. "It wasn't cool of this person to do that."

"Not cool," Brock agreed. He had downed the rest of the first sandwich and was moving on to the second.

Curt squatted on his haunches and stared into my face. "We think it might have been you."

I forced myself to look him in the eye. "So what if it was?"

He laughed at me. "Oh, you are saucy. It must be the hair. It makes you spicy. I don't think your little Amish friend would talk that way. What was her name again?"

"Becky." Brock spoke with a mouth full of food.

Curt whistled through his front teeth. "That's right. Becky. Pretty girl that Becky. And yeah, she does look a lot like Cassie."

Brock reached into the cooler for the bag of cookies and let go of my shoulder. I jumped off the bench before he could stop me. "Leave Becky alone."

Laugh lines creased the skin around Curt's eyes. "Or what?"

"I'll have a restraining order placed on both of you."

Brock puckered his mouth and looked at Curt. "Dude, your uncle wouldn't like that."

Curt glowered, and Brock popped a cookie into his mouth. "This cookie is amazing," He mumbled, spitting cookie crumbs into the air. "Curt, you want one?"

Curt shook his head and shifted closer to me. I could not only smell the tobacco juice on his breath, but I could see it on his teeth. "How about this, Red? You stop talking to the cops about us, and we leave the Amish girl alone." He shrugged, his pointy shoulders resembling triangles in his cut-off black T-shirt. "You talk to the cops, and we have a problem."

I tried to keep the quiver out of my voice. "Just leave her alone."

A grin spread across Curt's face. *Must have heard my voice shake.* He stepped so close that if I took another step back, I would have fallen into the pond. He pinched my cheek. "That's good, Red."

Then they turned and walked away.

I shivered, my cheek aching. I watched the two men stalk in the direction of the woods on the south side of campus and disappear behind the tree line, my lunchbox tucked under Brock's arm.

Gently, I wiped the back of my hand across my cheek, longing to wash Curt's filth off my face pronto. Instead, I reached into my skirt pocket and pulled out my cell phone, scrolling through my contacts until I found Chief Rose's number. I hesitated, my fingers hovering over the keypad, then stuck the phone back into my pocket.

I jogged up the small hill to Dennis. Outside, Joel sat in the sunshine sipping from a can of Diet Coke, as if he didn't have a care in the world. He had an unobstructed view of Archer Pond. The thought of Joel watching my confrontation with Brock and Curt made me sick to my stomach.

I speared him with a look. "What are you doing out here?"

He slurped from the pop can. "I'm on my lunch hour. Is that a crime?"

I inhaled and let it go. "No." I started toward the building's entrance, but glanced back to see him grinning.

"Interesting crowd you pal around with, director."

I spun on my heels and faced him again. "They are *not* my crowd."

He shrugged. "If you say so. Who knows what company you keep aside from that Amish girl who plowed into her boyfriend's father?"

I crossed my arms in front of my chest. "Joel, if you talk to me like that again, I will report you."

He crushed the Diet Coke can with one hand. "Knock yourself out."

Chapter Twenty-Eight

When Timothy showed up at my office at four o'clock, I leapt from my office chair, never so glad to end a work day in my life.

He grinned at my reaction. "Ready to go?"

I nodded and started to gather my things.

Miller and Clark sat at the conference table again, in the middle of inventorying the college's media equipment. Miller told me earlier in the afternoon that one of the digital camcorders was bad, and I asked him to try to fix it. The camcorder lay in pieces on the table. I frowned at the mess. If Miller was unsuccessful, the camcorder was yet another item I would have to find the money for in my withering budget.

Clark shook a kink out of a USB cord. "Hey, man," he said to Timothy. "How's the college's barn coming?"

"We should be done by the end of the day tomorrow."

Joel poked his scowling face out of his cubicle. "You would probably have finished earlier had you not been distracted."

Timothy frowned and tilted his head at Joel, but didn't retaliate.

Clark shot a look up at the ceiling. "Don't mind Joel. He got up on the wrong side of the bed this morning."

"Every morning," Miller muttered into the camcorder parts in front of him.

I grabbed Timothy's arm and pulled him toward the door. "Let's go."

When we were in the hallway, Timothy paused. "What was that all about?"

"Bad day. I can't talk about it here, though."

Mabel jumped up from the cement walkway in front of Dennis when she saw us coming. Timothy slapped his thigh. "Come, Mabel."

She trotted over, her black plume of a tail wagging happily. She woofed at me, and I scratched her on the top of her head.

When we were in Timothy's truck, he turned to me. "Do you want to tell me what happened?"

I groaned. "Budget cuts." As he pulled out onto the street, I relayed the conversation I had with Dean Klink "And . . ."

"And what?" Timothy asked.

Mabel flopped her furry head over the bench seat, her mournful eyes staring up at me. *She'd much rather have ridden shotgun.*

I sighed and told him about Curt and Brock's lunchtime visit.

Timothy jerked to a stop. "What?" He gripped the steering wheel tighter. "Why didn't you tell me about that right away?"

I shook my head. "I don't know." I didn't add that Joel had witnessed the whole thing and had done nothing. I don't know why I protected him. He didn't deserve it.

Timothy gunned the engine. "We have to go to the police station and report this."

"No." I crossed my arms, hugging myself. "They said they'd leave Becky alone if I didn't go to the police."

Timothy shook his head. "Guys like Brock and Curt don't keep their promises, Chloe. Becky's my sister. This is the best thing for her." He paused. "And for you. The police need to have this incident on file in case something happens."

"Something like what?"

"I don't want to think about it." His voice sounded gruff.

"Okay." I slowed my breathing and gazed out the window. "I hope Chief Rose keeps it quiet though."

Timothy gave a rueful laugh.

"What's so funny?"

He shook his head, and again, I wondered how he knew Appleseed Creek's police chief.

Timothy drove around the square, quiet on this Monday afternoon except for a few tourists strolling around, visiting the Amish shops. He turned into the parking lot behind town hall. Unlike Saturday when I had visited there with Chief Rose, the parking lot was almost full. Village officials were on the job. Timothy backed his truck into a space between a low-hanging buckeye tree and an SUV.

Mabel nudged my shoulder with her head, and I felt a twinge of pain. I pressed a hand to my left shoulder and rubbed the beginnings of a bruise.

Timothy scrutinized my face. "What's wrong?"

"Brock pinched my shoulder. I'm sure it's just a bruise."

He gasped. "Let me see that."

Gently, Timothy tugged my shirt collar away from my neck. My breath caught as he touched me just above my clavicle bone. Unlike Curt's, the sensation of Timothy's breath on my neck soothed me. What time did this happen?" he asked.

"Noon." My voice came out like a squeak. I shivered.

He pulled away and smoothed my collar back down.

I began to breathe again.

Timothy's forehead creased. "It's already turning purple. You will have to show that to Chief Rose." He opened the cabin door. "They should have some ice inside too."

Timothy and Mabel hopped out of the truck, and I followed. Inside the police station, a woman with snow white hair and a cameo pin that held together the collar of her blouse greeted us. "Timothy, I haven't seen you around here in a while. That's a good thing."

Mabel trotted over to the woman. She opened a desk drawer and pulled out a dog biscuit. "There you go, sweets."

Mabel ate the biscuit in one gulp and stared at the woman. "That's all you get." With a whine, Mabel lay down on the floor and put her head on her paws.

Why were Chief Rose's receptionist and Mabel old friends? I glanced at Timothy, but he kept his gaze ahead.

"Hi, Fern. We'd like to talk to Chief Rose, please," Timothy said.

"She's out in the field." She smiled at him. "Is there something I can help you with?"

"Yes." Timothy stepped up to her desk. "We'd like to file a complaint in conjunction with the Glick case."

Fern sat up straighter. "Officer Nottingham is here and can talk to you. Have a seat." She picked up her circa 1980 black phone and punched in a number.

Timothy and I sat on plastic chairs, and after about three minutes, I wished for a seat cushion. At least the uncomfortable seat kept my mind off my shoulder, which kept my mind off Timothy examining my shoulder. *I'm sure he does the same thing for his siblings when they get hurt. That's what big brothers do.*

Minutes later, a boy about a year older than Becky stepped into the waiting room. "Mr. Troyer. Miss Humphrey. Can you follow me?"

He opened the door to the room where I'd examined the mug shots on Saturday. *Had that really only been two days ago?*

"I'm Officer Nottingham," the boy, or rather, the *police officer* said when we were seated. "Fern said this had something to do with the Glick case."

I nodded. "It's related."

Timothy squeezed my elbow. "Tell him what you told me."

I took a deep breath and told him everything.

Officer Nottingham took furious notes. "I'll tell Chief Rose all of this. She will most likely want to talk to you."

I bet she will.

The boy-officer's mouth was a grim line. "Can I see the bruise?"

I pulled the collar of my crewneck shirt away from my throat to reveal the bruise forming on top of my shoulder. Officer Nottingham examined it from across the table. "There are definite finger marks there." He made another note. "I'm going to need to take a photograph of it. Be right back." He stood and slipped through the inner office door."

I curled my lip. "Is this really necessary, Timothy?"

"Yes." Timothy's eyes were soft. "I'm taking every step to protect you."

Before I could respond, Officer Nottingham came back with an SLR digital camera. He circled me like a scientist inspecting a bug and took shots of my shoulder from every angle. After the fifteenth shot, I smoothed my shirt collar back into place. "I think you got it."

He set the camera on the conference table. "Miss Humphrey, would you like to file an official complaint?"

Timothy started to nod, but I smacked one hand on the table. "No."

"I think you should," Timothy said.

But maybe Curt and Brock will leave Becky alone if I leave them alone. "I appreciate you documenting this, Officer, but I'm not filing a complaint."

Officer Nottingham ran a hand back and forth through his boyish hair. "I'll let the chief know. She's not going to agree with your decision."

Timothy shook his head slowly, his voice a murmur. "And neither do I."

Chapter Twenty-Nine

Back in the pickup, Timothy glanced at me. "I'd like to stop at a friend's farm."

I settled into the bench seat. *You won't hear me complaining about spending more time with you.* "Whose farm is it?"

He pulled the truck onto the street, his gaze fixed on the road. "Deacon Sutter's."

I sat straight up. "What? Are you crazy?"

He glanced at me. "No."

"They're going to kick us off the farm. Why would they let us in there?"

He shot me another glance. "The deacon won't be there."

"How do you know that?" I leaned back again the seat.

"The Sutters own several businesses in town. The deacon won't be home for at least another hour."

"If he's not home, what's the point of going?" I peered into the side door mirror and watched Appleseed Creek recede.

His mouth quirked in the corner as if he were holding back a smile. "You'll see."

I pursed my lips. This wasn't a good idea.

The Sutter home was fifteen minutes outside of town, and to get there we drove by the same gravel road the Troyers lived on. I hadn't realized that the Sutters and Troyers were next-door neighbors—at least in rural terms.

We rode the rest of the trip in silence, neither one of us willing to change our minds. Mabel slept in the pickup's backseat. Just how many dog biscuits had Fern given her? Timothy turned the truck onto a long gravel and dirt lane, and we both took in the scene. To our left a soybean field lay in ruins. Tire tracks crisscrossed the plants.

Timothy slowed the truck, and squinted through the windshield. "It's worse than I thought it would be."

A natural gas well bobbed up and down slowly, the shape and movement reminding me of a great blue heron dipping its beak into Lake Erie for a fish. I tilted my head, examining it from afar. "Is that pump on the Sutter's property?"

Timothy sped up. "Yes. It's a natural gas pump-jack. It belongs to the deacon's family."

My forehead wrinkled. "That's allowed?"

He nodded. "You saw all the appliances in my parents' house that run on natural gas. It's a valuable commodity to the Amish."

"But does it need electricity to run?"

He laughed. "You'd be surprised what the Amish can get to work without electricity. I believe that pump is powered by propane."

"Oh."

The lane ended in front of a two-story house that had a wide wooden ramp connecting the front door to the driveway. Before we were even out of the truck, the front door opened. I cringed, hoping it wouldn't be the deacon who greeted us. It wasn't. A man close to Timothy's age rolled out of the house in a wheelchair. He turned the chair so he rolled down the wooden ramp and waited for us.

Mabel didn't stir when we climbed out of the truck. Must have been some dog biscuits.

He wore plain clothes but his chair was titanium. Black hair stuck out from under his straw hat. "Where have you been, Tim?" His hazel eyes sparkled.

Timothy shook hands with the man. "Working." He glanced back over his shoulder. "I saw the handiwork of visitors in the soybean field."

The man in the wheelchair grimaced. "I wish I had seen who did it. I'd tell you so you could tell the police." He grinned. "Since as an obedient Amish boy I can't talk to the cops. I wish we could put a stop to it." His hazel eyes turned to me.

Timothy placed a hand on my back. "Chloe, this is my friend Aaron."

"Nice to meet you," I said.

Aaron's smile grew wider. "Pleased to finally meet you."

My brow wrinkled. Had his father said anything to Aaron about me? Whatever it was couldn't have been good.

Aaron turned his attention back to Timothy, his smile now a frown. "How's Becky? She must be devastated."

"Fine, considering," Timothy said. "She started a new job today."

"Really?" Aaron said. "Good for her. Tell her I asked about her."

Was that a blush?

Timothy smiled. "I will."

Aaron flicked his chin in the direction of the barn. "Timothy, there are a couple of milk stools by the barn. Can you go grab them? You two shouldn't have to stand."

As Timothy left for the stools, Aaron watched me, curiously. "I'm really glad to meet you, Chloe. You've made a big difference."

Before I could ask him what he meant by that, Timothy had returned with the milking stools. He placed one on the ground for me, and I watched him fold his long frame onto the other one, which was only six inches off of the ground. I bit back a smile.

Timothy gave Aaron a mock scowl. "This was the best seating you could come up with for us?"

Aaron chuckled before his expression sobered. "It's a shame about the bishop. He's going to be missed."

"He will," Timothy agreed. "He was the best bishop we ever had."

"Has your father said anything about the accident?" I asked.

Aaron squinted in the sun. "A little." He swung his gaze to Timothy. "You know how closemouthed the deacon can be."

Timothy screwed up his mouth. "Unless you are doing something wrong."

Aaron's head bobbed. "That's a fact."

I scanned the grounds as if the deacon would jump out from behind a bush at any second. "Is your father here?"

"No. I'm the only one home. I'm the youngest of twelve children, but all of my brothers and sisters live on their own farms with their families. My parents are in the next county visiting my sister since her husband's having a barn raising today." He tapped the side of his chair. "You can see why I wouldn't be much help in that situation." He gave Timothy an apologetic smile. "Even in Holmes County, I'm sure you and your family are the main topic of conversation, Tim. Most of the time barn raisings are huge gossip sessions, especially for the women."

"I heard your father paid a visit to my folks yesterday," Timothy said.

Aaron nodded. "He and Preacher Hooley did." He laughed. "I suspect my *daed* did most of the talking, though. Only time Preacher Hooley opens his mouth is on Sundays, and that's because he has to."

"The deacon told my family to stay away from Becky and Chloe." Timothy gave me an apologetic smile.

"He wouldn't want me to talk to you either." Aaron frowned.

Timothy looked sad, almost remorseful. "He hasn't wanted you to speak to me in years."

"That's true, especially now that you've gone *Englisch* on us." Aaron flashed a smile and rolled his chair back and forth in place. "So why are you here? I know it's not just to say hello."

Timothy groaned, then proceeded to tell Aaron about the cut brake line.

I shot him a look. *He didn't tell me he would share this with anyone.* "Tim—"

Timothy reached out a hand to calm me. "Don't worry, Chloe, we can trust Aaron."

Aaron rubbed his hands up and down the armrests of his chair. "He's right. I may be the deacon's son, but I don't agree with everything he does."

I pressed my lips together before speaking. "Could the bishop have been the intended victim?"

Aaron thought for a minute. "That's hard to believe. Everyone loved Bishop Glick." He tipped his straw hat back. "How would the person cutting the brake line know that Becky would meet him on the road?"

"We thought of that too. Right now, we are eliminating all the possibilities," I said. "Did you know the bishop well?"

"As well as most folks, I guess. I may have seen him more often than others in the district because of my father's position. He and the preachers stopped by our house many times to talk about goings-on in the district."

I leaned toward him, listening. "Would anyone want to hurt the bishop?"

Aaron shook his head. "I can't think of anyone."

The ladies gossiping at Young's sprang to mind. "What about your father?"

Timothy frowned.

If he thought we could trust Aaron, this was a question that needed to be asked.

"*Daed* and Bishop Glick didn't always see eye-to-eye, that's true. The deacon thought the bishop wasn't as strict as he should be, especially with the young people in the district." He clenched the arms of his wheelchair. "If it were left up to my father, all we would do is work, eat, and sleep. It was how he was raised. Before Bishop Glick, the deacon's father was the bishop until he died."

Timothy shuddered. "Bishop Sutter was a tough man."

Aaron gave a mock shiver. "You don't know the half of it. I think my *daed* always wanted to follow in his father's footsteps, but the Lord had another plan for him." He removed his hat, ran a hand through his thick black hair, and plopped it back on his head. "I do know someone who would know if the bishop had any enemies."

I straightened. "Who?"

"Hettie Glick. She knows everything that's going on in the district. She also happens to be the bishop's aunt. If someone wanted to hurt the bishop, Hettie would know." He gave a determined nod. "*Daed* complained to our family numerous times that the bishop had to run everything by Hettie before he came to a decision. Drove my father up the wall."

"Why's that?"

"For one thing Hettie's unmarried, and for another, she's a woman. In the Amish world, her opinion doesn't amount to much outside of the home." Aaron gave me an apologetic smile.

I held up my hand to block a sun ray that broke through the clouds. "Why did the bishop put so much weight on her opinions then?"

Aaron shrugged. "You'll have to ask Hettie that."

Timothy winced. "I don't know if she'd want to talk to me."

Aaron laughed. "You broke the picture window in the front of her house ten years ago. I'm sure she has forgotten by now."

"I don't think so," Timothy said, grinning. "She mentions it every time I see her."

My gaze swiveled from Timothy to Aaron. "Would she be willing to talk to us right now? She must be brokenhearted over her nephew's death."

"She might." Aaron spoke thoughtfully. "I'll find out, and I'll call you to tell you what she says."

My eyes widened. "You have a phone?"

Aaron laughed again. "There's a phone shed at the end of the road. We share it with three other farms, including the Glicks and Troyers. It's supposed to be reserved for emergencies and business. I think this would qualify as a little bit of both." Aaron peered up at the sky as if judging the time by the location of the sun. "My parents will be home soon. I doubt you would want to run into the deacon."

Timothy stood up from the milking stool and shook his friend's hand. "I'll stop by more often."

Aaron frowned up at him, but then he smiled. "You always say that. Don't forget to tell Becky I'm praying for her." He angled his chair in my direction. "It was nice to meet you, Chloe. Your hair is as pretty as I've been told."

Timothy's mouth fell open, and Aaron chuckled, shooting me a wink.

Chapter Thirty

"My parents' farm isn't far from here. Do you mind if we stop?"

I peered at Timothy at the wheel of his pickup. My mind whirred from our conversation with Aaron, so I was glad for the distraction. "No. It will be nice to see the kids again and your grandfather. I like him a lot."

"He likes you too. I can tell."

Unlike the first time we arrived at the Troyer farm, there were no children to greet us. The front door was closed, and everything was eerily quiet.

"Is something wrong?" I asked.

"I don't know." Timothy spoke barely above a whisper. "Mabel, stay in the truck."

The canine rolled over, kicking her legs in her sleep.

We stepped through the open screen door and onto the front porch. Timothy knocked twice on the wooden door that led into the house, but no answer. He tried the knob, and shrank back. "It's locked."

The third time he knocked with force, and we could hear Naomi crying on the other side of the door. Angry voices spoke back and forth in Pennsylvania Dutch.

Finally, the door flung open and Grandfather Zook stood there on his metal crutches, his face drawn. "Timothy, your father said this isn't a *gut* time."

"What's going on?" The color in Timothy's face had deepened.

His grandfather just shook his head.

"I'm going inside." Timothy glanced at me. "Chloe, can you stay out here?"

As Timothy disappeared inside the house, Grandfather Zook hobbled out onto the porch. "It's a nice evening. I'd rather be outside. Can you walk with me a bit, Chloe?"

Our walk went as far as the pine bench overlooking Mrs. Troyer's vegetable garden. Grandfather Zook lowered himself onto the bench and removed his braces, placing them on the ground beside him. "Why don't you come over here and take a seat?"

I sat next to him.

Grandfather Zook sighed, and for the first time he seemed like the old man that he was. "My family is from Lancaster, but my wife is from Knox County originally. I met her once when I visited Knox as a young man. I fell in love the minute I met my Louise." He shook his head and gave a small laugh. "It took lots of letter writing to convince her to love me back and to move all the way to Lancaster. She finally did it even though her family would have preferred she marry a local boy."

He smoothed his beard over his shirt. "Martha, Timothy's mother, is my oldest daughter. We had trouble with her from the get-go. She was rebellious from the day she was born. Louise and I were at our wits' end. We were afraid for Martha, afraid she'd leave the Amish way. When she was seventeen, we shipped her to Knox County to live with my wife's family." He laughed again. "We wanted to scare her straight. Although I am Old Order Amish, my district back in Lancaster is much more relaxed than the one here. Much to our surprise, Martha met Simon and fell in love. She told us she was going to marry him and stay here. We were happy she was staying within our faith. Yes, the congregation here was stricter, but it seemed to be what she needed."

I tried to imagine Timothy's quiet mother as a rebellious Amish teenager. The image of the demur woman acting out didn't fit. "The rest of your family is in Lancaster, then?"

He nodded. "They are. I have eight other children. They all have families with children."

"Why did you move here?"

He picked a twig off the bench and rolled it back and forth between his fingers. "Many Amish families have more than five children. Martha and her husband could have had more, but my daughter was plagued with miscarriages. I've told her a hundred times it wasn't true, but she feels those miscarriages were punishment for her rebellious years."

"That's awful."

"After my beloved wife died, all of my children asked me to live with them, including Martha. I decided to move here because she was pregnant with Naomi at the time. This was three years ago. I wanted to be with her in case the worst would happen again. The best person to be with her would have been her mother, but the Lord had already called her home." He smiled. "Naomi was born, and she was perfect. I never went back to Lancaster. I liked the slower, quieter pace here. It was a nice place to retire and spend my final years on this earth."

He sighed then winked. "You can take the Amish man out of Lancaster, but you can't take the Lancaster out of the Amish man. My son-in-law has been a good husband and provider for Martha and their children, but he's a stern man. He listens to his bishop, his preachers, and his *deacon*." He stressed deacon at the end of the sentence.

A row of pumpkin vines in the garden were flowering. It wouldn't be long before those flowers turned into fruit. Before we knew it, fall would be upon us. It would be my first fall in the country. I breathed it all in and turned to Grandfather Zook. "And what did those men tell him?"

His eyes drooped, as if filled with sadness. "He should stay away from Becky and you until the business with the accident is over. He should keep the younger children from you and Becky."

I bit the inside of my cheek. "What about Timothy?"

"The deacon didn't mention Timothy in particular. However if Timothy continues his contact with you and his sister, I wouldn't be surprised if the deacon returned and added that warning onto his list."

"Why are you telling me this? I assume the deacon gave you the same warning."

"He did." Grandfather Zook stared at the whitewashed farmhouse as if trying to see through it. "I've learned that what is right for me is not right for my daughter. Now my son-in-law and daughter must learn that what is right for them may not be right for their own children. Louise and I had been so afraid Martha would leave the Amish, and I still believe that leaving would have been a mistake for my daughter. However, I've since learned there is not one right way to be obedient to the Lord."

The screen door slammed shut, and Timothy stormed down the steps. "Chloe," he called. "I'm ready to go."

Grandfather Zook bumped my shoulder. "You should go."

I leaned over and gave him a hug.

Timothy was silent the entire ride back to Appleseed Creek, even though I wanted to ask him what happened inside his parents' house. What did they say? What did they not say? How did it all affect Becky? Him? And even me?

It was nearly six when he turned into the driveway. I hoped Becky hadn't waited for me to eat supper. For the first time that day, I wondered how her first day at the greenhouse had gone.

Timothy didn't turn off the truck.

I opened the passenger side door. "Good night."

He laid his hand on my forearm. "Thanks for coming with me today, Chloe."

I blinked. A tingle radiated from where his hand touched my bare arm. "You're thanking me? I was the one who asked you to get involved in this investigation."

"I was already involved whether you asked for my help or not."

The door stuck. He leaned across my body and pushed it open. "Good night. Take care of your shoulder. I'll let you know when I hear from Aaron about Hettie Glick."

Chapter Thirty-One

As soon as I entered the house, Becky was ready to tell me all about her first day at Little Owl Greenhouse. "Chloe, I had the best day. Scotch and Cookie are so much fun." Her face glowed. Despite working all day, Becky had managed to make a shepherd's pie for dinner. She warmed a piece for me in the oven as she told about her day, then she kept me up until past eleven with stories about the greenhouse owners. I was glad to see her so happy and saw no reason to ruin it with news of my day.

At midnight my cell phone rang, and I almost fell off my bed. I'd been asleep less than an hour.

"Chloe?" Tanisha's voice sounded as if she was across the room from me—not across the world.

Guilt washed over me. I'd promised Tanisha I would call her back the night I had dinner at the Troyer's farm, and that was three days ago.

"Did you lose my phone number or something?" She sounded hurt. Apparently, *she* hadn't forgotten.

I rubbed my eyes. "I'm sorry, Tee. How are you?"

"Awful."

I smiled at her bluntness. If I had been asked the same question under those circumstances, I would most likely have said "fine" or "okay," even if neither were true.

"Have you heard from Cole?"

"No, and I don't want to. What does he have to say to me other than that he doesn't love me anymore?"

"He *does* love you, Tanisha. I know he does. Maybe he's afraid you will find some hot Italian guy to fall in love with."

"I just might," she grumbled. "Anyway, that's a crock about him loving me. If he loved me he would understand why I have to stay here. I committed to teach here for two years. If he had a problem with it, why didn't he say something before I signed the contract?"

I couldn't argue with her there. "What can I do? Other than flying to Florida and telling Cole what a huge mistake he's making, that is."

Her laughter sounded rough, harsh. "Be there. I need my best friend right now."

I gripped the phone and nodded. "I'm here for you, Tee."

"You are? Then why am I the one calling you? *I'm* the one in the middle of a crisis here."

I didn't correct her, nor did I tell her that I was in the middle of a crisis of my own. What could she do thousands of miles away but worry?

To her credit, Tanisha was much more intuitive than given credit for. "What's going on? I know something is up."

My mind searched for the words to tell her. "Umm . . ."

"Is this about that hot buggy boy? Weren't you at his parents' home when I called?"

I sighed. "It's complicated."

"Good, because I need someone else's complications to think about right now. Don't let me wallow in self-pity and snotty tissues."

I shook my head, smiling at my friend's invitation, then heaved a heavy sigh. "Okay. I hope you're sitting down." I proceeded to tell her everything that had happened since Becky called me about the accident on Friday. Even as I spoke the words, they sounded unbelievable to me. And I'd lived them.

Tanisha groaned more than once during my story. "Where does the hot buggy boy fit into all of this?"

"You mean Timothy."

"Duh."

"Becky is his sister . . ."

"And?"

"He agreed to help me find out what really happened. If we can find out who cut the brake line, we will know who the intended victim was."

"Do you think it was you?" She sounded incredulous.

I hedged. "Why would it be me? I just moved here."

"You're right." She was quiet for a minute. "If I didn't know better, I'd say he liked you. Why else would he agree to help you investigate?"

"Umm, because his sister's in trouble, his family is not talking to Becky, and the younger children are being affected."

"Naw, it's because of you."

I had to laugh. Tanisha laughed too.

We talked until I was too tired to string together a full sentence. As I drifted off to sleep, I found myself wondering if Tanisha might be right.

Chapter Thirty-Two

Hettie didn't want to meet us at her home. Instead she agreed to meet us at a coffee shop in the neighboring town of Mount Vernon during lunchtime the next day. Timothy picked me up from my office again.

Joel sneered at him as we left the department. "Is this going to turn into a regular thing, boss, with your boyfriend?"

Timothy gave him a glare that could have turned sand to glass, and Joel didn't say another word.

Even though I had been to the outskirts of the town, this would be my first visit to downtown Mount Vernon. Just like in Appleseed Creek, the heart of the town was a square. However, this town was clearly English, as no Amish businesses were in sight, and a memorial statue of a Civil War soldier dominated the center of the square.

Timothy parked on one of the side streets, and we entered Rita's Coffee Haus. Tanisha would call the décor shabby chic.

An elderly Amish woman sat in the front of the shop near the large picture window. She wore silver wire-rimmed glasses, a dark navy dress, black apron, and a black bonnet tied securely under her wrinkled chin. Even if she'd been sitting in the back of the shop, she would have been easy to pick out. Clearly, the rest of Rita's diners were business people in khakis and suits on their lunch hours. As well as a coffee bar, the café had a full lunch menu of specialty sandwiches.

Timothy approached the elderly woman. The pair spoke in quiet tones. I stood off to the side, waiting. She peeked around Timothy. I wiggled my fingers at her and felt like I was being inspected by a mother superior. She ducked her head back behind Timothy and said something else in Pennsylvania Dutch.

"Thank you," Timothy said. He waved me over to the table.

"Sister Hettie. This is Chloe."

She examined me. "You're a redhead."

I blushed. I don't know why. Having red hair was nothing to be ashamed of, yet I wondered for the nine millionth time why people thought it was unusual enough to comment on. There were millions of redheads in the world. Did my redheaded brethren in Ireland have the same problems? "I am."

"My oldest daughter had red hair when she was younger. She's old now and it's all white. Your hair is almost as lovely as hers was." She bobbed her chin. "I have a soft spot for redheads."

I smiled. For once in my life my hair color worked to my advantage. "Thank you."

She pulled out a seat. "Sit here next to me."

I sat next to her while Timothy took a seat opposite us. He leaned forward. "I told Hettie why we are here. I—"

"Can I take your order?" A college-aged girl with a side ponytail and hoop earrings large enough for my cat's head to fit through had stepped up to our table. Timothy sat back while I ordered an iced mocha. He and Hettie both asked for black coffee.

I listened while they chatted about people in the Amish district until the girl returned with our drinks. When she did, I took a big gulp of the iced mocha. *Heaven.*

Hettie watched the waitress go. "Aaron tells me you want to know if anyone wanted to kill my nephew."

I nearly choked on my mocha. Timothy appeared unfazed by Hettie's directness.

I wiped my chin with a napkin and peered at Hettie. "We are so sorry for your loss."

Hettie nodded. "The Lord giveth; the Lord taketh away."

"Thank you for coming out to meet us," I said. "Aaron said you and the bishop were close, and that the bishop had consulted you often."

"Members of the district may believe I could sway my nephew's opinions, but that isn't true. I was someone he knew he could talk to without being questioned. That was all." Hettie didn't add cream or sugar to her coffee. "My nephew was a fine man and one of the best bishops we've ever had. He was strict but fair. No one had a bad thing to say against him."

If that were true, this was a dead end.

"What about Deacon Sutter?" Timothy asked.

Hettie stopped just short of taking a sip of her coffee. "Why do you ask about him?'

"Everyone in the district knows he thought he'd make a better bishop than Bishop Glick did."

"Which is exactly the reason he has never been one. The Lord wouldn't allow a pushy man to be bishop." She peered over her mug at me. "Rarely do the ambitious rise to places of importance among the Amish. You have to remember our culture is much different than your politics. My nephew told him this many times. I even heard them discussing it once when the deacon visited my nephew's farm."

"How did the deacon take it?"

"Not well."

"What does that mean?" I asked. "Did he yell, stomp his feet, or argue with the bishop?" My palm made a handprint on my glass.

"The deacon was angry, and their conversation was heated. However, neither man stomped or yelled. As I told you, no one in the district would want to hurt my nephew."

Timothy watched Hettie intently. "What about outside of the Amish?"

She sipped her coffee. "There may be one man."

"Who?"

"An *Englisch* developer. His name is Grayson Mathews."

I almost dropped my mocha. "I met him on my first day at the college. He was meeting with Dean Klink."

Hettie wrinkled her nose. "Striking some kind of deal, I'm sure."

"Who is he?" Timothy asked.

"He's a local football hero from Appleseed Creek, or at least, that's what Dean Klink said." I set my drink on the table. "Don't you know of him?"

Timothy gave me a half smile. "I grew up Amish, Chloe. We don't really follow football."

"Oh."

"Hettie?" Timothy turned his attention to her. "Why do you think this Mathews person would want to hurt the bishop?"

"He wants to buy several homes in the district to build what he calls a planned community."

"You mean like homes for *Englischers*?"

She nodded.

"Not one of the families is willing to sell, but he's relentless. He makes everyone uncomfortable. My nephew's farm was one that Mathews wanted the most. He stopped by my nephew's house many times, more often than the others. Mathews is not stupid. He knew if he could convince my nephew to sell, the other families would likely sell, too."

I turned to Timothy. "Did you know about this?"

He frowned. "No."

"I'm surprised." She set her mug on the table. "Your father's farm is one of those Mathews wanted to buy."

Timothy's eyes narrowed. "No one in the family told me this."

Hettie folded her napkin. "You are no longer part of the farm. It is not our way to tell outsiders our personal business."

Timothy's face reddened.

"Your father would have told you had you stayed in the faith." Hettie pursed her lips. "The farm should have gone to you and would have if you stayed in the faith. Now, I suppose it will go to Thomas, unless he falls away too."

Timothy's jaw twitched. "I didn't fall away. I found another way to believe."

She shook her head and finished her coffee.

I cut in. "Do you know how we can find Mr. Mathews, or where his offices are?"

She wagged her head. "I think my nephew said that he was from Columbus, but that's all I know."

If Mathews was a legitimate developer in Ohio, it should only take a couple of minutes to find everything I needed to know about him online. What was his connection to Harshberger?

The bell above the door rang, and Isaac stepped inside.

"That's my great-nephew. He's here to take me home. His mother needs me to help with the younger children. They are all taking this so hard." A tear rolled down her cheek, and some of her toughness faded. Instead of an austere woman, I saw a grieving aunt.

She started to stand, and Timothy rose and held her chair. Isaac's glare spoke volumes. Had Becky tried to contact him since the accident?

Hettie's eyes cleared. She straightened her spine and scrutinized Timothy. "I trust you haven't thrown any more softballs through anyone's front room window, have you?"

The color red tinged Timothy's cheeks. "No, ma'am."

She nodded as if satisfied with his answer.

After Isaac and Hettie had gone, we watched as their two-seater buggy passed in front of the picture window.

I let out a slow breath. "What do you think about this Grayson Mathews angle?"

Timothy looked stricken, his eyes wide, sad. "My father didn't tell me."

"Maybe he didn't want to upset you. There was no chance he was going to sell the farm, so why should he worry you?"

He shook his head, his face grim. "That's not it. Hettie was right. He didn't tell me because I'm not Amish." He stood up. "Let me take you back to campus."

I grabbed my purse and stood. "Can you take me to pick up my rental car on the way? The insurance company finally agreed to pay for one."

Timothy smiled, although it didn't meet his eyes. "Sure, where are you picking it up?"

I reached into my purse for the scrap of paper I had jotted the car dealership's name and address on. "It's called Uncle Billy's Budget Autos." I showed him the paper. "Here's the address."

Timothy laughed now, and the cloud that had settled on his face when we started our conversation with Hettie lifted. "I don't need the address. I know exactly where that is."

"Why is that funny?" I dropped the piece of paper back in my purse.

"You'll see."

I didn't like the sound of that.

Chapter Thirty-Three

Uncle Billy's Budget Autos was a mile outside Appleseed Creek. The front lawn resembled an auto graveyard. The sad remains of hoods, engines, and truck beds covered the ground, which was mostly weeds and crab grass. A large white sign on a pole read UNCLE BILLY'S BUD.

"Uncle Billy's *Bud*?"

Timothy glanced at me. "It used to have the whole name, but a storm came through here and tore most of the sign away."

"When was that?"

He grinned. "Fifteen years ago."

"Oh."

A huge man with bushy red hair and a beard stepped out of the body shop as Timothy turned his truck into the pothole-ridden parking lot. "Hello there!"

I climbed out of the car. "Are you Uncle Billy?"

"Just call me Billy. I'm nobody's uncle. Uncle Billy sounded more businesslike, you know?"

Businesslike where? Mayberry?

"Hey there, Timothy. In the market for any new truck parts? I'll give you a great dealer on a carburetor."

Timothy shook his head.

Billy shrugged his massive shoulders. "You must be Chloe Humphrey. Got your rental car right here." He pointed to a compact car that had been red in a former life.

"What is that?" My voice shot up an octave.

Billy didn't seem to notice my alarm. "It's a 1990 Chevrolet Prizm. Isn't it a beaut? I've kept her running long after her expiration date."

No kidding. The car looked like it was held together mostly by duct tape and prayers.

Billy moseyed over to the car. I stepped up for a better look. I touched the driver's side mirror, and it fell to the ground.

"Not to worry," Billy said. He produced a roll of duct tape as if from thin air. "We can fix that in a jiffy." He then proceeded to tape the mirror back to the side of the car.

I leaned close to Timothy, lowering my voice to a whisper. "Is this car safe?"

Timothy nodded, and whispered back. "It might not seem like much, but Billy keeps all of his cars in working order."

Billy dropped the side mirror on the ground. "Whoops!"

"Are you sure about that?" I stared at Timothy.

My new car wasn't the only item on Billy's property covered in duct tape. So was his screen door, his mailbox, a line of milk crates that doubled as chairs, and his tool cabinet.

"You must like duct tape," I said.

"I love the stuff," he said. "I even made my wallet out of it." He removed a duct tape-covered wallet from the back pocket of his low-slung jeans. "See. I only use the silver kind. It comes in colors now, but I'm a purist."

"Wow." It was all I could manage.

I circled the car. The bumper was held on by what else?

Duct tape. "Are you sure this is the car my insurance company approved?"

"'Course it is. Then again, it was the only one I had available. Not too many people rent cars around here. Everyone has a junk truck or two they use for backup, and the Amish aren't interested in my cars." He laughed. "Timothy was the exception. He was over here all the time poking around in my shop even before he gave up his suspenders."

"Billy taught me everything I know about cars."

"Of course I did." Billy chuckled. "Glad to see we have another redhead in town. We look enough alike to be brother and sister."

I don't think so. I smiled.

"If this is the only car you have, I guess I'll take it." I made a mental note to call my insurance company that night to straighten this out. The sooner I was away from the Prizm, the better. "Where is the paperwork?"

"Oh right," Billy said. "Be right back. I'll step into the office and grab the forms for you. We have to make sure we charge your insurance company."

"We do." After sending me to this dive, they deserved every surcharge Billy tagged on the bill.

Billy disappeared inside the shop, and I turned to Timothy. "Seriously, is this safe? Because I've had enough car accidents in my life and don't need another one."

"Another one? Has there been more than one?"

I stared at him.

The duct-taped screen door slammed shut. "Got your paperwork right here, Miss Chloe." He handed me a duct tape-covered clipboard with the documents clipped to the front. He pointed to the papers. "If you could sign here, and here, and initial here." He left a greasy mark every spot he touched on the paper.

I signed, and Billy fished a set of keys out of his pocket. "She's all yours. Treat her well. She's one of my favorites."

I looked at the previously-red car. "I'll try."

"Shame about the accident. I read about it in the Mount Vernon paper." He rubbed his beard with the back of his hand. "Real sorry your sister's in this mess, Tim."

Timothy thanked him.

"Does she need a lawyer? I've got a good one. He's real good and cheap to boot."

Timothy started to shake his head, but I interrupted him. "She does need a good lawyer. They assigned her a public defender, but I'm worried that person won't fight hard enough for her."

"You're probably right about that. My lawyer's name is Tyler Hart. His office is just outside of Mount Vernon. He's helped me out of a jam or two."

I wanted to ask Billy what those jams were but thought better of it.

Timothy pursed his lips. "My father wouldn't like it."

"Your father's not talking to Becky right now, and he's hardly speaking to you. We have to think about what is best for your sister." I faced Billy. "Do you have his phone number?"

"I know it by heart." He tore a scrap of paper from the bottom of my rental form and scribbled a phone number onto it. "That's his cell."

An alarm went off in the shop.

"Whoops!" Billy jumped into action. "Nothing to worry about! That's just one of the compressors. I'll see you all later." He galloped toward the shop.

"Are you going to call that lawyer?" Timothy asked me over the alarm.

"Yes." My firm tone left no room for argument. "And we need to pay a visit to Mr. Mathews. It may turn into another dead end, but we have to check it out."

Timothy agreed. "I have a job in Sunbury tomorrow. I can't go until Thursday."

"I could go myself or take Becky." I was eager to talk to the developer. The sooner I did, the sooner I could cross him off my list.

"I don't think so. It won't hurt to wait a day." He inspected my "new" car. "There is no way this thing will make it all the way to Columbus and back."

I poked a fist into my hip. "I thought you said it was safe."

"Not *that* safe."

I sighed. "Okay, Thursday it is. I can get off work early. I'll be ready to go at three." I thought of Joel's smart remark back in the office. "I'll meet you in the parking lot."

He nodded. "Why don't you drive off first? I want to make sure the car will make it all the way to Harshberger."

I gave him a look.

"You can never be too careful." Timothy grinned.

I climbed into the car. The interior smelled like wet socks. I leaned over the seat and rolled down the passenger side window. Then, I rolled down the window on my side of the car. I turned the key in the ignition, and surprisingly the car started right up. I waved to Timothy, who watched me through the windshield of his truck, and eased the Prizm onto the road. I tapped the brakes a few times, and the car reacted as it should. Timothy may have been curious about my stop-and-go driving, but I wasn't taking any chances.

The car had a couple of hiccups on the road but did not stall. I supposed I could make do with Billy's work of art until my insurance company sent me a check to replace my totaled car. Who knew how long that would be? I certainly wouldn't be making any trips out of Knox County until I had some new wheels.

Timothy followed me all the way back, and I was comforted by his presence. As I turned into campus, he beeped his horn and waved before driving off.

Chapter Thirty-Four

After returning to my office, I went online to find Grayson Mathews's company website. Most of it crowed about his victories as an Ohio State football star back in the late 1980s, the colors scarlet and gray prevalent on his site. If all the hype could be believed, Mathews was a savvy businessman.

I clicked on a link called *Success Stories*. He developed a planned community south of Columbus and another in Licking County, just west of Knox. Were there really enough people to live in all the mini-mansions Mathews planted across central Ohio?

The plans for the Knox County Community sat dead center on a page called *Future Communities*. It boasted a clubhouse with gym, swimming pool, and even a general store. The fine print at the bottom of the plans read, "pending." Pending what? Pending because he didn't own the land, that's what.

I clicked on an aerial view of the planned community. I zoomed in to find the Troyer house and the Glick farm. My jaw clenched. I'm sure Mathews knew there was no risk of the Amish seeing his master plan since they had no access to the Internet. I printed the pages and tucked them in a folder. I had a feeling I'd need them for our meeting with Mathews. I also e-mailed his Web site link to my phone for good measure.

Next, I checked the Knox County bar association website for information about Billy's attorney recommendation, Tyler Hart, and found glowing references—even one from Chief Rose. I removed the scrap of paper Billy gave me from my purse and called Tyler Hart's office. My call went to voicemail, so I left a message and asked him to call me back.

I looked out my office doorway to see the conference table still littered with camcorder parts.

Miller caught my eye. "It's a goner, boss."

"I know. We'll get a new one." I made the promise not knowing if I could keep it.

Joel peeked out from his cubicle and scowled. "With what money? Or are you too busy with your boyfriend to read campus e-mails."

"Man," Clark said. "Lay off."

Joel scowled at him, but to my relief, he slid back behind his fake wall.

I shook my head and called Becky at work.

"Little Owl Greenhouse. How may I help you?" Becky's voice held a slight tremor, as if unsure of herself.

"Hi, Becky."

"Chloe!" She sounded relieved. "Cookie asked me to answer the phone, and I've been dreading the calls all day. You were my first one."

The greenhouse's first call was at four in the afternoon?

"How'd I do?" she asked.

"Excellent." One call or not, I hoped I reassured her. "I got my rental car and thought I'd pick you up from work tonight."

"Really? That's great. I'm off at four thirty."

Instead of avoiding Butler Road as Timothy had, I let Pepper take me that way to the greenhouse. I pulled over on the side of the road before reaching Becky's work. "Continue one point two miles." Pepper's instructions came with her usual irritation.

"I'm glad you didn't lose any of your spunk in the accident." I exited the car. *Didn't everyone talk to their caustic GPS guide?*

The tree that the bishop hit was badly damaged. Most of its front bark had been torn away, revealing soft white wood underneath. A bright orange spray-painted *X* marred the wood, indicating that the county thought the tree, which I guessed by its broad leaves to be a sycamore, had suffered too much damage to be saved.

In the mud below the tree, I saw what looked like hundreds of shoe prints. *Probably police and other first responders.* There were hoof prints there, too, and two deep ruts cut into the earth where the buggy's wooden wheels had been pushed off the road.

Nothing else from the accident remained, not even a shard of glass. I wasn't surprised. Chief Rose was very good at her job. I wasn't a crime scene tech and wouldn't know a clue if it sat up and said, *Look over here! Clue!*

And yet I couldn't stop searching.

A chill ran down my spine as I remembered another accident scene. My mother's. On the day of her funeral, my father drove to the scene. A condemned tree marked with orange paint had stood there as well. Nothing else about the scene would tell you there had been an accident. As a family, we hadn't placed a white cross with ribbons as a makeshift memorial on the side of the road like so many others had done. Dad would not allow it.

My father turned off the car. We sat there on the side of the road, snow falling. Cars blared their horns at us as we sat in my father's car on the other side of the curve. The curve that had been covered in black ice the day my mother died, sending her small car spinning into the tree.

"Daddy?"

He didn't look at me. "This is all your fault."

I started to cry. "Daddy. I didn't—I'm sorry."

"We won't speak of this again." He started the car.

I shook the memory from my head and concentrated on the scene in front me. Could Grayson Mathews have had something to do with the accident? It seemed far-fetched. Surely there was enough countryside in central Ohio to satisfy his craving to develop if the Amish in Knox County wouldn't sell.

There was also another small fact I kept coming back to. If the bishop was the intended victim, how could the perpetrator know Becky and the bishop would be on the road at the same time? Who knew about her interview at the greenhouse? The police said the brake line had been recently cut. What if someone knew Becky would be the next person to drive the car?

At four thirty on the dot, I turned into the empty parking lot next to Little Owl Greenhouse, my mind still whirring. Scotch was out front watering the hanging baskets. He put down his hose as I exited the car. "From Uncle Billy's?"

I nodded.

"Been there." He removed a red bandana from his overall pocket. "Phew, it's a hot one today. Big storm is comin'. You can bank on that."

The sky was periwinkle blue without a cloud in sight. "Did you hear that on the news?"

"Naw, I don't put much stock in weathermen. Bunch of suits sitting in the air-conditioning. What do they know? The plants tell me, and they say a big storm isn't that far off."

O-kay.

Becky walked out of the greenhouse store wearing dark blue eye shadow from her eyelashes to her brows, hot pink lipstick, and red blush. She could double as a circus clown. Cookie followed her out.

I gasped. "What happened to you?"

Her face fell. "You don't like it."

I glanced over at Cookie. She folded her arms over her ample chest. *The Cookie makeup treatment.* I plastered a smile on my face. "It's colorful."

Cookie nodded. Her oversprayed, overdone hairdo attracted a bee, and she swatted it away. "That's right. I thought I should teach Becky the way around a makeup counter, seeing how she's never worn any before. I think she came out real good. I did the right side of her face, and she did the left. You can't even see any difference, and she did it with her left hand too."

"I don't notice any difference at all," I said.

Becky stared at the Prizm sitting in the parking lot. "Chloe, is that your car?"

I nodded.

"Wow."

That pretty much sums it up.

Scotch hooked a thumb at the car. "One of Uncle Billy's."

"Thought so," Cookie replied.

"Since I have a car now, such as it is, I can pick up Becky from the store each day. Can you still give her a lift here? I leave for work much earlier than she does."

"No problem at all," Scotch said. "Becky is a real delight to have around the shop. We are real proud of her."

Becky still beamed under his praise as we left the parking lot. "We deserve a girl's night out," I said.

She bounced in her seat. "Really?"

I nodded. "We need to celebrate your new job and my new car."

She scrunched her nose. "This thing is worth celebrating?"

"Sure. It is has wheels. It moves. What more do you want?" I grinned at her, then turned in the opposite direction from Butler Road, hoping Becky didn't notice. "But," I added, "before we go anywhere, you need to wash your face. I'm not going out on the town with you looking like that."

She examined her reflection in the visor mirror. "You don't like it."

I bit my lip. "Let's just say it suits Cookie, not you."

Chapter Thirty-Five

Becky glowed as we stepped out of the only department store in Mount Vernon. It wasn't Neiman Marcus or even Macy's, but it worked in a pinch. Becky's cosmetics had been professionally applied by a woman at the makeup counter, and she wore jeans and a blue knit top, which matched her eyes. "Chloe, I can't thank you enough. I will pay you back as soon as I get my first paycheck."

"Don't worry about it," I said. "It was a gift."

"I mean, Chl . . ." She pulled up short.

"What is it?"

She pointed at my car. Chief Rose sat on the hood.

"Nice car." Chief Rose swiped a hand across the hood. "I like the duct tape. It's one of Uncle Billy's, I presume."

"I'd be careful if I were you." I ignored the smug look on her face. "You might be stuck there."

She hopped off the hood.

"Are you following me, Chief Rose?" I walked around the car and unlocked the trunk. It sprung up, nearly hitting me in the face.

Becky placed our purchases inside.

"You can call me Greta. How do you know I'm not following Becky?" She nodded at Becky. "Nice makeover," she said. "Jeans too. I like it."

Becky blushed.

I rested a hand on my hip. "Are you here to talk to me or Becky?"

"You. Nottingham told me about your little run-in with Curt and Brock on Monday. I would have tracked you down sooner, but I was assisting the sheriff's department on another case over the last couple of days."

Becky slammed the trunk shut. "Curt and Brock? What's she talking about, Chloe?"

"She didn't tell you?" The police chief crossed her arms at her chest and asked. "Okay, Humphrey, I want to see your shoulder."

I backed away from her. "You have the pictures."

"I know, but it's been a couple of days now, so I expect it to be nice and purple."

Becky's eyes were wide. "What's wrong with your shoulder?"

"It's nothing."

"Let me see it," Chief Rose said.

The sun had begun to fall behind the department store. "It's getting too dark to see it."

The police chief took a step toward me. "There's still enough light left."

"Fine." I pulled at the collar of my yellow T-shirt to show where Brock had pinched the upper part of my shoulder.

Becky gasped.

Chief Rose whistled. "That's quite a bruise."

I gave my head a tight shake. "It's because I'm so fair."

Becky wrapped her arms around herself. "What happened?"

Chief Rose answered for me. "Your roomie here had a little run-in with Curt and Brock." She folded her arms over her chest. "I thought I told you to call me if you saw them again."

I bristled. "I reported the incident to the police." I didn't want to share my real reason in Becky's presence.

"The way Nottingham tells it, you only did that after Timothy Troyer made you."

"Timothy knew about this?" Becky started to shake. "Why didn't anyone tell me?"

"Becky, you have enough to worry about."

She glared at me. "There you go protecting me again. I'm an adult. I don't need it."

You do, too. But I didn't bother to argue with her. She didn't need to know that I didn't tell Chief Rose right away because Curt had threatened her.

"Nottingham tells me that you haven't filed an official complaint." With the fading sun, the lightbulbs in the parking lot's lampposts flickered on one by one. Chief Rose's peculiar green eyes reflected the yellow light like a cat's.

I held my ground. "No, I didn't. I see no point in aggravating Curt and Brock. They promised to leave us alone."

Chief Rose started to respond, but I jumped in. "If they bother Becky or me, I will report them, but I haven't seen them or their pickup since. I have to believe they are keeping their word." I calmed myself with a deep breath. "It's getting late. If there's nothing else, Becky and I would like to head home."

"Not so fast," the police chief said. "I have something else to talk to you about."

"Can it wait until tomorrow?"

She shook her head. "No, because you're the key to this whole case. You're the one who is going to lead me to the killer."

I watched her. "How am I going to do that?"

"I saw your little meet-and-greet with Hettie Glick this afternoon. I know you're poking your nose in where it doesn't belong."

Becky's mouth fell open. "You spoke with Isaac's *aenti*?"

I shivered as the sunlight and air temperature fell in tandem. "Yes, Timothy and I both met with her."

"Good, you admit it." Chief Rose placed a hand on the side mirror, but it popped off and fell to the ground. She picked it up and handed it to me. "You'll want to get that fixed so I don't have to write you a citation."

I ground my teeth.

"I'm impressed by the way you've been able to insinuate yourself with the Amish in the county even though you've only been here a short time. A meeting with Hettie Glick is the Amish equivalent of an invite to the Vatican."

I rolled my eyes. "That has to be an exaggeration."

"Not by much," she said. "I've been the chief of police in Appleseed Creek for five years and haven't got so much as a 'hello' from her."

"She was willing to talk to me because I was with Timothy. I doubt she'd speak to me if I had been alone."

"Regardless, I need your help."

I smirked. "Why? You're the chief of police."

She wagged her head, her eyes fixed on me. "I may be able to get the townsfolk to talk to me, but the Amish are a whole other story. You can."

"What makes you think that?"

She pointed a thumb at Becky. "They seem to like you."

Becky rubbed her hand up and down her arm. I handed her the car keys. "Becky, you can get in the car if you are cold."

She took the keys and climbed into the passenger seat. The Prizm door groaned as Becky shut it.

Chief Rose glanced at Becky through the glass. "Now, I can speak more freely,"

"What can you say to me that you can't say to Becky?"

"She wouldn't understand what I'm about to say." The chief didn't budge. "You will."

My forehead wrinkled.

"You're in a profession like mine."

I laughed. "I'm a computer programmer. You are a cop. I don't see the similarity."

"We both work in a man's world. I'm sure you have to fight for your place among the computer geeks, and I have to fight for my place among the cops." She smoothed the front of her neatly-pressed uniform. "I need to save my department. You're going to help me."

"Save it from what?"

Through the windshield Becky watched us. I noticed what the chief apparently did not—the passenger side window was open. Becky could hear every word.

"Village council wants to shut the police department down. They think Appleseed Creek is too quiet and peaceful to need its own police force. They believe the sheriff's department is enough protection. We both know that's not true, don't we?"

"What does that have to do with me?"

"The sheriff gave me this case. He thought it was a simple open-and-shut thing. If he had been running the show, Becky would have been charged with vehicular manslaughter the day of the accident."

I glanced at Becky. She placed her hand to her mouth. *She can hear us all right.*

The chief continued. "Like you, I think there is more to it than that. I was vindicated when the forensic mechanic found the cut brake line." She leaned forward, and the yellow light from the parking lot lamp cast shadows on her sharp features. "If I solve this case, I will save my department. How could the village council say we don't need a police department when there has been a murder in Appleseed Creek?"

I shivered. It was the first time the accident had been called murder. In my mind, it had always just been an accident. "What do you want me to do?"

"Same thing you have been doing: checking in with the Amish, following leads I can't. Oh, and I need you to report back to me."

"The Amish I speak to don't expect me to turn around and tell the police. The Troyers are my friends."

She cocked an eyebrow at me. "All the Troyers? I heard Becky's parents weren't speaking to her."

Becky appeared to gasp.

"Timothy and Becky are my friends." My tone was sharp.

Chief Rose took a step closer to me and whispered, "I'd be careful with Timothy Troyer if I were you."

I shrank back. "What does that mean?"

She eyed me. "He's not the perfect Amish boy he'd have you believe."

"He's not Amish anymore."

A sly smile played on her face. "I wondered if you noticed that. Now, do we have a deal?"

I agreed to nothing.

Chapter Thirty-Six

On Wednesday afternoon, butterflies somersaulted in my stomach as I crossed the campus to Dean Klink's office. He wanted a report on how I planned to cut spending in my department. I had one. Would he like what I came up with? Probably not.

I stepped through the glass doors that led to the administrative building. It was strange to think I had only been working at Harshberger for two weeks. It seemed like so much longer.

Dean Klink's secretary, Irene, raised one of her penciled-on eyebrows as I entered her office. She picked up her phone. "Miss Humphrey is here to see you, sir."

"Chloe, so good to see you!" The dean spoke as if he hadn't just seen me a few days earlier. "Let's go to my office." He pointed to the open doorway.

I sat on one side of a paper-covered coffee table, and Dean Klink sat on the other. Behind him a bookshelf filled with management and higher-education tomes lined the wall. A three-by-four wooden shadow box hung next to the only window, hundreds of fishing lures decorating its shelves.

He stood and removed a dragonfly lure from the box. "Aren't they beautiful?"

"They are." The detail and bright colors of several of the lures surprised me.

"Here." He handed it to me. A serious-looking hook sat at the end of the lure. *Is this for shark fishing?*

"That one's for salmon fishing. I used it two years on a fishing trip in Alaska. I reeled in a forty-pound King Chinook with that one." He clapped his hands, and I returned the lure. With care, he set it back into place. "Have you thought anything about our last meeting?"

Did our discussion on the softball bleachers qualify as a meeting? It felt more like an ambush to me. "I have." I handed him a proposal of several areas the computer services department could cut back.

He flipped through the pages. "There aren't any personnel reductions."

I folded my hands in my lap.

"This only cuts seventeen percent from the budget. I asked for twenty and would love twenty-five."

"Dean Klink, I've only been here a few days. I don't feel that I know the staff well enough yet to let anyone go. I'm still learning everything each person does. Can I have until the end of the fall semester?"

He shook his head. "The college can't afford it. You have until the end of this week, or I make the decision for you."

"That's not enough time. I—"

"It will have to be because I have to answer to my boss, the college president, about how I'm going to reduce the budget." He sighed. "I know these are tough decisions, Chloe, but they are the ones you were hired to make. Now bring me something I can use tomorrow morning."

I left the dean's office deflated.

From the green, I could see the hood up on my rental car. I

increased my pace. A man was bent over the engine. I called out before reaching the car. "What are you doing?"

Joel pulled his head out from under the hood. "I saw this death trap out here and wanted to make sure it had all its moving parts."

I furrowed my brow, and something in me snapped. "I didn't ask you to do that."

"Excuse me for trying to help. Is taking care of cars something else you're so good at? Considering the dead Amish bishop, I don't think so."

"What do you know about cars?" I peered under the hood, my arms crossed, checking to see if anything had been tampered with. The brake line looked fine. Good thing I had seen those photos on the Internet that showed how to cut one.

Joel glowered at me. "I work on antique cars, which this contraption doesn't qualify for. This is just junk."

"You work on cars?" *Could Joel have cut my brake line?*

"Does it surprise you that I have a life outside of Harshberger?" Joel released the prop rod and let the hood slam shut. "We both know that most of your interests are off campus."

I stumbled out of the way and watched him lumber toward Dennis. I stood in the parking lot a few minutes, waiting for my heart rate to come back down. My cell phone rang, and I jumped. It was a local number but not one I recognized. "Miss Humphrey?" The male voice sounded like it could be on the radio.

"Yes." I took a seat on a bench outside my building.

"I'm Tyler Hart," the radio voice said. "You called my office yesterday. I'm sorry I wasn't able to answer. I was in court, and I can't seem to keep a secretary on my payroll." He laughed. It was a rich deep laugh that reminded me of Santa Claus.

"Thank you for returning my call." I walked over to a nearby park bench and sat.

"You need a criminal lawyer," the Santa Claus voice said.

I dropped the stack of files onto the bench beside me. "Yes—I mean, no—I mean not for myself, for a friend who is in some trouble."

"What kind of trouble?"

"She was in a car accident and the person in the other . . . um . . . vehicle died."

I heard the lawyer's deep intake of breath. "That is serious. When was this?"

"Last Friday."

"She was driving the car?"

"Yes." I paused. "And she doesn't have a license."

Hart clicked his tongue. "This doesn't sound good for your friend."

"I know." I straightened the files sitting next to me on the bench, but only succeeded in making the stack less tidy.

"Was the accident in Knox County?"

"Yes."

The sound of typing came though my cell phone. "I'm at a computer now, and the only fatal accident that happened in the county last Friday was an auto-buggy collision."

"That's the one."

He whistled. "Her name is Rebecca Troyer."

"That's right. Will you take the case? Billy from Uncle Billy's Budget Autos recommended you."

He laughed. "Billy's one of my best clients. I wish he was able to stay out of trouble though. I'll tell you what, why don't you and Miss Troyer stop by my office later today?"

"Are you available after five?"

"Sure. I'm usually in the office well past seven." He rattled off the address.

I hung up my cell and gathered the files into my lap. I would need to do more research on Tyler Hart before our meeting. I wanted to make sure he was the right lawyer for Becky. I stood, trying to concentrate on the different places that I could search for Hart online, but thoughts of Joel peering under the hood of my rental car hood weren't far from my mind.

Chapter Thirty-Seven

Before I left campus to pick up Becky from the greenhouse, I drove a lap around campus, testing my brakes. Testing the brakes every time I started the car had become a habit. They seemed fine, and the telltale brake light was unlit. Then again, I wasn't entirely sure the Prizm had a functioning brake light.

Could Joel have really been the one who cut the brake line?

At the greenhouse, I inched through the glass door. No one was at the cash register. "Becky?" I waited. "Cookie?" No one replied.

Crash! The sound came from the hothouse.

I ran through the shop to find Becky standing over a broken ceramic pot. Dirt scattered across the cement floor, and a cactus stalk lay in pieces.

I rushed toward her. "Are you okay?"

Her eyes were wide, sad. "I can't do anything with this stupid cast."

I pulled a large garbage can close to the broken pot and started tossing pieces of broken pottery into it.

"Careful," Becky said. "Don't let the plant stick you." She grabbed an extra pair of heavy-duty leather gloves off the utility shelf and tossed them to me.

I put them on, but because my hands were so small, the fingertips extended an inch past where mine ended.

Becky also wore a glove on her good hand and began throwing broken pieces in the can. She groaned. "Cookie and Scotch left me in charge of the store. They had a meeting at the bank. I knew Scotch wanted to change this display table to highlight our cacti, so I wanted to do it before they got back as a surprise. I should have known I can't do anything right."

"That's not true." I examined the cactus. "But I don't know why you tried to move such a huge plant by yourself. That pot must have weighed thirty pounds."

"I've carried things much heavier than that."

I glanced up at her from where I crouched on the cement. "Not with a broken arm."

Becky took a deep, staccato breath as if she might start crying again.

I offered her a smile. "When will they be back?"

Her eyebrows inverted. "I don't know. They've been gone for three hours."

"And you watched the store by yourself the entire time?"

She shrugged. "It wasn't hard. I had one customer, and she only wanted to buy fertilizer. Yesterday we only had four customers all day."

That didn't sound good. Again, I wondered why Cookie and Scotch hired Becky. They didn't have the foot traffic to need the help.

Becky and I cleaned up the rest of the mess, and following her direction, I arranged the plants on the display table. By the time we finished I was covered in sweat.

Cookie's voice floated into the hothouse. "Hello?" She and Scotch entered the room.

Scotch used a cane to support himself. He examined the display table. "Becky, did you do this?"

Becky swallowed, and nodded, her eyes still wide. "I know you wanted to do it, Scotch, but I thought it would be a nice surprise for you and . . ."

"It is a nice surprise." He clapped his hands together. "You're a jewel, Miss Rebecca."

Becky beamed.

Cookie perched on a gardener's stool. "Chloe, you didn't like the makeover I did on Becky."

I licked my lips. "Well, it's not that I didn't like it—"

"You think she looks better now?"

I glanced at Becky's outfit. She wore a plain pink T-shirt, her first pair of jeans, and light makeup. I looked back to Cookie. "She looks more like herself."

Cookie sniffed. "I suppose you are right. Not everyone can pull off my style." She removed a compact mirror from her long skirt pocket and admired her reflection. In the muggy hothouse, her eye makeup ran down her cheek. She powdered her nose and seemed unconcerned by her reflection.

"That's so true," I said.

Becky bowed her head to hide a smile.

Scotch hooked his thumbs through the belt loops in his overalls. "Any customers?" Scotch sounded hopeful.

Becky nodded. "One."

Scotch's face fell. "It is toward the end of summer. The planting season is over. I'm sure it will pick up in the fall when people plant bulbs and need supplies to overwinter their plants."

Cookie sighed. "You must be right, dear."

"How was the bank?" Becky asked.

Scotch and Cookie shared a grimace.

Becky frowned. "Did I ask something wrong?"

Cookie forged a smiled, but didn't answer the question. "The display is wonderful. Thank you, Chloe, for helping her." Cookie's overplucked eyebrows shot up. "Scotch, it's already after five o'clock. We don't want to keep the girls. I know they have lots of things they'd rather be doing, and you need to get ready."

Scotch's brow drooped.

"For the *thing* . . ."

"Oh! Oh! The *thing*," Scotch said. "That's right. Yes, you girls run along." He stepped behind Becky and me and pushed us toward the exit. "Becky, we will pick you up tomorrow at nine like always."

I dug my toes into the cement to slow the pushing. "I have an appointment after work tomorrow. Can you drop off Becky at our house, too?"

Scotch continued to usher us out. "Of course, of course. Now, run along."

When Becky and I stumbled through the greenhouse's front door, Scotch closed and locked it behind us. I scrunched my forehead. "What was that about?"

Becky shrugged. "They needed us to leave." *The girl doesn't have a suspicious bone in her body.*

As for me, suspicion ran deep. "I guess . . ." I mirrored her shrug and together we walked to the Prizm.

Inside the car, I programmed Pepper to find Tyler Hart's office.

Becky cocked her head. "This isn't the way home. Where are we going?

Hands on the wheel, I turned to meet her gaze. "To meet your lawyer."

Chapter Thirty-Eight

Tyler Hart worked out of a barn. At least I think he did. There wasn't a sign, but the address was right. Becky and I stood outside the white barn, waiting for the attorney to reply to my knock.

"Are you sure this is the right place?" Becky asked. "Maybe that GSP thing broke in the crash."

"The *GPS* is working fine, and this is the address he gave me."

"It's a barn."

Just then, the barn door slid open. A stocky man a few inches taller than I grinned at us. "You much be Chloe and Becky." He laughed his Santa laugh. "Don't worry, you are in the right place. Come on inside."

The outside of the structure may have resembled a barn, but the inside had been completely transformed into a respectable office. The ceiling's exposed wooden beams were the only rustic remnant inside.

"Thanks for coming all the way out here. The farm belonged to my grandfather. I inherited it when he passed away seven years ago. I never thought much of manual labor, but I saw the barn's potential for a law office."

"Is it hard being so far away from town?" I asked.

"It's only seven miles as the crow flies, and the location hasn't hurt my business. Then again, my clients would rather others in town not know they need a criminal lawyer." He pointed to a seating area that I suspected used to be a horse pen. "Let's get started."

Becky sat on the edge of her high-back armchair and clasped her small hands tightly in her lap.

"Before you got here, I read all the newspaper coverage of the accident, and I called your public defender, Becky, to get his take on the case. I have to say he was not especially helpful and seemed relieved when I said I was considering taking your case." He leaned forward. "But I want to hear everything from the beginning from you. From the moment you decided to take the car until the collision."

Becky looked to me, and I nodded to let her know it was okay.

As she spoke, I examined the lawyer. He had light brown hair, blue eyes, and he wore black plastic-rimmed glasses that made him look more like a high school chemistry professor moonlighting as a body builder. As Becky spoke, he tapped notes into his tablet.

Tyler examined his notes, then looked up. "The police said that the brake line was cut."

"Yes," I answered. "They believe the cut was recent, at least since the last time I had driven the RAV4."

He peered at me over his glasses. "When was that?"

I thought for a minute. "Last Wednesday was the last time. After work."

"Where did you go?"

"The small market in Appleseed Creek. Becky and I went grocery shopping."

"Did you see anything out of the ordinary? When you came out of the grocery store was anyone hanging around your car?"

"No. Becky, did you notice anything?"

She shook her head.

Tyler sat back. "The good news is the police have decided not to charge Becky with vehicular manslaughter."

"Chief Rose already told us that."

His eyebrows shot up. "You've spoken to Greta?"

"Yes." *More often than I would have liked to.*

"Does she have any suspects?"

"She did, but they have an alibi." I told him about Curt and Brock.

"I know them well."

I pulled back.

"Don't worry," he said with that Santa Claus laugh, "I've never represented either of them."

I relaxed. "What kind of charges will Becky face?" I reached over and squeezed my young friend's hand, and she in turn gave me a brave smile.

"She is charged with driving without a license, without insurance, and there is a chance she can be charged with auto theft."

"But she didn't steal the car. I told the sheriff and the police chief that."

He adjusted his glasses. "Did you give her permission to drive it?"

"No, of course not."

He replaced the cover on this tablet. "It's up to the prosecutor, then."

I bit the inside of my lip.

"Don't worry. If you are unwilling to press charges about Becky taking the car, it's not likely he will charge her."

"What happens now?" Becky's voice quavered.

"I decide whether or not to take the case." He remained silent for a full minute.

I glanced at Becky, then again at Tyler. "Well?"

A smile broke across his face. "I'll take it. I can't turn down a friend of Billy's."

Billy and I were barely acquaintances, but I didn't correct him.

"Now, we need to devise a strategy."

"A strategy?" *What is this, playing chess?*

He leaned his chin on his fist as he thought. "My advice is to plead guilty to driving without a license and without proper insurance."

"I am guilty," Becky whispered.

"What will happen if she pleads guilty?"

"The judge may be more lenient. I'm not sure though. I know all the prosecutors in this county." He laughed. "Not all of them like me, but they respect me. I will ask for probation and community service. Also, I can guarantee you won't be able to apply for a driver's license in the foreseeable future."

"I'll never drive again," Becky mumbled.

"What kind of community service will it be?" I asked.

"It can vary, but don't worry, there are many options, and we will find what Becky might enjoy."

I allowed myself a deep breath. "What's your fee?"

"I'll take this one pro bono."

Becky's brow knit together.

I caught eyes with her. "He means he won't charge us anything."

Becky's shoulders relaxed.

I was skeptical. "That's kind of you, but why would you do that?"

He smiled. "My grandfather, the one who left me this farm, grew up Amish. Since I'm no use in farming, this is something he'd want me to do."

Tyler removed the cover from his tablet. "Chloe, I want you to go home and write down everywhere your vehicle might have been over the last week and a half. Even if you stopped at the post office for two minutes, I want to know about it." He pointed at Becky with the edge of his tablet. "I want you to write down everywhere you've been in the last week and a half. I want to know who you think might have a reason to sabotage Chloe's car."

"I haven't gone many places," Becky said.

"Everything counts. Did you tell anyone you planned to borrow Chloe's car last Friday."

Becky rung her hands.

"Did you, Becky?" I asked.

"I told my sister Ruth. She called the house from the shed phone. The phone is only for business or emergencies, and she surprised me when she called. I saw Ruth in town the Tuesday before the accident and gave her the number in case of emergency." She paused. "Ruth's upset I left home. She said I abandoned her."

The phone call was news to me. "When did she call?"

"Thursday, while you were at work."

"And you told her about your interview?" Tyler asked.

Becky nodded. "I didn't mean to tell her. It just came out. I wanted to show her I was doing okay."

"She didn't see a problem with it?" I asked.

Becky flinched. "She knew I could drive. My friend Isaac taught me."

"Isaac Glick?" Tyler asked.

Becky nodded.

Tyler wrote something down. "Would she tell anyone?"

"Who would she tell? She's only twelve," Becky said.

"You need to find out if she told anyone." He plopped his pen into the holder on his desk. "It could have something to do with the accident."

"Ruth would only talk to someone in the district."

"Do you think that person who tampered with my car was Amish?" I asked.

Tyler shrugged. "We can't rule it out at this point." He leaned forward, his hands clasped on his desk. "It's too circumstantial that the intended victim was the bishop. It's too unlikely the car and buggy would converge on Butler Road at the exact same time. My gut feeling is one or both of you was the intended victim. The question is, was the saboteur's intention to scare you or hurt you?"

I tasted blood from biting down on the inside of my lip too hard.

Outside, Becky closed the door to the Prizm carefully so that the duct-taped side mirror would not fall off again. "Let's just go to the farm and ask Ruth if she told anyone."

I sighed. "It's not that easy."

"What do you mean? It's suppertime. Everyone will be home now. *Mamm* would love to feed us."

"Your father doesn't want us there."

"Why not?"

I told her what happened when Timothy and I stopped by the farm on Monday. Tears gathered in the corners of Becky's eyes, and she turned her head toward the window.

"Your family loves you. I'm sure this is hard for them. The deacon forced them to choose between you and the district."

"They chose the district." The hurt in her voice cut deep. It was the hurt of a rejected child. I knew it well.

"If they loved me, they would help me. Instead, they've turned their backs on me."

I didn't know what else to say.

She took a deep breath. "If *Daed* won't let Ruth speak to me, call Timothy. He can talk to Ruth." Her tone was bitter. "They still accept him."

"Timothy was in Sunbury today. I'll talk to him when I see him tomorrow."

"Tomorrow? What are you doing tomorrow?"

I told her about Timothy's and my meeting with Hettie Glick. "Tomorrow, we are going to Columbus to talk to the developer."

"Why can't I go?"

I started the car. "We're leaving before you get off work."

"That's right. I forgot." She wiped her face with a handkerchief. "What's going on between you and my brother?"

I watched her out of the corner of my eye. "What do you mean?"

"You're spending a lot of time with him."

I kept my eyes on the road. "To help you."

Becky leaned back in her seat. The duct tape holding the headrest together squeaked. "I'd watch out for Hannah if I were you."

My body tensed. "What does any of this have to do with Hannah?"

She frowned. "Forget I mentioned her."

That made me worry even more. I opened my mouth to ask her what she meant, but her expression, reflected in the window, was crestfallen, so I decided to drop it. For now.

We were silent for a few minutes, then Becky started squirming in her seat.

"Are you okay?"

"I was thinking about what Mr. Hart said, about me needing to write down everything I've done the last few days and everywhere I've been. It reminded me of something."

"What?"

A loud sigh escaped her. "Ruth wasn't the only one I told about my interview."

We were approaching the square. The center of the town was empty and many of the Amish and English shops were already closed for the day. An elderly Amish man in plain clothes and a young English man in shorts and a T-shirt strolled down the street, chatting with each other.

I took my eyes off the road for a second. "Who did you tell?"

"Hannah," she whispered.

I nearly drove off the road. The men glared at me as my tires screeched on the pavement. I took a deep breath. One car accident at a time was more than enough to deal with.

We drove in silence until I pulled into our driveway and shifted the Prizm into park. It shook, then settled. "When?"

Becky didn't answer me. She stared straight ahead.

"Becky, when did you talk to Hannah?"

"Isaac is here."

Through the windshield, I saw Isaac sitting on the uneven front steps of our house. His eyes downcast, he held his black felt hat in his hands and waited.

Chapter Thirty-Nine

I unbuckled my seatbelt, but Becky didn't move. "Becky?"

"Huh?" She clung to her hot pink cast as if it offered protection from the man sitting on the front porch. Was she afraid of Isaac or of what he might say?

"Are you going to get out of the car?"

"I don't know."

I couldn't help but smile. Becky was honest to a fault.

"Don't you think you should? Isaac is here for a reason. He wants to talk to you."

"Why? Why would he talk to me after what I did to his family? He must hate me."

"There's only one way to find out." I placed a hand on my door handle.

She shivered. "I'm afraid."

"I know, but so is he." I juggled my car keys in my hand.

She turned her chin in my direction. "He is?"

"I'm sure of it." I tucked the keys into my purse.

She nodded and opened the door. Isaac stood up, and I followed Becky up the cracked walkway to the house. Isaac nodded at me. "I see you saw Uncle Billy about a new car."

"You know Uncle Billy?"

"I did." He frowned.

I hurried up the porch steps and unlocked the front door. "Becky, I'll be in the house if you need me." Gigabyte meowed at me from his perch on the back of the couch, his new favorite place. I ignored him and opened the front window a crack. I told myself I needed to hear their conversation for Becky's sake, but deep down knew I wanted to hear it for myself, too.

"How did you know where I live?" Becky's voice quavered.

"Everyone knows where you live. Appleseed Creek is too small to hide."

"You think I'm hiding?"

Isaac didn't reply.

"I'm happy to see you, Isaac. I know this must be hard for you." She took a shuddered breath. "I'm so sorry. I never meant to hurt your *daed*. I would never want to hurt you or anyone in your family. You know how I care about all of you."

"What about your own family? They are hurt too."

"I know." Becky's voice was low. "Can you forgive me?"

There was a pause. "How's your arm?" Isaac asked.

"It's better. The doctor said the cast can come off in six weeks. It doesn't hurt much but itches like crazy."

"You broke your right arm." Isaac stepped out of my view. I heard his footsteps travel to the far side of porch.

"Yes," Becky said. Through the curtain, I saw her cradle her arm to her chest.

"Don't you think *Gott* wanted to tell you something?"

"Like what?" Becky sounded close to tears.

"Your *art* is wrong." His voice cracked like a whip. "Since you chose it over obeying your parents, you have been punished."

I shivered.

"Why are you here, Isaac?" I could hear tears in Becky's voice. Her back was to me now. I wanted her to turn around so I could reassure her that Isaac was wrong. *Should I go out there? Should I defend her?* I was afraid my intervention would only make it worse for Becky. Surely Isaac blamed me to some extent too.

"You dress like an *Englischer* now." Isaac sounded sad. "The woman who lives here gave you those clothes."

"Chloe is my friend."

"You hardly know her. We've known each other our entire lives. That meant nothing to you. You turned your back on me and ran away."

"I couldn't stay, Isaac. I know that's difficult for you to understand, but I wanted to be my own person. I wanted to draw and not be judged for what I drew. How can my portraits be wrong—"

"Because they are!" His voice thundered. "Because the bishop said they were wrong. That should be enough reason for you. You should have accepted his decision."

Becky stumbled back and almost collided with the window.

Gigabyte batted his paw at the glass and hissed. He wasn't a fan of Isaac's.

"You are your own person now." Isaac voice was still sharp. "You were wrong to leave. Because you did, my father . . ." His voice caught.

I placed my face closer to the window. I wanted to see Becky's face, but her back was still toward me.

Isaac added something in their language, and Becky gasped.

Gigabyte jumped off the sofa and leapt onto the windowsill. "Shh," I warned him.

He yowled in return.

"I'm sorry." Becky spoke in English.

"You made your choice, Becky. Now we both have to live with it."

Isaac hurried down the rickety porch steps and along the walk.

The front door opened, and Gigabyte and I jumped away from the picture window. Becky ran across the room and fell onto the couch. Tears covered her face.

I took tentative steps toward her. "Are you all right?"

She cradled her broken arm, and I sat beside her. I pulled my knees up under my chin and rubbed her back just as Mrs. Green did when I had nightmares after my mother's accident.

She gripped her cast with her left hand. "I can't paint because of my arm. The reason I left everything behind is broken. Isaac is right, I have been punished."

"Isaac is wrong. God loves you. He would never punish you like this."

Her large blue eyes swam in tears. "Then why did this happen?"

I rubbed her back and thought. I wished Mrs. Green were here. She would know the right thing to say. I tried to remember what she said to me the many times I cried over my mother's accident. "Because bad things happen. Bad things happen because there is sin in the world. Jesus saved us from sin when He died on the cross and rose again. Just because we're Christians doesn't mean bad things won't happen to us while we are still on earth." I fumbled over my words.

She looked unconvinced.

"I think—" The sound of my cell phone ringing interrupted me.

"Go ahead and answer, Chloe. I think I'd like to be alone for a little bit."

"Okay."

By the time I dug it out of my purse, the phone had stopped ringing. I checked the missed call. *Sabrina.* I grimaced and debated calling her back. Before I could make up my mind, the phone rang in my hand. I almost dropped it.

"Hello?"

"Chloe!" Sabrina's voice snapped in my ear. "Why didn't you answer my call?"

I slipped out the front door and onto the porch. "I—"

"I don't want to hear your excuses. Your father is furious."

I sat on the bench. "With me?"

"Of course with you! Who else would it be?"

I should have known that was a dumb question. "What did I do?"

"You are harboring a murderer."

"What?" I stumbled into one of the porch posts. It shifted under my weight. Timothy hadn't been able to mend it yet.

"We know about that girl killing the Amish judge or whatever he was."

"He was a bishop, and it was a horrible accident." I stepped away from the rickety post and sat on one of the brown folding chairs.

She huffed. "If it's an accident, why are the police investigating it?"

"Becky's part in it was an accident," I said firmly.

"Is she still living with you?"

I bit my lip. "Yes. How do you know all this?"

"One of your coworkers e-mailed your father the newspaper story. You can imagine his surprise when he's in a board meeting and reads a story about his daughter in the middle of a murder investigation."

I shook my head. "All of that wasn't covered in the paper."

"Thank goodness it wasn't. Your father e-mailed the man back and asked for more details."

My mouth hung open, my forehead creased. "So instead of calling me, his daughter, he e-mails a perfect stranger to find out about my life." The corners of my eyes itched, but I refused to cry. I had wasted too many tears over my father—a lifetime's worth. "Who?" I demanded.

"Who? Your father, that's who!"

"No. *Who* told you about the accident?"

"Does it matter?" she practically growled.

"It matters to me." I scooted to the edge of the chair and tipped forward ever so slightly.

Her dramatic sigh sounded like an airplane landing. "It was something with a J, like John or Jason."

I grew still. "Joel."

"That's it. He said he was looking out for you. As a friend, he was worried about you and wanted your father to know about it."

I leaned back into the chair, and its back legs hit the porch's warped wooden boards with a thud. "Looking out for me? A friend? Nothing could be farther from the truth."

"The point is your father is upset, and rightly so; you never stop and think how your behavior will reflect on your family. Your father's opponents would love news like this to use against him."

I clenched my jaw. "My family? Is that what you are? You could have fooled me."

"I will tell your father you spoke to me like that."

"Go ahead. I'm not a child anymore." I lowered my voice. "Have a nice time on your Thanksgiving cruise." And then I hung up on her.

Chapter Forty

The next morning, the house was silent. Becky wasn't moving around in the kitchen making an enormous breakfast as she had every other morning. When she wasn't up by the time I was about to leave for work, I knocked on her door. She didn't respond. In the short time I had known Becky, she'd always gotten up with the sun. I opened her door and almost tripped over Gig as he wove around my feet to get inside. He jumped onto her bed, but she didn't stir.

She lay under a pile of blankets, only her foot peeking out from under the yellow-flowered comforter. "How can you sleep under all those covers? You must be burning up." I tugged on her toe.

She retracted the foot as if I pricked it with a needle. "Go away." She pushed her face deeper into a pile of pillows.

I checked my cell phone. Seven forty-five. I needed to be at work by eight if I wanted to take off early with Timothy. Today we were going to talk to Grayson Mathews. "Get up!" I felt like Mrs. Green when she tried to convince Tanisha or me to get out of bed. "Cookie and Scotch will be here in less than an hour to pick you up."

"I don't care," the muffled voice said.

My brow shot up. "I thought you liked your job."

She rolled over onto her stomach. "It doesn't matter. I ruined my life. I ruined Isaac's life. Why should I bother?"

"Because that's what Isaac thinks."

She opened one bloodshot eye. Gigabyte jumped on the bed and began kneading her hair. She swatted at him, but he moved out of range.

I smacked her on the back. "Now, get up!"

As I left, I heard the shower running.

Emotions were high at work as well. Clark and Miller waited for me in the Computer Services office. "Good morning."

Miller fidgeted in his seat and turned a flash drive over and over again in his hands. He gave Clark a look.

Usually low-key, Clark seemed tense, but he sat still.

I stood there, watching them both. "What's going on?"

Clark opened his mouth, but Miller blurted out, "Is someone going to get fired?"

I put one hand on my hip. "Where did you hear that?"

"Chloe, Harshberger is tiny." Clark eyed me and opened his laptop on the conference table. "Everyone knows everything. Word on campus is that you have to reduce our budget by twenty percent. That can only mean someone's going to get the ax. There's no way you can cut that much from services. It's true, right?"

It made my stomach turn that they knew the exact amount I must reduce my budget. "I can't answer that."

"That's boss talk for yes," Clark told Miller.

The nervous programmer dropped the flash drive onto the table. It bounced off the table and onto the floor. "I'm doomed. I have the least seniority."

I picked the flash drive off the floor and handed it to him. His hands were shaking. "Miller, if I have to make this decision, and I promise you I am racking my brain to find a way to avoid it, I won't base that decision on seniority."

Joel stepped into the room with a smirk on his face. "If she was going to make the decision on least seniority, boys, she'd have to fire herself." He glared at me.

My back stiffened. "Joel, can I talk to you in the hallway, please?"

His smirk faded a little, but then he shrugged and followed me out of the office. I shut the office door behind him and walked a little way down the hall.

"Where are you going?" Joel followed me at a distance. "Are you going to fire me?" There was laughter in his voice.

When we were out of earshot of the office, I spun around. "Did you e-mail my father?"

A grin spread across his face.

I took that as a "yes." "Why would you do that?"

"I'm a father myself, and I would want to know if my daughter was in trouble."

I gritted my teeth. "I'm not in trouble. How did you find my father anyway?"

"Do you Yahoo?" he quipped. "Who knew your father was some big shot California executive. He made it clear in the emails that we exchanged that he's a very important man."

I wanted to slap Joel across the face just like in a movie, but I put my hand in my pocket. "I don't want you contacting anyone in my family again." I tried to keep my voice even, but I heard the quaver in it.

"Sure thing, boss. Like I said, I was just looking out for you." He winked at me. "I'm going to take my break now if that's okay with you."

As he walked away, he looked over his shoulder, "Sorry about your mother's *accident*."

I felt like I might be sick.

At three o'clock, Timothy picked me up in the parking lot outside Dennis. I jumped into the truck, thrilled to escape campus. I had spent most of the day worrying over my budget. I examined my funds from every angle, desperate to find a way to save my employees' jobs. There was nothing. Dean Klink was right. The only way to reduce the budget by twenty percent was to let someone go. Now I had to decide who that would be.

Timothy smiled. "I hope you don't mind Mabel coming along. She was with me on my job in Sunbury, and I didn't have a chance to take her home."

I twisted around in my seat to pet the dog's ruff. She *woofed* in return.

"I don't mind. She will make nice company for the trip. How long will it take?"

"About sixty minutes if we beat rush hour."

As Timothy pulled out of the lot, I buckled my seatbelt, "I did some research on Grayson Mathews. He was a huge football star, a quarterback. He took Ohio State to the national championship his senior year, and even played pro for a few years. He retired because of a knee injury." I frowned. "I couldn't find any online connection to Harshberger though. I wonder what he was doing talking to Dean Klink."

Timothy gave me a gloomy look. "How did you learn all of that?"

"It's all on the Internet."

He shook his head. "I can barely send an e-mail."

"You have to remember I grew up with computers. I think I had my first computer when I was six. It was an enormous beige box, and I loved it. I wish I still had it."

"Our childhoods could not have been more different."

I thought of Timothy's close family, and then of Sabrina and my father. Timothy had no idea how true that statement was, and it had nothing to do with my ability to build a motherboard from scrap parts.

"What else did you learn about him?"

"The planned community in Appleseed Creek isn't his first. There are two others on the south and west sides of Columbus."

I paused. "According to his Web site, the Appleseed Creek project will go through. He has all the plans posted online. The only caveat was the plan is currently 'pending.' Did you ask your father why he didn't tell you about Mathews's offer?"

"No."

"Why not?"

"Because I already know the answer. Hettie Glick spoke the truth. My father didn't tell because I'm not Amish anymore. If I'm not Amish, I don't have any right to know."

"Why wouldn't your grandfather tell you though?"

Timothy shrugged. He didn't have an answer for that question.

We were on US 36 leading out of town. "Becky and I went to see Billy's lawyer yesterday."

Timothy watched me out of the corner of his eye. "I thought we agreed, she didn't need a lawyer."

"You agreed. I never did."

Up ahead an Amish buggy came into view. Sunlight reflected off the bright orange triangle in red outlined on the back of the buggy. Timothy slowed as his drove around it. I waved at the elderly couple in the buggy's front seat as we passed. They didn't wave back. "Do you know them?"

Timothy checked the rearview mirror. "Yes, but you are changing the subject. We were talking about the lawyer. We can't hire him because we don't have the money."

"He said he'd take the case for free."

Timothy's eyebrows shot up. "Why?"

"His grandfather grew up Amish."

Timothy pursed his lips. "Let's hope he's sensitive to Amish ways, then."

Twenty minutes later, Timothy merged onto Interstate 71, and before long, the cityscape came into view. Columbus wasn't the size of Cleveland, but a familiarity washed over me as I watched cars swerve in and around the beginnings of rush hour traffic.

Timothy glanced at me. "You miss it."

"Miss what?" I hadn't made a sound.

"City life."

I thought for moment. "I miss parts of it. Yes."

"Like what?"

"Silly stuff, like being able to run to a mall or have every store I could possibly think of only minutes away, and being able to walk to a museum on a whim."

"You don't plan to stay in Appleseed Creek long." There was no question in Timothy's voice. He stated a fact.

Mabel made a snuffling sound in the back. I used my apparent concern for the dog to cover my confusion. *How would he know that?*

Timothy slowed the truck as traffic increased. It was four thirty, and rush hour had begun. He idled in his lane while waiting for traffic to clear around Interstate 270. "I don't miss city traffic, though."

"What do you like about living in the country?"

You. I caught my tongue before it escaped from my mouth. A blush crept up my neck. I was grateful the traffic occupied most of Timothy's attention. I breathed in and out. "I like the scenery. I like how friendly everyone is. I've only been in Appleseed Creek two weeks, and I feel like I belong. A large portion of that is because of you and Becky." I turned to him. "Could you ever live in the city?"

He changed lanes. "It wouldn't be my first choice, but I might for the right reason."

My stomach flipped. I wanted to ask him what the right reason would be, but chickened out.

Mabel snuffled in her sleep again and kicked her front paws back and forth as if she were chasing Gigabyte in her doggy dreams.

Timothy took the Greenlawn Avenue exit, and before long we were on High Street, one of the main roads that bisected downtown Columbus. He turned right, away from downtown. Grayson Mathews's office sat south of the city. Scarlet and Gray was out in force on every street, even though Ohio State's fall quarter was weeks away.

Four blocks south of downtown, Timothy turned into a narrow alleyway that led to a parking lot behind Grayson Mathews's office, a two-story glass and brick building. Mathews Real Estate Development was emblazoned on the side of the structure.

"I've seen that logo before," I said.

Timothy parked under a large shade tree. "On the Internet, right?"

"No. I saw it on a utility truck the day of the accident, when I took Ruth home. It wasn't far from your parents' house."

"I guess someone from Mathews's office was surveying the property."

Mabel jerked awake and followed us out of the truck.

I glanced at Timothy's precocious pet. "Something tells me this place has a no-dog policy."

Timothy opened the truck bed. "Mabel. Up!" The shaggy dog jumped into the back of the truck and curled into a ball on top of a painter's tarp. "She'll be fine here. We won't be long."

I grinned. "I guess she wasn't done with her nap."

Timothy laughed. "I swear that dog is part cat with how much she sleeps." He filled a plastic bowl with water from a disposable bottle. The August air was too hot and humid to leave the dog in the truck even with the windows down. My heart melted a little as I watched the concern he showed his dog. "Stay," he told Mabel. She didn't even bother to raise her head, but fell fast asleep.

Timothy and I walked around the building. He tried to open the door, but it wouldn't budge. I reached around him and hit the buzzer. He frowned. "Why don't they just leave the door unlocked?"

"This is the big city, remember?"

A woman's voice came over the intercom. "Mathews Real Estate Development. How can I help you?"

I told her who we were and that we had an appointment with Mr. Mathews. I'd called earlier in the day, telling the secretary that I was a resident of Knox County interested in the planned community he was building outside of Appleseed Creek. She had said Mr. Mathews could meet with me at four forty-five today.

Mathews's office spoke of his success, with understated, expensive furnishings that reminded me of my father's office in California—the one I had only seen once. A blonde woman sat at a cherry wood desk angled in one corner of the room. She smiled brightly at us from behind a laptop, a telephone, and a huge vase of sunflowers. "Miss Humphrey?"

"Yes."

"Won't you and . . ." she looked at Timothy.

"Timothy Troyer," he said.

Her smile grew, and Timothy smiled back.

I frowned at the display.

The blonde showed us to the waiting room. I took a seat on one of the leather-padded chairs, and Timothy sat next to me. Now it was the blonde's turn to frown.

Chapter Forty-One

We didn't wait for Grayson Mathews long. He entered the room and snapped his fingers, his football ring reflecting the light from the chandelier overhead. "Humphrey? Don't I know you from somewhere?"

Timothy and I both stood.

"Harshberger College," I said. "I met you in Dean Klink's office."

"That's right. You're the computer whiz. Welcome, welcome. Benni told me that you are here about the Appleseed Creek project. Are you looking to buy a home?"

I stifled a laugh. There was no way I could afford one of Mathews's homes.

He didn't wait for an answer, but instead shook Timothy's hand. "Your last name is Troyer?"

"That's right," Timothy said.

"Do you have any connection to the Troyer Farm in Knox County?"

"It belongs to my family."

Mathews's smile grew wider. "Wonderful. I have been having

trouble connecting with you and your family. Your name's not Simon, is it?"

"That's my father. I'm Timothy Troyer."

His grin lit up his face, showing off his ultrawhite teeth. "I'm happy someone from the family is here to talk about the project. Let's go back." He waved at his secretary. "Benni, hold all of my calls."

Mathews's office was three times the size of Dean Klink's. A chrome and glass meeting table that could comfortably seat ten dominated half of the space. Black leather executive chairs encircled the table. Mathews sat on one slightly larger than all the others. Timothy and I sat across from him, our backs to a window that overlooked High Street.

Mathews folded his hands on the tabletop. "I'm so glad you stopped by. I hope this means your father has changed his mind and is willing to sell. Like I told him, I don't want to push him off of his land. He's welcome to live there and sell me a portion. What I'm offering will give him a comfortable retirement."

Timothy's jaw twitched. "The Amish don't retire. At least not in a way you understand."

Mathews's expression fell. "If he would like to continue to farm, he will have plenty of room for it." He wrinkled his nose. "I would have to ask him to remove the cows though. The smell would upset my clients."

I tilted my chin. "He's a dairy farmer. How can he do that without cows?"

"He won't need to. I will pay him more than the cows are worth." Mathews stood and picked a long tube from a rack beside his desk. He opened it and removed a map of Knox County that covered a third of the table. He ran his fingers along the map until he came to the location of the Troyer farm, outlining it. "This is how much land your father would be able to keep. We are considering purchasing three quarters of your father's property, which will leave him with over fifty acres of land, more than enough to keep him occupied for years to come."

Timothy's jaw twitched again.

"What about the Glick farm?" I asked.

Mathews traced that area and frowned. "The Troyer Farm is on the outskirts, but the Glick Farm is right in the middle of our development plan. We hope to purchase the entire thing." He rolled up the map. "You know the family, I assume."

I nodded. "Yes."

He dropped the map back into the tube, and it made a *pop* when it hit the bottom of the container. "It's such a tragedy what happened to the family. I saw it in the Mount Vernon newspaper. However, with what I'm offering, there is an opportunity for the widow and her children to move to town. That must be too much land for them to care for."

"The bishop has sons. The farm will go to them." I sat rigid in my chair. "Why would the widow sell it?"

Mathews wrinkled his forehead. "Young men don't want to be held back by a farm."

I coughed out a laugh. "I don't think the Amish agree with you." *When did I become an Amish expert?* Two weeks ago I knew virtually nothing about them.

Timothy remained silent, but his strong jaw twitched every time the old football hero spoke.

I continued with my line of questioning. "If the Glick family doesn't sell, will you be able to develop in Knox County?"

Mathews's perpetual smile tightened. "Under the circumstances, I believe the widow will sell. It is in her best interest—and in the best interest of her family. This can make her a wealthy woman. She has no idea how much money she's sitting on."

"What if she doesn't want wealth?" I asked.

Mathews looked at me like I was crazy.

Timothy broke his silence. "So the bishop's death worked to your advantage."

Mathews's head snapped up. "No, of course not. His death is a tragedy. I've already shared my condolences with the family. I am only offering a way for the widow and her children to rebuild their lives."

Timothy shook his head. "The Amish rebuild their own lives. They don't need your help or money."

I folded my hands in my lap. "You argued with the bishop about the land not long before he died."

Mathews jumped from his seat. "What are you getting at?"

I shivered inside, imagining what Mathews looked like as a formidable force on the football field. He glared at Timothy. "I thought you were here to discuss my offer for your father's farm."

"It's not my place to speak for my father," Timothy said. "But he won't sell. My father won't want to quit farming. Working on the land is all he knows."

Mathews's smile faded. "Why are you here?"

I spoke up. "Do you know anything about the accident?"

Mathews stepped back. "The one that killed the bishop?" His eyes narrowed. "Of course not. You came all the way to Columbus to ask me that?"

"I saw one of your utility trucks outside of the town the evening after the accident."

"So? I have dozens of employees with responsibilities all over central Ohio. One of them must have been out there on a job. Is that a crime?" He set the tube containing the Knox County map on his desk.

"Depends on the job," Timothy said.

Mathews drew in a sharp breath between his perfect white teeth. "I'm offended by what you are implying. I think we are through here. Benni will show you out. I have work to do." He opened his office door and slammed it behind Timothy and me.

As we returned to the truck, the sky darkened in the west. Mabel stood in the back of the pickup and barked.

"What's gotten into her?" I asked. The usually lazy dog stood ramrod straight as if mimicking a pointer. As soon as Timothy lowered the tailgate, she jumped out and ran around, circling the truck.

Timothy grabbed her collar and pointed to the sky. "The weather's got her spooked. A storm must be coming. She's terrified of them." He laughed. "She's not cut out to be a country dog." He opened the door to the cab, and Mabel jumped inside without being asked. She wiggled into the backseat and made three loops before finding a spot that suited her. Finally, she lay down, but this time she didn't fall asleep. Her eyes stayed wide open and worried.

I climbed in too. "Scotch said a big storm was coming."

"He was right." Timothy started the truck.

We battled gridlock all the way to US 36, and the sky grew darker with each passing minute.

Timothy leaned out of his opened window. "I hope we can get off the interstate before it hits."

"How far are we from Appleseed Creek?"

Timothy gave me a small smile. "Depends on the traffic." He reached into the back of the truck, pulled out an old sweatshirt, and handed it to me. "You look tired. Why don't you take a nap?"

"I'm not tired." I rolled it into a pillow anyway. As I drifted off to sleep, I wondered if Grandfather Zook would talk to us about Grayson Mathews's offer to buy the farm.

A huge clap of thunder startled me awake, and I banged my head on the passenger side window. The sweatshirt I had been using as a pillow lay on the floor. Mabel whimpered in the backseat.

"It's okay, girl." Timothy tried to soothe Mabel, but he could've been speaking to me.

A lightning bolt sliced through the dark sky in front of us. Timothy sat up straight in his seat, his tanned hands white at the knuckles.

"What time is it?" I asked.

He kept his eyes on the road. "Six thirty."

"It looks like midnight." I leaned forward for a better view of the sky. A large wall cloud floated just west of the truck over a cornfield. The Kokosing River was to our east, its usually clear water churning and foaming.

Fat rain drops began to fall from the sky. Timothy wagged his head. "I don't like that sky." In one motion, he turned on the wipers and the radio, tuning it to the local Mount Vernon station.

> Until eight p.m. Knox, Richland, Ashland, and Holmes counties are under a severe thunderstorm warning. Knox and Richland counties are under a tornado watch until seven p.m.

Another lightning bolt. Another crack of thunder.

Timothy's leg flexed as he pressed down on the gas pedal.

I stared at the sky. "I've never seen a cloud like that before."

"I have."

I didn't find that comforting.

Another crack of thunder and rain started to fall in sheets. The truck began to slow.

I stared at Timothy. "Why are you slowing down?"

He kept his grip on the steering wheel. "There's water on the road. We could hydroplane."

We were on a downward slope to the river. Water had formed puddles in the dips and ridges of the road.

"This road floods frequently." Again, he spoke calmly.

I swallowed. "How far are we from town?"

"Ten miles."

The emergency warning sound came through the truck speakers like a foghorn.

> Knox County is under a tornado warning. It has been confirmed a tornado is on the ground.

My stomach clenched. Mabel leaned her head over the seat, and I stroked her cheek with my hand.

> Eyewitness accounts spotted a twister making its way up Glenn River Road. If you are in this area, please take cover!

Through the sheets of rain cascading down my window, I caught sight of a street sign. I only caught the first word: *Glenn.*

I shouted above the din. "Timothy, what road are we on?"

Timothy hit the brakes and did a U-turn in the middle of the road. My seatbelt tightened across my chest. I tugged it away from my throat.

Mabel started barking, and I clapped a hand over my left ear. Abruptly, Timothy pulled the truck to a stop and threw it into park. "We have to get out of the truck."

"Out of the truck? Are you crazy?"

Lightning flashed and made the inside of the truck cabin as sunny as a summer afternoon. I could see the distress etched on Timothy's face.

> Please take cover, folks! This is a tornado warning. A tornado is on the ground in Knox County. The twister is headed south on Glenn River Road.

"Get out!" Timothy shouted

I fumbled with the door handle. As soon as I opened the door, I was soaking wet. My sneakers swished as they hit the wet asphalt. I could barely see beyond my hand. Timothy touched my arm, and I jumped as another clap of thunder shook the earth.

Timothy pointed to the side of the road. "Get in the drainage ditch."

Rain ran down my face and into my eyes. *Is he serious? Dear God, help us!*

He reached into the truck and pulled Mabel out by the collar. She fought against him and barked hysterically. "It's okay, girl. It's okay." He coaxed her out of the truck.

The dog's nails scraped across the wet pavement as Timothy

dragged her by the collar. He grabbed my hand on the way and pulled me with him. We stumbled down a slick grass bank. Two inches of muddy water filled the ditch.

Timothy shouted as he pushed me into the ditch. "Keep your face out of the water." Rocks dug into my palms and knees. Mud splattered my face. A twig dug into my side.

"Lay down, Mabel."

I felt the large dog press against my side. Then Timothy lay on top of both of us, covering our heads. Harsh breaths puffed out of my chest. Mabel whimpered, and her doggie breath puffed into my face. A horrible sound like tearing metal shrieked all around us.

I closed my eyes, buried my face in Mabel's wet shoulder, and waited for it all to be over.

Chapter Forty-Two

Timothy touched my cheek. "Chloe, it's over."

I opened one eye. Timothy's bright blue eyes stared at me through a mask of mud. A leaf stuck to his forehead. I reached over and plucked it off.

He smiled at me. "You look awful."

"So do you."

Mabel sat beside Timothy also covered in mud. She howled and shook her entire body, sending mud and leaves flying all over us. A leaf landed inside my mouth, and I spat it out. "Yuck!"

Timothy started laughing.

I giggled, despite myself. He helped me up, and I stumbled, bracing myself on his arm. It was still raining, but not nearly as hard. Instead of bolts of lightning, the sky lit with white flashes. I sighed and counted. "Thirteen Mississippi. It's moving away."

In another flash of lightning, I saw his smile, but not the truck. My heart sank. "Did your truck get sucked up in the tornado? Can we get out of here?"

"It's still here. Just not exactly where I left it."

Mabel stayed close to my side as Timothy helped me up the

steep bank out of the drainage ditch. The truck had landed a few yards away, the powerful force turning it so it lay east and west across the road instead of north and south. In another flash of lightning, I saw the tornado's path. It had made a sharp turn east off the highway and into a cornfield. A line the width of a small house cut through the corn rows almost like a crop circle.

No one could blame this on E.T.

Timothy patted the dog's head. "Can you stay here with Mabel? I'm going to see if the pickup is okay and turn it around."

Mabel leaned against my leg as Timothy ran into the road. Rain, which was still coming down in sheets, dripped off the tip of my nose. Every so often the shaggy dog would shake off some of the water collecting on her fur. If it made her feel better, I didn't mind. It wasn't like I could get any wetter—or dirtier for that matter.

The truck stalled the first two times Timothy tried to start the engine. I shivered. The last thing I wanted was to be trapped on this lonely stretch of county road in the middle of a thunderstorm. The storm was moving away, but until it passed, there was always the potential for more tornados. Scotch had been right about the weather after all. I wondered how the greenhouse and Becky faired. Uncontrollable shivers tried to overtake me, and I dug my fingers deep into Mabel's fur.

The engine started on his third attempt, and slowly Timothy turned the truck in the right direction. Mabel and I ran to it and jumped inside.

"You okay?" he asked.

I started laughing even though it wasn't funny. "I can't believe we were just in the middle of a tornado. When I tell Tanisha, she'll be shocked."

"What about your family?"

I stared out the windshield. Rain rolled down the windowpane in waves.

"Did I say something wrong?"

I shook my head. "I don't have much family outside of Tanisha and her parents."

"No family is perfect," he said. "Not even an Amish one."

"Your family seems close to it."

He laughed. "My father would disagree since two of his five children have left the district."

I bit my lip. "Why did you leave?"

He wiped his muddy hands on the edge of his T-shirt. "I'm not good enough for that life."

"What do you mean?"

"I wasn't good enough in the eyes of my district. I made mistakes."

Chief Rose's warning about Timothy not being as good as he appeared came back to me. "Did something happen?" I shivered again.

He reached under his seat and pulled out an old sweatshirt. "Put this on. You must be freezing."

I wrapped the sweatshirt around my shoulders, convinced that he would never answer my question.

"I was in the middle of *rumspringa* and thought I was invincible. My carpentry skills were in high demand. I had jobs all over the county. Aaron is my closest friend, and I asked him to work with me even though I knew he wasn't a skilled carpenter." Timothy sighed. "He'd helped me on jobs and made mistakes, which I always covered up because I wanted to work with my friend. We were working on a house in Mount Vernon one morning. The *Englisch* family wanted a balcony to be built off the third-floor master bedroom. Aaron wanted to do it, and I let him."

"What happened?"

"When he was done with the project, I could tell right away it wasn't stable, and I told Aaron so. He got angry at me, and we fought. I told him, 'If you're so sure it's safe, go jump on it.'" Timothy shuddered, his voice grew thick. "Aaron will do anything to prove a point, and he jumped on it. At first it held . . ." Timothy stopped in the middle of the trail again.

"You were right about the balcony," I whispered.

He nodded. "He fell twenty feet, and broke his back."

I cupped a hand to my face. "Aaron was paralyzed from the fall."

He nodded his head. "It's my fault." Rain coursed down the windshield.

I squeezed his hand. "It's not your fault," I whispered. "Even if you don't believe that, Aaron has forgiven you."

"I know." He didn't let go of my hand.

We listened to the rain hit the roof of the pickup's cabin for a minute. I broke the silence. "Thank you for telling me."

"I wanted to tell you because you think you have no family." Timothy rubbed his thumb along my wrist. "You have Tanisha and her family, and you have Becky too." He paused. "Look at me."

I turned my head to look into his face.

"And you have me."

After a few seconds, he let go of my hand, switched on the wipers, and shifted the pickup into drive. The sensation of his touch stayed with me.

By the time we drove into Appleseed Creek, the sky was starting to lighten, and the heavy rain transformed into a fine mist. Tree limbs were down around the town, and a park bench on the square overturned. All minor damage when it could have been so much worse.

In bare feet, Becky ran to the truck to meet us. "Timothy! Chloe! I was so worried!" I climbed out of the pickup, and the teenager threw her arms around me. "I tried to call your cell phone, but it went right to voicemail."

I hugged her back. Timothy was right. I had Becky too.

Becky threw her arms around her brother next.

He hugged her back. "I'd better get going. Both Mabel and I need a bath." He caught my eye. "Chloe, remember what I said."

As if I could forget.

I removed my mud-soaked sneakers and left them on the front porch. I didn't have much hope for them.

"Becky, can you bring me a towel? I don't want to track all over the house."

Inside the door, I stripped down to my underwear and wrapped the towel around my body. "There, I feel better already. Where were you during the storm? Were you already home?"

She nodded. "Scotch closed the greenhouse at two because he said a storm was on the way. He and Cookie dropped me off here around two thirty. I thought he was crazy because it was fine until six, and then the storm broke loose."

"How did you know there was a tornado?"

"The tornado sirens went off. I took Gigabyte and went down into the basement." She shivered. "If you think the upstairs of the house is bad, don't go down in the basement. It's a hundred times worse."

Why am I not surprised?

I let my gaze wander around the room. "Where's Gig?"

"Hiding. He was terrified." She showed me an inch-long scratch on her arm.

"Ouch. Are you okay?"

She shrugged. "He didn't mean it."

"Still, you should put something on that."

She wiggled her fingers sticking out of the hot pink cast. "I'm worried about my family. I tried to call the shed phone, but a voice said the line was disconnected. What if that tornado hit the farm?"

Through the window, the sky was clear and blue. At only eight o'clock, the sun hadn't yet set.

"I won't be able to sleep until I know they are okay. I should have asked Timothy to take me there before he left." She picked up the cordless phone. "I'll call him and ask him to take us."

"No." I wasn't ready to see Timothy again so soon. I needed to sort out what I thought about our conversation in the pickup. *Did he care about me? Am I reading too much into it?* "Timothy must be exhausted from driving to Columbus and back. Let me take a quick shower and change. We can take my car. I'm sure everyone is fine, but I know we will both feel better when we are absolutely certain."

Chapter Forty-Three

As we drove to the Troyer farm, the countryside glistened in the setting sun. We turned onto the road to the farm, but within a few yards of the driveway, could go no farther. An enormous pine tree lay across the lane. I stopped the Prizm, the long branches scratching the hood of the car. I stared at the scene. "Wow."

"The tornado passed through here," Becky whispered. She jumped out of the car and ran through the wet grass and disappeared around the base of the tree.

"Becky!"

She didn't even pause. I jumped out of the car and jogged after her. As I rounded the tree, I saw the Troyer house unharmed by the storm. The only other sign that bad weather had passed through was an overturned bench, the one I sat on with Grandfather Zook a few days earlier.

Becky froze in front of the house. Her chest heaved up and down.

The screen door opened, slamming against the house. Mr. Troyer stomped outside. Becky stepped toward him, but pulled up short. In three strides her father stood in front of her and pulled his eldest daughter into an embrace, the deacon's warning unheeded. She buried her face in his shoulder and cried as any little girl who needed her father would.

Naomi, Ruth, and Thomas ran from the house and wrapped their small arms around their sister and father. Even Naomi's faceless doll was squashed in the embrace. Grandfather Zook followed them at a much slower pace, the old man grinning from ear to ear. Mrs. Troyer stood in the doorway, watching her husband and Becky holding each other, a hand to her mouth.

Grandfather Zook hobbled in my direction. "Timothy is okay too," I said. "Becky and I saw him after the tornado." I decided not to mention the trip to Columbus or about my being trapped in a drainage ditch with his grandson and Mabel. Grandfather Zook may be more lax than his brethren, but he was still Amish.

"*Gut.*" The old man's eyes twinkled as if he knew there was more to the story. He leaned heavily on his crutches and seemed more stooped over than usual. His crutches left deep indentations in the saturated earth. He smiled. "Don't give me that worried look. I'll be fine. The change in weather always affects my old bones, and crawling in and out of the root cellar to avoid a tornado is more activity than I'm used to." He examined the overturned bench, pointing a crutch at it. "Can you pick up the bench so we can sit?"

I did as asked.

Grandfather Zook settled onto the bench with a sigh. "Much better." He exhaled a deep breath and looked to me. "Thank you for bringing Becky here. Her mother was beside herself. This was the first tornado we've had since both Timothy and Becky left home. It's hard on my Martha."

"How did you know it was tornado?" I asked. "You don't have TV or a radio. Can you hear the sirens all the way out here?"

He laughed a deep belly laugh. "What do you think people did before all those gadgets? Long before television and radio, farmers learned to read the sky." He pointed at Becky with his crutch. "I see Becky went shopping."

I glanced at Becky in her T-shirt and jeans. "Maybe she should have changed before we stopped by."

He laughed again. "I know her father doesn't approve, but right now, he is happy she is alive. He will grumble about it later."

I twisted a determined glance in his direction. "Grandfather Zook, have you ever heard of Grayson Mathews?"

He squinted at me. "Grayson Mathews? Why would you ask about that fool?"

"You know him?"

"I wouldn't say that, but he's been by the farm a few times. I wouldn't mention his name to my son-in-law if I were you." He smoothed his beard over his shirt front. "How do you know his name?"

"Hettie Glick said he offered to buy several farms in the district. He wants to build *Englischer* houses."

Grandfather Zook nodded. "I'm surprised Hettie spoke to you. She doesn't think much of the outside world."

"Timothy and I both spoke to her."

Grandfather Zook rooted around in the hip pocket of his trousers and pulled out a gray linen paper business card. "This is the man you mean?" He handed the card to me. "You can keep that."

Grayson's name and company information was embossed on the card in black lettering. "Yes, this is it."

"He gave me that card the last time he stopped at the house. Happily, it was a time when Martha, Simon, and the children were away. He wanted me to talk my son-in-law into selling to give us all a good retirement. I'm in retirement." He waved his hands around. "How can it be better than this?"

"When was this?"

He thought for a moment. "It was the day the company comes and picks up our milk, so it must have been last Thursday."

"Before Becky's accident?"

"Yes, I'm positive it was before the accident." He watched me. "You've spent a lot of time with my grandson."

My cheeks grew hot.

He grinned. "Ah!"

"He told me about Aaron's fall." The words popped out of my mouth before I could stop them. My face grew even hotter. *It must be the same color as my hair now.*

"That's a start," he said.

What did that mean? "Could Deacon Sutter still be angry enough over Aaron's accident to have something to do with the buggy?"

Grandfather Zook examined my face. His white beard reminded me of Saint Nick's, and his assessing expression made me wonder if he tried to determine if I was naughty or nice. "Deacon Sutter is a hard man, and he and I certainly don't agree on most things. He already hurt Timothy as much as his power would allow."

My brow wrinkled.

"Promise me you will remember that we've all made bad choices."

"Are you talking about Timothy? Asking Aaron to jump on the roof was a bad choice. Is there something else?"

Grandfather Zook shook his head.

"Are you saying that leaving the Amish was a bad choice?"

Grandfather Zook adjusted his crutches on his arms. "You will have to ask him that for yourself. However, I think now he would say 'no.'"

Across the lawn, Becky beamed at us. Grandfather Zook waved her over. "Come give your *grossdaddi* a hug too!" Becky hurried over and threw her arms around her grandfather. The business card felt heavy in my hand, and I stepped away so that the two could speak.

Ruth twirled Naomi, and the three-year-old squealed in delight. Her faceless doll peeked out of the pocket of her white apron. The sisters slipped on the wet grass in their bare feet and fell in a laughing heap. I helped them up. Naomi gave me a bright smile, and I could tell she would look just like Becky when she was older.

Seeing Ruth reminded me I needed to ask her a question. "Ruth, can I talk to you a minute?"

She cocked her head at me. "Okay."

"Becky told you about her interview last Friday, the day of the accident, right?"

Ruth checked to make sure her parents were occupied. "Yes."

"You called her on the telephone."

She glanced around again. "Yes," she whispered.

"Ruth, did you tell anyone about Becky's interview?"

Ruth scrunched up her nose. She nodded and thought for moment. "I didn't tell anyone at home because then they would know I'd been using the shed phone, and I would get in trouble." She angled her head toward her father.

"Did you tell a friend?"

"Not a friend exactly." She brushed wet grass from her skirt. "I told Esther Yoder."

"Who is Esther Yoder?"

"She's the girl Isaac's going to marry because Becky's not Amish anymore."

I took a sharp breath. "Did you tell anyone else?"

"No."

"Why'd you tell Esther?"

"I saw her in town when I made a delivery to the bakery. She asked me all these questions about Becky. She wanted me to say something bad about my sister, but I wouldn't." She rolled a blade a grass between her fingers. "Instead, I told her about the interview and that Becky was driving herself to it. I wanted to show her Becky was fine."

"Did you tell anyone else this?"

"No." She shot a nervous glance at her mother who strolled toward us. "Don't tell her."

I nodded.

Mrs. Troyer placed a gentle hand on my arm. "Chloe, would you and Becky come inside for a piece of peach pie?"

"Of course."

Mrs. Troyer's smile lit up her entire face.

An hour later, Becky finally said good-bye to her family, and we walked back to the Prizm. Becky carried an Amish woven basket full of home-canned pickles, jams, and Amish bread in her hand. I carried Grayson Mathews's business card.

Inside the car, I stuck the card in my visor so that I would remember to take it in the house. I needed to talk to Timothy about this latest development—and about why he left the Amish. *Was there more to it than Aaron's accident?* Grandfather Zook was confident Timothy would tell me, but I wasn't.

I did a U-turn in front of the tree and headed back home. "Becky, who is Esther Yoder?"

My question woke Becky from her happy daze. "Esther Yoder?"

I glanced at her.

She folded her hands in her lap. "How do you know about her?"

"Ruth told her about your interview."

She gave me a sideways glance. "Esther wouldn't have messed with your car. She wouldn't even know how to open the hood, much less cut the brake line."

"You're probably right, but she may have told someone that could. Who is she? Why are you avoiding my question?"

Becky wrinkled her nose, making her look just like her twelve-year-old sister. "Her family owns the bakery downtown."

"The one where you couldn't get a job?"

She nodded.

"Do you think Esther had anything to do with that?"

She leaned her head on the window, her eyes downcast.

"Ruth said Esther would marry Isaac if you didn't." I took my eyes off the road for just a second to look at her.

She sighed. "Isaac can marry whomever he likes. It doesn't have anything to do with me."

I wasn't so sure of that.

"Turn here," Becky said when we approached an intersection. "This is a shortcut home."

We drove onto another nameless county road with crop fields on either side. Half a mile ahead, we spotted a pickup truck on its side in the drainage ditch on the opposite side of the road.

Becky's voice was distressed. "Chloe, the truck is green."

I gripped the steering wheel so hard my knuckles ached.

Chapter Forty-Four

I slowed down and turned on my headlights. Dusk had begun to fall. "It doesn't look like anyone is there."

Becky pressed her nose against her window. "We have to stop."

I bit my bottom lip.

She turned to look at me. "We have to see if they're okay."

I nodded. "I'll call the police and report the accident. Can you hand me my cell phone from my purse?"

Becky gave me the phone. *No service.* I groaned.

"What's wrong?"

"No reception here."

Becky put her hand on the door. "Chloe, we have to stop. What if they're hurt?"

"Okay." I stopped the Prizm next to the truck. "Do you think they are still in there?"

Becky unlatched the passenger side door, her eyes wide. Something moved on the other side of the overturned green pickup.

I placed a hand on her shoulder. "Don't get out."

Curt and Brock climbed out of the ditch and stumbled across my headlights, covered head to toe in mud. It was like watching a clip from a swamp monster movie. *Timothy and I had probably looked much the same.*

I shifted the car into drive. "See, they're fine. Let's go."

Becky put her hand on the dashboard. "Ask them if they're hurt."

My brow shot up. "Are you serious?"

"Please."

"Fine." I opened the window halfway. "Are you okay?"

Curt ambled over and leaned against my car. "Brock! Look who's here. Our Red!" He twisted a glance in my direction. "Red, I didn't know you cared."

Brock wiped mud from his face with a filthy bandana.

"See." I spoke through gritted teeth. "They're both fine. I'll call the police when we get back into town."

Curt stood a foot from my car, his arms outstretched. "Red, are you here to rescue us?"

Brock folded his arms in front of his barrel chest and smirked at his scrawny friend. "Maybe you're right, Curt. Maybe she likes you more than the Amish dude."

Curt smiled, his teeth mottled. "I always knew Red wanted a real man."

I started manually rolling up the window, but Curt reached through it. I jerked away from him, and he knocked the visor down. "Get out!" I screamed. He pulled his hand away and I finished rolling up the window.

I pressed the gas pedal to the floor and swerved around the truck. In my rearview mirror, I could see Curt and Brock doubled over in laughter.

When we were close enough to town to get a cell phone signal, I called the chief. She picked up on the first ring. "What do you have, Chloe? I'm in the middle of storm cleanup right now." Chief Rose's voice sounded sharp. "This better be good."

I told her about Brock and Curt's accident.

She groaned into the phone. "I'll send a tow truck out there to pick them up. Not that they deserve it. Did they say anything to you?"

"Nothing important." Appleseed Creek's square came into view.

"Hmm." She murmured as if she didn't believe me. "All right. We'll talk about this later." Then she hung up.

In our driveway, I reached up to the visor for Grayson Mathews's business card. It wasn't there. A streak of dirt marred the cloth roof of the Prizm.

Becky had stepped out of the car. "What are you looking for?"

"Mathews's business card. I put it in the visor."

She pressed her lips into a line. "It must have gotten lost when Curt reached into the car.

I shrugged. "I don't need it. I know how to find Mathews."

Chapter Forty-Five

A cowbell on the glass door rang when I entered Amish Bread Bakery early the next morning. It was a little after seven o'clock, and the bakery shelves were fully stocked with fresh breads and pies for the day. All of the shelving was blond wood and glass, the only decoration a bouquet of wildflowers on the counter next to the cash register.

Two young Amish women stood behind the counter filling the glass-domed display case beneath with cookies and treats. The girl with dark brown hair and wire-rimmed glasses gave me a shy smile. I floated around the room, trying to decide what to buy, hoping the boys in the office would be surprised and pleased if I showed up with treats. I settled on sugar cookies and a strawberry pie. A short line of shoppers purchased pies and bread as the girls behind the counter chatted with them.

Finally, it was my turn. I placed my purchases on the counter. "Is Esther here?"

The girl wearing glasses glanced at the other young Amish woman further down the counter. "That's Esther." Esther wore a white prayer cap over her dark blonde hair. Her hair was the same shade as the maple tables and shelves in her shop.

I paid for my purchases and moved down the counter to where Esther was helping an English woman wearing flip-flops, large hoop earrings, and a maxi dress select a tray of cookies.

"I'll have the raisin cookies—wait—no the oatmeal. Wait no." She tapped her nose with her index finger. "They all look so good. It's impossible to decide."

Esther smiled. "We have oatmeal raisin baking in the back. They may be done by now."

"You do? Those would be perfect."

"I will check for you." Esther slipped through a swinging door that led to the back of the bakery.

I checked my cell phone for the time. A minute later Esther returned with a white bakery box. "Here you are, ma'am. I put two dozen in there for you."

"Thank you." The woman gushed, her maxi dress swishing around her feet as she moved down the counter to pay for her purchases.

Esther's smile faded when she spotted me. "Do you need something else?" She scowled at my shopping bag.

"Are you Esther Yoder?"

"Yes." She folded her arms across her chest.

"I'm—"

"I know who you are."

"Oh." I couldn't hide my surprise.

"I will sell you anything in the shop, but I won't talk to you about the Glick family or that girl."

"That girl? You mean Becky?"

She ignored my question. "If you don't need anything else, I would like to help my next customer, please."

I glanced behind me. I was the only customer left in the store. "I don't mean to upset you."

The dark-haired girl at the cash register adjusted her glasses. She opened the counter display case and rotated the trays of cookies. With each tray turned she got closer to Esther and me.

"Becky and her family may think it is all right to talk about our ways with you, but I don't." She wiped the counter. "Please leave."

The dark-haired girl walked over and said something in Pennsylvania Dutch to Esther. Esther shook her head. Abruptly, she turned and went through the swinging door that led to the kitchen.

I held up my shopping bag. "Thank you for these. I'm sure they will be a big hit at the office." I stepped outside and the cowbell clanged after me. *Hmm, that went well.* I sighed and headed in the direction of the college.

The cowbell on Amish Bread Bakery rang behind me. "Miss!" A voice called. I turned to find the girl with the brown hair and glasses running down the sidewalk after me.

"Did I forget something?" Mentally, I checked for my purse, the cookies, and the pie.

"No." She tried to catch her breath. "You wanted to talk to Esther about Becky Troyer?"

"Yes."

"This is about the accident?"

I nodded. "Yes."

"Good! I've been waiting to talk to someone. Esther may not speak to you, but I will."

I blinked at her. "Why?"

She adjusted her glasses. "Not now. I have to get back to the bakery. I can talk to you when I'm finished with work."

"When is that?"

"Two o'clock. You work at the college, right?"

I nodded.

"I'll meet you by the campus entrance at two thirty."

Before I could answer, she bolted back for the store. My heart lifted as I continued my way down the sidewalk, until Chief Rose sidled up next to me. I jerked a look over one shoulder. "Where did you come from?"

She smirked. "You don't look too happy to see me."

"I don't like how you appear out of thin air."

She shrugged. "It's a special talent of mine. Now, tell me more about the attempted rescue last night of Buckley and Fanning."

"Are they okay?"

"Sure. Their truck wasn't too bad off. They'll be back on the road by the end of the day." She folded her arms across her chest.

I wasn't so sure that was good news.

She cocked her head. "So what did they say to you?"

"Nothing important. Just like I told you last night. They cracked a few jokes." I didn't mention that Curt had reached into the car.

"Good. It was nice of you to stop, but in the future, you will be better off if you stay away from those two."

I picked up the pace. "I plan to. I can't help wondering what they were doing out that way, since they're all Amish homes there."

"You think they are the ones harassing the Amish?"

I nodded.

"I agree, but I need concrete proof."

I frowned. "Did the tornado do much damage?"

"It destroyed some outbuildings around the county, but no homes. No one was seriously hurt."

"Thank God for that." The college came into view.

The chief kept up my pace. "I heard you got caught on the road in the tornado last night."

I stopped. "How'd you hear that?"

She laughed. "I don't think you understand how life in a small town works." Chief Rose removed her mirrored sunglasses. I wondered, for the second time, if she chose those to wear while in uniform because they were so popular on cop shows. Maybe she thought the sunglasses would make her more attractive to the sheriff's department as a deputy.

I shook my head and started walking again.

"And Timothy Troyer was with you."

I froze. *How could she know that?*

The police chief put her sunglasses back on. "I would be careful about how close I got to the Troyer family, Chloe. You may think they've let you into their world, but you will never completely fit. Trust me. I have lived around the Amish my entire life. What makes you think you can break into their family in such a short time?"

That is none of your business. I gritted my teeth. "Is that all?"

She tipped her hat at me, that smirk still squarely on her face. "For now."

Chapter Forty-Six

As I walked onto the Harshberger campus, my thoughts turned from Chief Rose to the Computer Services Department.

My cell rang. "Miss Humphrey?"

"Yes."

"This is Tyler Hart. Becky's public defender brought me up to speed on her case. Her case is set to be heard at the Knox County Courthouse on Tuesday."

"So soon?"

"There was a cancellation on the court's calendar, so I was able to get her in. It shouldn't take long since she is pleading guilty to all the charges."

"There are no new charges?"

"No. She needs to be there at eight thirty Tuesday morning. I know the judge. He usually makes up his mind quickly. We should know her sentence within the hour."

I pressed my lips together, taking in all that Becky's lawyer told me. "What do you think it will be?"

"Like I told you and Becky in my office, I've asked for community service and probation. I think the prosecutor will go for it. He doesn't want to send an Amish girl to jail."

My breath caught in my chest. "Is jail possible?"

There was a pause. "If the prosecutor decides to add auto theft to the list of charges, yes, she would get at least six months in jail."

My knees went weak. "She didn't steal the car!"

"I know, I know. Don't worry. I've seen a draft of the charges. It wasn't on there. If it shows up, we'll fight that. Just make sure Becky's there on Tuesday. The best thing to do is keep the prosecution on our side and the judge happy."

I stepped into the department to find Miller and Clark hovering over their laptops at the conference table. Joel wasn't in the office yet. Why was I not surprised?

"Good morning," Clark said.

Beads of perspiration gathered on Miller's upper lip and the crease of his brow.

I put the cookies and pie on the conference table.

Clark eyed it. "Is this like a last meal before the execution?"

I sighed. "No."

Clark grinned. "I'm not saying I won't eat it. I love strawberry pie." He nodded toward Miller. "You can have the cookies. I'm not wasting my time on those."

Joel arrived as Clark was slicing the pie in half. He pointed at one half. "This is my share. You can divide the rest among yourselves."

Joel glared at the table, then at me. "Is that from your little Amish friends?"

I ignored his comment and went into my office.

"Dude," Clark said. "You're making it worse for yourself."

"I already know how this is going to go," Joel snapped.

So do I. The decision had been clear from the beginning. At ten o'clock, my office phone rang. It was Dean Klink's secretary, Irene. He wanted to see me again.

I walked to the dean's office as if to the executioner. Inside Dean Klink's office, fishing lures reflected colorful light around the room. He smiled at me from his seat. "You have to make a decision."

"I . . ."

"I know this is hard, Chloe, but we need to do this for the college."

The decision was made, but I had a question of my own before I gave the dean my answer. "Why did you hire me?"

The short man pushed away from his desk and peered at me with narrowed eyes, as if taken aback. "What do you mean?"

"There are plenty of qualified candidates out there looking for work who would love this job. Most of these people have much more experience than I do. Why did you choose me?"

He licked his lips. "I knew you were the best person for the job."

"How?"

He stood and began to pace. "Chloe, did you make your decision or not? Who is it going to be?"

I took a deep breath and told him.

He smiled. "I knew you would do the right thing. That's why I hired you."

I felt sick. As much as I disliked Joel, I knew he needed the job.

"I knew who you would choose," the dean said. "I've already spoken to human resources. The sooner we take care of this, the better. Let me call security."

My eye brows shot up. "Why do we need security?"

"It's a precaution, one we have to exercise with all our employees, especially considering his access to sensitive information. Joel works for you. You know he has access to everything."

I chewed off my lip balm. Dean Klink was right.

"You will have to kill his access to all the servers and computer networks. Can you do that?"

I inhaled another deep breath. "Yes."

Two hours later I watched as Joel cleaned out his desk. Clark and Miller sat at the table and solemnly watched too. The pudgy sunburned security guard observed Joel from the department's entrance.

Joel set a picture of his family into the box. My stomach clenched. "Do you need help carrying anything?"

He glared at me. Obviously not the right question.

Miller jumped up and picked up a box. "I'll help him."

I nodded and retreated into the doorway of my tiny office.

Joel picked up his briefcase, and Miller and Clark each took a box. After twenty years of working at Harshberger, his entire career fit into two boxes. Nausea overwhelmed me. Miller and Clark left the office first.

Joel turned at the doorway. "Klink didn't make a mistake when he hired you after all. You did exactly what he wanted. The only surprise is that you don't scare easily."

He left, and the security guard closed the department door behind them. I pushed the taste of bile back down my throat and erased Joel's access from every part of Harshberger's computer system. *You don't scare easily* resounded in my head with each click of the mouse.

Chapter Forty-Seven

At one o'clock, Clark peeked into my office. "I'm going to run to the cafeteria for lunch. Do you want anything?"

I tore my eyes from my computer screen. "No, I'm all right."

He leaned against the door. "You don't look all right. Why don't you come with me? It will be good for you to get out of the office, away from the place of execution."

"I wish you'd stop calling it that."

He grinned. "So, how about it?"

"All right. Can Miller come too?"

"Naw, he already left. He usually goes home for lunch. Poor guy is pretty shaken up."

I gave him a pained expression. "Is that supposed to make me feel better?"

"Don't worry about it. Miller will be fine by Monday. Now, let's go."

Clark and I walked in companionable silence across the green to the cafeteria, which was located directly across from Dennis. The only students on campus were volleyball and soccer athletes here for practice. Harshberger was too small for a football team. The students elbowed each other as they moved down the line to fill their trays. At twenty four, I was only a few years older, but felt worlds away. The teams sat together on the far side of the cafeteria close to the entrance to the college bookstore.

Staff and faculty dotted the rest of the large room. None of them seemed to relish their meals. The culinary options were a salad bar that could double as a biology experiment—I bypassed that—greasy pizza, or overcooked hamburgers and limp french fries. I settled on the hamburger and fries, hoping a thick layer of ketchup would overpower the burnt taste.

Clark was already seated at a table by a window that overlooked the gymnasium and student dorms when I paid for my lunch. As a staff member, the whole meal only cost me two dollars, so it certainly had price in its favor. I slipped into the beige plastic molded seat across from Clark.

Clark sawed his hamburger in half with a white plastic knife. "What do you think of the food?"

"Well . . ."

He laughed. "You don't have to pretend to like it. No one does. When the semester starts, it will be fifty percent better. Notice I didn't say one hundred percent. However, fifty is a marked improvement."

After slathering the burger with ketchup, I took a bite. It tasted like charcoal dipped in ketchup. I set it back on the ceramic plate.

Clark put down his burger. Despite his complaints about the meal, most of the burger and fries were gone. "Can I ask you a question?"

"Sure." I popped a soggy fry in my mouth, swallowing hard to force it down my throat.

"How long are you going to be here?" Clark squinted in the sunbeam that cut through the window. The legs of his chair made a horrible screeching sound as he scooted away from the glare.

"What do you mean?"

"Dean Klink may look harmless, but he's done this many times before."

"Done what?"

"Restructured a department." He made quotation marks with his fingers when he said "restructured." "Not that firing Joel was wrong. The dude had a chip on his shoulder the size of Mount Rushmore."

"Joel wasn't fired," I corrected. "He was let go,"

"Whatever. We knew when our old boss resigned that it was just a matter of time for us." He sipped from a paper cup. "Klink hires some young hotshot like you—someone who won't be here too long—to take over a department.

"Then the hotshot leaves for bigger and better things, and the department is how Dean Klink wants it. Now he hires the person he really wanted for the job because having fired one or two people means he can now afford the expert with more experience."

The bite of french fry lodged in my throat. I took a big gulp of water.

"So how long are you going to be here?"

I didn't answer right away.

"Your silence is all the answer I need." He popped another fry into his mouth and chewed thoughtfully. "What, one year? Two years?"

"I don't know." After meeting the Troyer family, leaving after two years didn't sound as good as it once did.

He wiped mustard off his chin. "At least Miller and I know what to expect."

I leaned forward, unable to eat another bite. "Are you going to tell Miller about this conversation?"

He thought for a long minute while dragging the tip of his knife along the rim of his plate. "Naw. The kid is spooked enough as it is."

"Can I ask you a question now?"

He nodded.

"What can I do to make it better for you guys at work?"

He dropped a french fry. "No one has asked me that before."

I pushed my plate away. I would eat the lunch that Becky packed for me when I got back to my office.

"I don't know. I'll have to think about it."

I gave him a nod. "Ask Miller to think about it too."

AT A QUARTER AFTER two, I waited at the entrance to Harshberger, checking my cell phone for the time every few minutes. *Will the girl from the bakery show?* I wished I knew her name.

"Miss Humphrey?"

I turned to find the girl from the bakery. "I'm so glad you came."

She nodded, her expression shy. She was still wearing her apron from the bakery. A smudge of chocolate marked her pocket. She picked at it with her thumbnail.

"Do you want to sit down?" I pointed to a bench.

She glanced inside the college's grounds. "No, I can't stay long. My brother will be showing up to the bakery soon to take me home."

"I'm Chloe." I held out my hand. She squeezed my fingers but didn't shake my hand. "What's your name?"

"Sadie Hooley."

"What did you want to tell me, Sadie?"

"I haven't seen Becky in awhile, not since she left home. My family wouldn't like it if they thought I was talking to her." She adjusted her glasses. "But I know Becky and know she could never hurt anyone, especially Bishop Glick. Some of our customers at the bakery say it wasn't an accident. They think Becky hit the bishop's buggy on purpose. I know that's not true."

"I know it would mean a lot to Becky to hear you say that."

"Can you tell her for me? I can't talk to her. I shouldn't even be talking to you."

"I will," I promised.

"You came to the bakery to talk to Esther."

I nodded.

"Esther and Becky don't get along. They never have, even when we were in school. It has always been over Isaac." She picked at the chocolate smear on her apron.

"Does Esther plan to marry Isaac?"

Sadie nodded. "She always planned to marry Isaac, even when he was courting Becky."

"Isaac courting Becky must have made Esther mad."

Sadie laughed. "It made her furious. I don't know how many times I had to hear her rant about Becky in the bakery. Once I told her she should be more upset with Isaac because he chose Becky over her. She didn't talk to me for a week after, which was a relief really. Esther can talk a person's ear off, especially if she's angry."

"Could Esther be angry enough to want to hurt someone?"

Sadie removed her glasses and cleaned the lenses on her apron. "No."

"Then why are you telling me this?"

She thought a moment. "Esther can be bristly, even short with people, but I know she could never hurt anyone just as I know that Becky couldn't. I wanted to talk to you to tell you that. It's the truth, no matter what you might hear around town."

"Are there rumors going around about her?"

Sadie shrugged. "People coming into the bakery like to talk. It doesn't matter if they are Amish or *Englisch*. They want the news, and the biggest news in town now is the bishop's passing."

"Thank you for telling me, Sadie."

"I should go. My brother must be waiting for me."

I nodded.

She placed her glasses back on her nose. They didn't look any cleaner than before. A bit of chocolate marred the edge of one lens. Just before she started down the sidewalk, she turned. "You seem like a nice girl. Becky can use all the friends she can find right now. I'm glad she found you."

As she walked away, I whispered, "Me too."

Chapter Forty-Eight

After work, a black buggy sat in front of my rented house. Had Grandfather Zook brought the children? As I got closer to the buggy, it became clear it wasn't Grandfather Zook's. This buggy was smaller, and dust covered the back end. Grandfather Zook would never drive his buggy if it was less than pristine.

The main tip-off, though, was the horse: a black and brown mare. No white star on the forehead. Definitely not Sparky. I walked around the empty buggy, and then glanced at my house, seeing no movement. To my right, the crunch of coarse gravel caught my attention—as did Deacon Sutter stomping down my driveway.

I crossed my arms. "What are you doing here?"

"Looking for you, Miss Humphrey."

He took a few steps closer to me, but I held my ground.

He towered over me, deep sun lines etching his face. "You have no place to speak to the people in the district."

My brow furrowed. "What are you talking about?"

"Did you stop in the bakery in town today?"

"I did." I held up my chin. "I bought some cookies. Is that a crime?"

"You weren't there to buy cookies."

I didn't deny it.

"My brother-in-law told me how upset my niece Esther was by your visit."

"You're Esther's uncle?"

"Yes." He glared at me.

I blew out a breath. "I'm sorry I upset her, but I wanted to know what she may know about the accident."

"So you admit it."

"I never denied I want to know how my car was sabotaged."

His eyes bored into mine. "Did you talk to anyone else?"

Sadie came to mind, but there was no way I would tell the deacon about her. She took a big risk by speaking to me. "I don't have to answer that." I started for the front door, feeling for the cell phone in my purse.

The deacon reached out and grabbed my upper arm. His long slender fingers dug into my flesh. "Don't walk away from me."

I jerked my arm away and glared at him. "I thought the Amish were nonviolent. Maybe you should listen more closely to the rules that you preach."

His eyes narrowed, but he took a step back. "Stay away from my district. You've already tricked the Troyers into accepting you, but it won't work for anyone else. I blame their worldliness on Zook's influence. Simon Troyer would have never behaved this way before his father-in-law moved to the county. Perhaps they need to be reminded of the error of their ways."

"How would you do that?"

"That's a matter for the church."

I bit the inside of my lip and tasted blood.

He stopped and wagged his index finger at me. "Don't come around my family again." Then he climbed into his buggy.

As the horse pulled the buggy away, I wondered what he could do to me if I did. Nothing. I wasn't Amish. He had no control over me.

The Troyers were another story.

THIRTY MINUTES LATER, I parked outside Little Owl Greenhouse and found Becky sweeping the parking lot. Even with only one good arm, Becky's broom kicked up huge clouds of dust. There was mulch everywhere.

I hopped out of the car. "What happened?"

"One of the mulch bags broke open during last night's storm. I've been sweeping for two hours. Cookie asked me to finish it before I leave."

"You have a long way to go."

"I know."

I glanced around the lot. "Is there another broom? I can help."

She grinned and ran into the shop for a second broom. Heat rose from the pavement, and I was glad I had changed into shorts and a T-shirt. "Where are Cookie and Scotch?"

She handed me the broom. "In the hothouse."

I began sweeping. "I spoke with Sadie Hooley today."

"Sadie? How is she? I saw her when I stopped at the Amish Bread Bakery looking for work." She sighed. "I shouldn't have tried applying there."

"Why not?" I sneezed as a cloud of dust and mulch flew into my face.

"The bakery belongs to Esther Yoder's family. Why'd you talk to Sadie?"

"I wanted to talk to Esther."

"Esther? Why?"

"Just to see if she knew anything about the accident."

Becky stopped sweeping. "Why would she know anything about that?"

"Ruth said—"

"I know what Ruth said, but Esther wouldn't do anything to anyone. I already told you that." Before I could respond, she started one-handed sweeping again. "Esther doesn't like me. She never has, even when we were *kinner*, but she would never hurt me."

"Maybe she asked someone else to do it."

She looked up. "Why?"

"Isaac."

She dropped her gaze and shook her head. "The minute I left home, Esther won Isaac. Why would she bother?"

"I'm trying to be thorough. I'm not going to ignore a lead because it's uncomfortable. Are you more upset about this because of Esther or because of Isaac?"

"I don't want to talk about Isaac." She dropped her broom on the blacktop.

"Did you leave for art or did you leave to avoid marriage?" The question popped out of my mouth, and I immediately regretted it.

Her blue eyes filled with tears, and she fled into the greenhouse.

Why did I ask her that? I set both brooms against the front of the greenhouse, then found Becky with Cookie and Scotch in the hothouse.

"Hush! Hush!" Cookie allowed Becky to cry into her shoulder.

Scotch pulled a yellow bandana from his bib overalls and handed it to Becky.

Cookie's heavily made-up eyes turned on me. "Now, why'd you have to go and make her cry."

"I—Becky, I'm sorry."

Becky shook her head against Cookie's shoulder.

Scotch waved at me. "Come on, Chloe, let's give the girls a minute."

Helpless, I followed him back into the store. Scotch moved behind the counter. "Don't worry about Becky. Cookie will calm her down. She's good with our girls."

"You have daughters?"

He nodded. "Two. Both are grown. One lives in Seattle and

the other in Richmond. Cookie likes having Becky here so much because our girls are so far away. She misses mothering. Tell the truth, we both love having Becky here and would do anything for her."

"You've already done so much by giving her this job, and driving her back and forth to work goes way above that."

He waved away my praise. "We need to know she's safe." Scotch sat on a stool behind the cash register, clutching his cane. There were no cars in the parking lot and no customers in the shop or greenhouse.

What was Cookie saying to Becky in the hothouse? I hoped her motherly advice was better than her makeover.

Scotch looked around the rustic building. "This greenhouse was Cookie's dream. It's something she's wanted since I first met her more than thirty years ago. I knew I had to make it happen for her."

"How long have you been open?"

"Four years." He popped open the cash register and started counting the money in the drawer. There didn't seem to be much there, but most people shopped with credit cards now anyway.

"It must be hard to run a small business right now."

He nodded, keeping his eyes focused on the slim pile of bills. "It's hard to run any kind of business right now."

I thought about the unfortunate event at Harshberger earlier in the day.

"But," Scotch said, "in tough times, we have to make tough choices to keep things afloat."

"That's true." Again, Joel came to mind, ornery as he was. Silently, I prayed for him and his family, feeling guilty that it hadn't occurred to me to do so before.

"Sometimes, too"—Scotch said more talking to himself than to me—"you have to work with people you don't care for to save your business and protect those you love."

My brow wrinkled. "Like who?"

He laughed. "Look at me, an old man muttering about his troubles! It won't be long before Cookie'll be wheeling me into the nursing home and my diet will consist of gelatin and creamed carrots."

I thought there was more to it than that, but before I could ask him, Becky and Cookie entered the shop. Becky's eyes were dry, and she was smiling. I don't know how, at age twenty-four, I had a nineteen-year-old under my care. I was not equipped to be a parent and certainly not to someone so close to my own age.

"We're all better," Cookie proclaimed. "I gave her the old Cookie pep talk. Worked every time with my girls." She winked.

"I'll finish cleaning up the mulch, Chloe, and we can go home."

I followed her. "I'll help."

Becky shrugged, so we worked in silence.

Once in the car, I couldn't stand Becky's silent treatment anymore. "Becky, I said I'm sorry. If you don't want to talk about Isaac, I won't mention him again."

She let out a breath as if she'd been holding it a long while. "I'm sorry for being angry." She stared out her window. "I wanted to love Isaac as much as he loved me, but I loved my art more."

"Then you made the right decision."

Her eyebrows shot up into her hairline. "Really? Everyone told me the opposite."

"Marrying Isaac would be easier for you and for your family. You were brave to turn him down. Someday you will find someone you love more than art."

Her whole face lit up. "I pray so. Do you think you will find someone you love more than your computers?"

I laughed, but then grew serious. "Maybe . . ."

Chapter Forty-Nine

Saturday morning I woke up to find Gigabyte chewing on my hair. I swatted him away, and he yowled in protest. "Gig," I complained into my pillow. "This is the only day of the week I get to sleep in. Go away."

Another yowl.

I opened one eye and focused it on the wayward animal. "I'm sure Becky's up. Ask her to give you breakfast."

My bedroom door flew open, and Becky bounced onto my bed. "Chloe, get up. It's after ten o'clock."

"Wake me up for lunch," I mumbled.

She bounced some more. A headache formed at the base of my skull. Most of the time I appreciated her energy. Ten a.m. on a Saturday was not one of those times.

"You have to get up."

"Why?"

She let out a dramatic sigh. "Didn't you hear the phone ring?"

"No," I told the pillow.

"Timothy's coming."

I bolted upright in the bed. "What? Why?"

"He says he has a surprise for us, and he's bringing Aaron too."

I blinked the sleep from my eyes. "Aaron? Deacon Sutter's son? *That* Aaron?"

She frowned. "*Ya!* Now, get up!" She hopped off the bed and skipped out of the room. *She seems awfully excited to see her brother.*

I fell back onto my pillow.

By eleven when Aaron and Timothy rolled in, I was presentable in a pink T-shirt and khaki capri pants. Becky wore her jeans again. I told her at some point that weekend we would have to take them to the Laundromat since she was determined to wear them every day. That or we'd have to go back to the department store and buy a month's worth.

Timothy climbed out of the car, but Aaron waved from the passenger seat. "Climb in on my side," Timothy said.

Since I was the shortest, I climbed into the back with Mabel. The woolly dog flopped onto my lap. We had bonded during our tornado ordeal. "Where are we going? Does this have to do with the case?"

Timothy watched me in the rearview mirror. "I think we need a break from the case today. We are taking you to one of the best parts of Knox County: the Kokosing Gap Trail."

Becky beamed. "I love it there."

Timothy backed out of the driveway. "There's an entrance not too far from here."

My toes curled in my sandals. "Won't the ground be muddy?" In my mind, trail meant puddles and roots that trip.

Aaron laughed. "The trail is paved and follows the river through Knox County for more than thirty miles. Kokosing meant 'little owl' to Native Americans. Sometimes you can see an owl on the trail at night."

"Oh." Relief poured through me. One muddy adventure this week was more than enough.

Timothy turned into a nearly full gravel parking lot. Apparently, the trail was a popular place in the county. A family filed out of the minivan next to us.

Becky, Mabel, and I climbed out of the truck as Timothy removed Aaron's wheelchair from the bed and unfolded it. He then lifted his friend out of the truck and placed him on the chair. "Now, this is what I call service," Aaron proclaimed. "Onward!" He pointed up the ridge that led to the paved path. Timothy took it at a run, pushing the wheelchair up the side, with Mabel barking at his heels. On the path, Timothy clicked a leash on Mabel's collar, and she barked in protest. He pointed at the leash law sign as if she could read it.

I reached for the leash. "I'll walk her so you can push Aaron."

"No," Becky said. "I'll push Aaron."

Timothy pointed at her cast. "Can you with one arm?"

"Watch me," Becky said.

Timothy shrugged and let Becky take over the reins of Aaron's wheelchair. He fell back in step with Mabel and me.

"Becky looks happy," I said.

Timothy grinned. "Aaron, too."

We fell further back, and I glanced at Timothy. "Becky must think there is some sort of race."

He laughed.

Broad-leafed trees hung over the bark-topped path, birds twittering in their branches. I could hear the sound of the Kokosing rushing by behind the tree line. "It's beautiful here."

Timothy shortened his stride to meet mine. "It's one of my favorite places. I come here all the time."

I picked a leaf from Mabel's fur. "The deacon was okay with you picking up Aaron in your truck?"

"The deacon doesn't exactly know. If he had his way, Aaron would be hidden away at home all the time." Timothy's tone turned raw, almost bitter.

"If his father is so awful, why does Aaron stay?"

Timothy's brow wrinkled. "Each Amish person must make a choice. I made mine, so did Aaron. Neither of us is unhappy."

Ahead of us, Becky and Aaron laughed together, and Timothy turned to me. "Could he be happier?"

Suddenly Mabel jerked my arm to the left and started barking on the side of the trail.

Timothy reached for the leash, giving it a tug below where it wrapped around my hand. "It's just a squirrel, girl."

She barked an argument. Together, we were finally able to coax her away from the squirrel. By then Aaron and Becky were out of sight.

Timothy looked on ahead. "Knowing my sister, they are half way to Mount Vernon by now."

I fell into step beside him. "It's nice to see Becky so happy." Mabel tugged on the leash again. *These woods must be bursting with squirrels to chase.*

"Aaron, too."

"Was your family upset when you decided to leave the Amish?"

"Of course. Especially my father. However, I think they recognized the alternative was worse."

I stopped in the middle of the trail.

Timothy exhaled. "After the accident, while Aaron was in the hospital, I went through a bad time. I fell into the wrong crowd."

"The wrong Amish crowd?"

He gave a rueful laugh. "There are tough kids among the Amish too. I got arrested for drunk driving and robbery." He looked down at the ground, as if ashamed. "That's how I know Greta, or Chief Rose, so well. She's locked me up a few times."

"Oh." *This must me the reason for all of Chief Rose's cryptic warnings about Timothy.* "But you turned your life around."

He nodded. "Do you remember Hannah? You met her at church."

Oh, I remember.

"Her father is a carpenter too, and I worked with him a lot before the accident. He saw I was making a bad turn and invited me to their church. This was after my third arrest, third night in jail, and I was ready to turn back to *Gott*. I just didn't know how. Actually, I wasn't turning back to *Gott*, I was turning to Him for the first time."

"What do you mean?"

"John Hilty, Hannah's father, taught me there's a difference between Amish faith and *Gotte's* grace. Amish faith would not forgive me, but the grace of Christ would. I only needed to ask Him for it. This was so different from what I was taught by the leaders of our district. They taught us from a young age that you had to work for forgiveness. What John helped me realize is that I could never work hard enough to undo every wrong deed I had ever done. The rules that I followed or broke being Amish were not getting me any closer to *Gott*. For me, they were a form of separation because I knew I could never close the distance, so why bother trying. I left the Amish because I wanted to know I was forgiven. I didn't want to live in constant fear. I could not earn Christ's love and forgiveness, only accept it."

Could I ever be as confident about what I believed, enough to give up so much?

Timothy watched me for a moment, as if reading my mind. "That doesn't mean I don't have moments of doubt or even guilt. Every time I see Aaron's wheelchair, I feel guilt. Every time I run into the deacon, guilt is there."

"You didn't make Aaron jump on that roof."

"He's confined to a wheelchair for something I told him to do."

I grabbed Timothy's arm. "But he did it."

He shook his head, his expression sober. "It doesn't matter. He's a son. He cannot take over his family farm and may never marry. It's because of me."

I squeezed his fingers. "You don't know he won't get married."

"What Amish woman would want to marry a man who can't work? The father in the family is supposed to be the provider. Aaron can't do that."

"I don't believe that he can't provide for his family in some way. He might not be a farmer working in the fields, but there's other work he can do. A person's entire worth is not measured by the type of work they do."

I let go of Timothy, and started walking again. "I know what it's like to live with guilt."

He didn't say anything, but simply waited for me to continue. And yet, I saw the concern on his face.

I rubbed my eyes, remembering. "My mother died in a car accident when I fourteen, and it was my fault." I took a shaky breath. "It was late, close to one in the morning when it happened, and it was because of me."

He reached for my hand and squeezed it.

"I was at a friend's house for a sleepover and got sick." I winced at the memory. "Really sick. I must have had food poisoning. Anyway, the mom of the girl—not Tanisha, although Tee was there—called my parents and told them that one of them had to come get me. This was in January over Martin Luther King weekend. On the way to pick me up, my mother hit a patch of black ice that sent her car spinning into a tree."

Timothy squeezed my hand harder, our fingers intertwined.

"Mom died at the hospital from her injuries, and my father never forgave me."

He didn't let me go. "You were just a sick kid. How could that be your fault?"

I watched Mabel sniff her way down the path. "Within a year of the accident, my father remarried. My stepmother's not the easiest woman to get along with, and she pulled my father and me further apart. When I was fifteen, she convinced him to move to California and leave me behind."

"What do you mean 'leave you behind'? Why didn't you move with them?"

"Sabrina—she's my stepmother—thought she was doing me a favor. She said I wouldn't want to move and leave my life and friends in Cleveland. That was true to some extent. She asked Tanisha's family to take care of me, and even offered them money to do it.

They never took any money from her, but they agreed to let me live with them. I don't know what I would have done without them." I said all of this without tears. The tears I cried over my father were gone. Only a cold, hollow sadness remained. "I went along with it because my father never said a word about it. He never asked me to move with them. He never asked me to stay. He said nothing. That's pretty much how it's been ever since. Silence."

Timothy looked down at me, his eyes unwavering. "I told you, you had me the night of the tornado, and I meant it."

I smiled. A red-iron bridge that spanned the Kokosing River came into view. "Wow," I said. "It's beautiful." Trees heavy with bright green leaves hung heavy over the river. Becky parked Aaron's wheelchair so he could peer into the water. She sat next to him cross-legged on the bridge. I admired them from afar. "Clearly, Becky doesn't care if Aaron can run his family farm."

Timothy squeezed my hand one more time before letting go. "Clearly not."

The four of us and Mabel returned to the parking lot, then pulled up short. The green pickup was parked next to Timothy's truck.

Timothy picked up the pace and called to me over one shoulder. "You guys hang back until I unlock the truck." He marched toward his pickup, and Brock stepped out from behind it.

I noticed Becky grip the handlebar of Aaron's wheelchair with her good hand.

Brock didn't back down. "Well, look who's here, Curt?"

"Why it's Red and her Amish amigos." Curt pointed a thumb at us. "She even has a new friend. A cripple. My, Red, you know how to pick 'em."

I slipped my cell phone from my pocket to call Chief Rose, but the screen said, "Searching for service." Why did I still carry it with me? It was turning out to be nothing more than an expensive clock. I slid the phone back into my pocket.

Becky looked like she was ready to bolt down the embankment and kick Curt in the shin.

Timothy's voice was low and firm. "Please, leave us alone."

I helped Becky guide Aaron's chair down the embankment to the parking lot. "Let's stand by the exit," I whispered to her. "We can get into the truck when Timothy backs up."

Aaron used his arm to shift his leg in his chair. "Are these the knuckleheads who have been bothering you? They don't look so tough."

I glanced around for help. The parking lot was full of cars, but there were no people around. Their owners must have been on the trail.

"Sorry, buggy-rider, but we aren't going anywhere."

Mabel growled deep in her throat.

I took over pushing the wheelchair and pulled Becky to the getaway spot.

"Blondie doesn't want to go with you," Brock called. "Maybe you want to come home with us?"

"He's lucky I can't chase him," Aaron muttered.

Timothy seemed to grow taller. "Get out of my way."

"Or what?" Brock stepped up to Timothy's face. "Are you going to hit us, buggy-rider?"

"Aw," Curt said. "A good Amish boy wouldn't do that."

"There will be a point when we will have to defend ourselves against people like you," Timothy said.

Curt adjusted the dog tags around his neck, eyeing him. "What do you mean by that?"

Timothy's tone remained level. "We all know you two are behind the harassment of the Amish."

Curt spat. "You don't know what you're talking about."

Brock grimaced. "At least we aren't afraid to get our hands dirty to protect our family and our country." He turned to Becky. "So, blondie, the offer still stands. Want to lose these two and come with us?"

Becky recoiled.

Curt gave a fake pout. "Now you've gone and hurt my feelings. I thought we had something."

"We're leaving," Timothy said.

Brock sniffed. "Okay, run from a fight. That's what you Amish are good at, aren't you?"

Timothy's head snapped around. "Don't ever come around either of these girls again."

Brock snickered.

Curt laughed so hard he bent at the waist, gasping for breath, before recovering. "What are you going to do?"

Mabel growled again. I bent down and unhooked her leash. "Go!"

The dog was off like a shot, barking and snapping at Curt and Brock.

Brock jumped behind his friend and squealed. "It's Cujo!"

Timothy used the distraction to climb into the truck. He backed out of his space and stopped in front of us on the road. He then jumped out and lifted Aaron into the truck.

Curt kicked at Mabel, and she chomped on the end of his boot. He swore. "That thing has rabies!"

Becky and I jumped in through the driver's side door as Timothy placed Aaron's chair in the back.

He hopped back into the cab. As he pulled out of the lot, Timothy stuck his head out. "Mabel! Come!"

The dog spun around, ran full tilt for Timothy's truck, and jumped into the bed. I turned in my seat to see Brock make an ugly hand gesture at our truck.

A short while later, Timothy drove up to the house. He walked me to the door as Becky said good-bye to Aaron. Neither man had mentioned Brock or Curt again. "There is a picnic at the church tonight," Timothy said. "It's a celebration for the end of summer."

I wasn't eager to see Hannah again. "Does Becky know about it?"

"She should. You might need to remind her though."

"I can do that."

He paused. "Will you come?"

"To bring Becky? Sure, if she needs a ride."

"I don't want you to just drop her off."

"Oh, okay."

A slow smile grew on his face. "No. I want you to come."

I felt a blush spread across my face—and I forgot all about Hannah.

Chapter Fifty

I ran my hands along the skirt of my flower-print dress, unsure of what to wear when I visited Timothy's church again. Since the congregation was Mennonite, most of the women wore long skirts. I didn't believe Becky when she said anything I wore would be fine.

"You look beautiful. I don't know what you're so nervous about. I should be the one who is nervous. *I'm* the one everyone is talking about," Becky said. "I'd rather be home with Gigabyte watching Paula Deen."

Becky had recently discovered Food Network. She was obsessed.

"You're going as a favor to me. Timothy wanted you to come too."

Becky shook her head. "I don't think so. He likes you. I've never seen him act this way around anyone else, not even Hannah."

Did she have to keep bringing up Hannah? It was bad enough I knew she would be at the picnic that night.

The picnic area behind the church was filled with people and four gas grills loaded down with hotdogs and hamburgers. It smelled divine. These hamburgers would be much better than the one I gagged down in Harshberger's cafeteria.

Timothy stood next to a middle-aged man at one of the grills. He waved at us and jogged over. "I'm so glad you could come." He ran his eyes over me. "You look nice."

I blushed. Hopefully he'd think the redness on my cheeks was just a sunburn from the hike we took that morning.

He started back toward the grill, and gestured for me to follow him. "I want you to meet someone."

Becky bumped into me. "Don't leave me," she whispered.

I grabbed her hand. "Then come with us."

Timothy gestured to an older man at the grill. "Chloe, this is John Hilty."

I knew where Hannah got her good looks. John Hilty was a handsome man, with a tan from working outside and laugh lines that creased the corners of his deep-set eyes.

Mr. Hilty removed his oven mitt and held out his hand. I shook it. "It's nice to meet you. How do you know Timothy?"

I nodded to my housemate. "Through Becky."

"Hello, Becky," Mr. Hilty said.

From yards away, Hannah waved in our direction. "Daddy!" She wore a flowered dress similar to mine, but as my dress hung straight from my shoulders, hers hugged her curves. I wished I'd followed Becky's advice and worn my jeans. At least then it wouldn't look like I was trying to copy Hannah.

Kim and Emily followed behind Hannah at a respectful distance, as if they were ladies-in-waiting and she was the princess. Church members beamed as Hannah floated by. Maybe she was the princess.

Hannah fake pouted. "Timothy, I've been waiting for you to get here, and you go straight to my father instead of saying hello to me." Her pout morphed into an adoring grin.

The worst part? The affectionate expression he offered her in return.

Mr. Hilty pointed a metal spatula in my direction. "Have you met Chloe, Hannah?"

Hannah gave me the smallest of smiles. "Yes, we met last Sunday. It's nice to see you again, Chloe. Will you be attending our church on a regular basis?"

Not if you ask me like that.

Hannah put a hand on my wrist. "We shouldn't distract the men when they are cooking. Why don't you and Becky join my friends and me?"

I opened my mouth to make an excuse, but Timothy nodded. "That's a great idea. Have fun!"

Becky and I followed Hannah and her friends to a picnic table as if our shoes were full of lead. Suddenly Becky stopped. "Oh, I see someone I have to talk to."

"Wha—" I grabbed at her as she ran in the opposite direction.

Hannah glanced over her shoulder. "Are you coming, Chloe?"

I looked heavenward and followed. At the table, I perched on one of the benches next to Kim. She seemed the least ferocious of the group. Besides, from this vantage point I could see Timothy at the grill.

Hannah folded her hands on the table. "You seem to be spending a lot of time with Timothy and his family."

I decided to change the subject. "Becky told me that you knew about her job interview?"

Hannah arched an eyebrow at me. "I did. She mentioned it to me when we met in town one afternoon."

"She told you that she'd be driving my car."

There was a pitcher of lemonade on the table, and Emily poured us each a paper cup full.

Hannah took a sip. "She told me that she was driving a car. I didn't know it was yours. To be honest, I wasn't all that interested. You think a lot of the Troyers, don't you?"

I glanced at Timothy, who laughed with the other men around the grill. "They've been so welcoming."

"I'm surprised, considering . . ."

I looked to Hannah. "Considering what?"

"That you are an English girl."

I didn't rise to the bait. Instead, I watched Timothy flip hamburgers on the grill and laugh with Hannah's father. I could never imagine him doing that with my father. I could never imagine my father doing that with anyone, for that matter.

"For Amish, the Troyers are more accepting than others in their district. I'm sure it's the grandfather's influence." She took another sip of her lemonade. "After everything that's happened, they've come to accept me as part of the family too. I know his parents are Amish, but I think they now know that I'm a good match for Timothy."

I froze. "A good match?"

"Didn't Timothy tell you? We are a couple. We are practically promised to each other."

"Promised to each other? What does that mean?"

She laughed lightly, her eyelashes fluttering. "That we will be engaged soon."

My face grew hot. "A person is either engaged or not engaged."

"Why are you getting so upset?" She crushed her empty lemonade cup in her hand. "Emily, pour me another. I want a fresh cup."

Emily did as she was told.

I swallowed. "I've never heard the term before."

"It might not be something people say in the big city you're from, but in Knox County it's common."

"Oh." I took a deep breath. *Get a grip, Chloe.*

"You are getting so upset, I . . . well . . ."

"What?" My temper flared.

She gave her lilting laugh again. "I'd almost think you have feelings for him."

Her minions giggled.

She took a sip from her fresh cup. "That's silly. You have to know his family would never approve of you. You're English."

I cocked my head. "So are you."

"True, but I'm Mennonite. I guess his family feels if he's going to leave the church, I'm close enough. We share the same faith and values." She frowned. "I'm surprised he didn't tell you about me." She crushed the second empty paper cup in her hand. "I've heard all about you. You were trapped in the tornado together. No wonder you have a crush on him." Her eyes narrowed. "How cute."

"I've got to go." I got up from the table and walked away. How dumb of me to come. My version of plain clothing or not, I did not belong here. I was better off with my high-tech toys. Hannah was right; she was a much better fit for Timothy than I could ever be. If Timothy had been promised to her, it was no wonder he'd been reluctant to talk to me about his past. The question was, why did he bother to tell me at all? I knew I should go to Timothy directly and ask him. That's what Tanisha would have done. But I didn't have my best friend's nerve. I couldn't bring myself to do it at the picnic with Hannah close by. I needed to get out of there to clear my head.

I was almost to the parking lot when Timothy touched my arm. "Chloe, what's wrong? Where are you going?"

I tensed. "Nothing's wrong."

"You're upset."

"I'm not upset." I could hear my own voice catch, and took a breath. "I'm going home."

"What happened?"

"Ask Hannah."

His eyes were concerned. "Is Hannah all right?"

His question was like a punch in the gut. *Maybe she had been telling the truth.* "I have to go."

"It's late. How are you going to get there?"

"Same way I got here. I'll walk," I snapped.

He jerked back as if I slapped him. Then he let go of my arm and let me walk away.

As I walked home, I felt ridiculous for getting so upset. I let Hannah get to me without giving Timothy the chance to explain.

He deserved the chance to do that. As I walked along the sidewalk, a flush ran up the back of my neck into the crown of my head. *How could I be so stupid?*

As I made my way up the path to my house, a silver car drove by me very slowly. I tamped down a shiver. *I must still be spooked from today's encounter with Curt and Brock.* I put the key in the lock, then glanced at the silver sedan's taillights. At least it wasn't a green truck.

Chapter Fifty-One

On Monday afternoon, a reception was held in the cafeteria for summer staff. Dean Klink and the college president stood behind a podium in front of an unlit fireplace. The dean tapped his finger on the microphone. *Pop. Pop.*

Next to me, Clark winced, his voice a harsh whisper. "I hate it when people do that. Hurts the equipment."

The dean leaned into the mike. "Can you hear me?"

A shout came from the back of the cafeteria. "No!"

Clark groaned.

I elbowed him. "Go up there and help him."

"All right." He left his seat and wove through the chairs.

The dean clapped his hands. "Oh good, I see Clark's coming to help us."

Miller kept rearranging the salt and pepper shakers on the table. I fought back the urge to snatch them from him.

A cluster of secretaries stood in the middle of the room, blocking half of the stage. I stood up and took a few steps to observe Clark. His foot stuck out from the side of podium. An amp or speaker must have gotten unplugged. I was about to sit down when

I noticed a third person standing, waiting to speak. My back stiffened. Grayson Mathews. *What is he doing here?*

He made eye contact with me and smiled. A chill ran down my spine.

Clark crawled out from under the podium, said something to Dean Klink, and then hurried back to our table.

"Thank you, Clark," Dean Klink spoke into the microphone. "Thank you, everyone, for taking time from your busy day to come out and meet together as a campus this afternoon. We know you are all tirelessly working to make this the best year Harshberger has ever seen. As year-round staff, you're the wheels that keep us moving, and we thank you for that. Each and every one of you is important to the success of this college."

He waited for the round of applause to die down before he continued. "Since you work all year round, we only thought it was fair to share some exciting news with you first. We have a new partnership coming to Harshberger College, and we are thrilled to tell you about it." Dean Klink gestured to the president. "President Hammerstein, would you do the honors?"

I'd yet to meet the college president in person. He was an elderly man with a beaklike nose. His wide smile softened the severity of his features. "This school year we will be breaking ground for a new building: The Mathews Science Center."

The sound of clapping resonated through the room.

"The Mathews Science Center will have state-of-the-art labs for all our science majors, including nursing. Mr. Mathews and his company have made a generous two-million-dollar donation, and many other donors have also given gifts." He started listing the donors. As he did, I could not take my eyes off Grayson Mathews. When we met, I had told him I worked at Harshberger. So why didn't he tell me about this project? Was it because the college was keeping it a secret until details were finalized? What else didn't I know about him?

Mathews stepped up to the microphone. "Thank you, President

Hammerstein. Thank you, Dean Klink." He shared his toothpaste-commercial smile with the room. "I'm so grateful for this opportunity to partnership with Harshberger College. As many of you know, my father loved Harshberger and taught here for more than thirty years in the chemistry department. Even though I never attend here as a student—I might have if you had football . . ."

A chuckle rumbled through the crowd.

"Harshberger is as much my home campus as Ohio State is. I grew up here, and I know that the great work you do to educate and prepare young people for both their personal and professional lives is unsurpassed. This new building will be in honor of my father's memory, but also in honor of you, his colleagues and friends."

Clark shifted in his seat, muttering. "He wants his last name on the building. It will make it easier for him with the county."

"What do you mean?" I whispered.

"He's not just trying to buy Amish land, if you know what I mean."

I wrinkled my forehead.

Miller rotated the salt and pepper shakers again. "Strategic philanthropy."

"Or natural gas," Clark said.

"Natural gas?" The pump on the Glick farm came to mind.

"Oh, yeah. Knox is one of the top natural gas-producing counties in Ohio. I'm sure Mathews would love to get his hands on it. The Amish are sitting smack-dab on top of it."

"What about the planned communities?" I asked.

Clark shrugged. "He might want to do that too, but it won't make him the same kind of money the well will. I mean, who in Knox County can afford those huge houses he builds?"

Who indeed?

A woman sitting across from us made a shushing sound, and I realized I missed the end of Mathews's brief speech.

After the speech, Miller, Clark, and I got in line for cookies. "It was the weirdest thing," Clark said, "but I could have sworn I saw his car in the lot this morning. Later, I went outside to search for it, but by then, it was gone."

"You did?" Miller asked.

"What kind of car is it?" I asked, half paying attention as I watched Mathews work the room.

"A silver sedan."

My head snapped around. The car that passed me Saturday night was a silver sedan.

Clark's brow knitted together. "Did I say something wrong?"

"No. I'll see you guys back at the office." I made a beeline for the punch table where Grayson Mathews stood, shaking hands.

I waited in line as one of the vice presidents gushed over him. "Mr. Mathews, you don't know how much this donation means to Harshberger and our students."

Mathews smiled his perfect-teeth smile and patted the man on the back as if he was a member of the same team. *Old habits must die hard for the football hero.* The vice president, five foot one at best, had probably not been a former football teammate, yet he beamed.

At my turn, I held out my hand. "It's nice to see you again, Mr. Mathews."

He gave me the same smile he shared with the vice president, but this one didn't reach his eyes. "Oh, yes, Miss Humphrey. It's nice to see you again. Has Timothy and his family changed their mind about my offer?"

I shook my head.

He pursed his lips. "What a shame."

"It's nice of you to donate to the college. Very generous."

He smiled. "I have plans to be a large part of Knox County, and in particular, Appleseed Creek. It makes sense I would give back, and what better place to do that than to Harshberger? The college has been here for nearly one hundred years."

"How do you plan to be a large part of the Knox County? I mean, other than the development in the Amish district. You do know you will never convince all those Amish families to sell."

He set his punch on the table. The cup was full. I wasn't surprised. Grayson Mathews didn't strike me as a fruit punch kind of guy. "You may be right. Not all the families will sell—at least not right away. However, if I can convince a few strategic sales, we can move forward with our plans. The plans may have to be scaled back, but we can always add on later as more land becomes available."

I selected a sugar cookie from the tray. "Strategic sales? Do you mean the Glick Farm?"

"I appreciate your curiosity, but that's simply none of your business."

"Are you interested in the Glick's land or the natural gas pump on the property?"

His head whipped to one side.

"I'm guessing you would have to offer each family much more for their property if you took into account their mineral rights. Have you included that in the negotiations?" I folded the cookie into a napkin.

The developer's jaw twitched. "You don't know what you are talking about."

"True, I don't know much about it, but I do know real estate is not as profitable right now as gas and oil is." The cookie crumbled inside the napkin as I squeezed my hand around it.

"We are done here. Your college president wishes to speak to me."

I turned around to see President Hammerstein standing behind me. As I left, I tossed the mangled cookie and napkin into the trash.

At the office, Miller and Clark were already back at their desks. It was almost four o'clock. "You guys can go home early."

They peeked out over their cubicle walls and nodded in tandem. The two then grabbed their lunchboxes and made a dash for the door. I laughed. I couldn't believe how much lighter the mood was in the office now that Joel was gone. It had been difficult to let him go, but it was the best thing for the college and the department. I prayed that now Miller, Clark, and I could become a real team.

Alone, I logged onto the Internet and started researching Grayson Mathews. This time I would dig deeper. Considering his wealth and reputation, there was bound to be a plethora of information about him online. I wasn't disappointed. The first half-dozen articles talked about all the work that Mathews had done creating a planned community south of Columbus called Jeffersonville Village. Every article mentioned his record as an Ohio State football hero, as if that should give him the credentials to develop property.

I clicked a tiny icon, a logo of some type, at the bottom on the main page of his website. The logo led me to a new website called Buckeye Tree Companies.

The CEO of that corporation was Grayson Mathews. A long list of businesses fell under the corporation's control, from Jeffersonville Village to restaurants to a gas company—Buckeye River Gas. "Got you," I whispered. I couldn't wait to tell Timothy why Mathews was really interested in the Amish lands.

My stomach clenched when I saw the name of another company halfway down the page—Little Owl Greenhouse. I clicked on the link and found a photograph of the place where Becky worked. She was there now.

My heart revved. *Calm down, Chloe.* So what if Grayson's corporation owned the greenhouse? He owned half a dozen other small businesses in and around Knox County, too. There didn't have to be a connection with the greenhouse and his real estate or gas companies.

I couldn't let go of the fact that Scotch and Cookie had offered Becky a job she was clearly unqualified for. Yes, when she lived with her Amish family, she'd helped with the gardening. However her experience had been exclusively related to fruits and vegetables. She didn't know the scientific names of flowers; she didn't understand growing zones or how to landscape. She was a fast learner, but she still had a long way to go.

And then, there was her broken arm.

I clicked back to Buckeye Tree Companies and found the link to Jeffersonville Village, which had its own Web site. The people in the photos smiled, showing me right away that Jeffersonville Village was the best place to live in the entire state. The village had a swimming pool, tennis courts, and a clubhouse. The list went on and on.

I clicked on the listing prices. Houses were priced from two hundred thousand dollars to five hundred thousand. I stared at the screen. My father in California wouldn't blink at these prices. In fact, where he lived these homes would be considered cheap. However, in rural Ohio the prices didn't ring true. Who in Knox County could afford such an expensive home?

I sat back, stunned. Clark was right. It wasn't the land Mathews wanted. It was what was *under* the land.

It was after four, and Becky would be done at the greenhouse in half an hour. I thought about calling Timothy, but we hadn't spoken since the picnic. I held my cell phone in my hand. He was working in Sunbury again this week anyway. I slid the phone back into my purse, telling myself that not calling him had nothing whatsoever to do with Hannah Hilty.

With so much on my mind, I turned off the computer, grabbed my purse, and headed for Little Owl Greenhouse.

Chapter Fifty-Two

Cookie wasn't at the cash register when I stepped into the greenhouse, but that was to be expected. Cookie and Scotch were always wandering around. Usually Becky was the easiest to find, but I didn't see her either.

I cupped my hands around my mouth. "Becky?"

No response. That girl really needed a cell phone for times like this. I kicked myself for buying her jeans first. I stepped through the store and hothouse, the thick air greeting me. Still no Becky. I checked outside at the fenced-in part of the property. Becky should be here. She had told me the night before that Scotch was going to teach her how to prune the fir trees. How she planned to manage that with one arm, I couldn't understand. But I hadn't wanted to dampen her mood. She'd been upbeat ever since our walk on the trail with Timothy and Aaron.

I hurried down the long row of maples until reaching the fir trees. It felt like I'd stepped into a potted version of a Christmas tree farm. "Becky?"

Still no answer. The hairs on the back of my neck stood on end, prickling my skin. I turned around to head toward the exit.

Just then, Brock and Curt stepped out from opposite sides. They trapped me in the middle of a stand of pine trees. Curt's lip curled. "Red's back, Brock."

"Hello, friend." Brock clapped his hands, the sound of it like thunder. "We missed you."

"I can't say the same," I snapped. "Get out of my way."

Curt shook his head. "No need to get testy." He took a step toward me.

My breath caught, and I retreated, the sharp, spiny branches of a fir tree poking me in the back. "Don't come near me or I will scream. The people working here will hear me."

Curt snorted. "You mean Cookie or Scotch? They are old friends of ours. They won't say anything about your screams."

"Old friends? What are you talking about?"

"My goodness, Brock, she doesn't have it all figured out. I would have thought Little Miss Super Sleuth would know everything by now. You've been all over the county, poking your nose where it don't belong."

I clenched my fists. "Where are Cookie and Scotch?"

"They're here. Keeping quiet just like we told them to. They're good at following orders."

"Not all the time," Brock corrected.

"They are after we roughed up Scotch a little, you know, as incentive." Curt smirked.

My heart pounded in my chest, the sound exploding in my ears. "Where's Becky?"

"Don't worry. She's here. She's been spending some time with us. We've decided to put the past in the past. Now we're all chums." He nodded at Brock. "Aren't we, brother?"

"Totally," Brock agreed.

"You better not have hurt her." I removed my phone from my pocket, then swallowed a groan. *No service.*

Brock grabbed the phone from my hand. "There will be none of that. No calling for help, especially from that Amish boyfriend of yours."

Curt paced in front of me. "Why would you bother with some buggy-rider when you could have a real man like one of us?"

"Or both of us," Brock said, his grin sickeningly wide.

Curt narrowed his eyes. "That's an idea."

I leaned against the fir tree, its branches like knives in my back, and the pot it was planted in wobbled slightly. I threw all my weight against it, and the pot fell over. Tree limbs and needles covered the ground, and I lay in the middle of it. I scrambled to my feet, and ran down the next row of trees.

Brock stepped into my path, and I pulled up short.

Curt ran up behind me and yanked my right arm behind my back. "Now you've made me mad."

Tears sprang to my eyes. "Get away from me. Where's Becky?" I glared at Brock. *Dear Lord, help me through this. Please protect Becky.*

Curt sighed as if my reaction was a disappointment. He tightened his grip. "We'll take you to her."

Brock grabbed my arm, knocking Curt out of the way. "She's in the roses."

I attempted to yank myself from his grasp. "I know where that is. I can walk there myself."

"True, but then you would try to run away again," Curt said. "Brock could use the exercise by chasing you, but he's not in the mood for it tonight. Are you, big guy?"

"Naw, I'm not much for running."

Brock dragged me toward the rose garden where I found Becky seated on the floor, her unbroken arm tied to her ankles.

Cookie and Scotch were on the cement next to her. Their hands were tied as well. Scotch had a gash over his left eyebrow.

I knelt in front of him. "Are you okay?"

"We're sorry," Cookie said.

Tears rolled down Scotch's face and onto his overalls. "We tried to protect Becky. That's why we drove her back and forth from the greenhouse. We had to know she was safe all the time, so they wouldn't try to hurt her."

Brock grabbed the back of my shirt and pulled me away from them. "You can see how well that worked out."

Curt pulled something out of his pocket. A handgun. "Don't try anything stupid, Red, or I'll shoot all of them, starting with the girl."

Becky's body shook uncontrollably.

"What time is your uncle going to be here?" Brock asked.

Curt kept his watch on us. "Any minute."

Brock hopped from foot to foot. "He's going to be impressed with this." He towered over me. "You're not going to mess it up for us *this* time."

"This time?"

"You snatched the girl from us on Route 13. Then we couldn't grab her. You or that buggy-rider was always with her."

I scrunched my forehead. "Why did you want to kidnap Becky?"

"Someone needed to show the Amish who is in control of this county. They'd sell their land to his uncle if we held the girl." A smile spread across Brock's face. "And I wanted to have a little fun with her."

Curt grinned, giving me a full view of his tobacco-dip stained teeth. "He will no longer see me as a screw-up. I got it right this time."

"You have to let us go," Cookie said.

"Shut up," Curt barked. "My uncle owns this place. You should be grateful for everything he's done for you."

My stomach dropped. "Grayson Mathews is your uncle?"

Curt glared at me. "Shut your mouth! Sit down next to the girl." He pointed the gun at me. "You do anything stupid, I shoot the Amish girl."

I sat on the cold cement next to Becky. "Becky, did they hurt you?" I whispered.

"No." Her voice was a hoarse whisper.

Relief washed over me. "God will protect us."

Curt's head snapped around. "I said shut your mouth."

A voice called from deep in the greenhouse "Curt!"

Curt gestured with the gun. "That's my uncle. Go get him."

Brock disappeared into the maze of plants. He returned with Grayson Mathews following behind him. "Curt, this better be worth me delaying my trip back to Columbus. I can't stand all this country life. Those idiots at Harshberger bought my—" He saw Becky, Scotch, Cookie, and me sitting on the ground. His jaw twitched, and he swore. "What is this?"

Curt melted under his uncle's glare.

"Curt, what did you do?" His voice was thunderous.

"I'm helping you. She was going to connect you to the accident that killed that Amish guy."

"Connect me to the accident? I had nothing to do with it. That was another one of *your* mistakes. I gave the police an alibi for you, and you pull this stunt?"

Curt removed something from his pocket. I flinched, afraid it might be another gun. Instead, he removed a dirty business card. "She had your card in her car. She knew you asked us to mess with the Amish."

I do now.

Mathews closed his eyes.

I squared my gaze on him. "You killed the bishop."

Brock squeezed my arm and hissed, "The bishop was a lucky casualty."

My eyes ran across the three of them. "One of you cut the brake line."

"Yeah," Brock said. "We meant to get you out of the way so we could get the girl"

Hot bile rose in my throat. I swallowed hard to force it down,

"If we had the girl, the Amish would sell the land to Curt's uncle."

I glared at Mathews. "You asked them to do that?"

"I'm not that stupid," Mathews snapped.

Brock pulled his chin into his chest, his expression confused. "But you asked us to convince the Amish to sell, whatever it took."

Mathews ran a hand through his JFK Jr. hair. "Next time, I'll make a list of do's and don'ts."

"It's because of the natural gas, isn't it?" I said.

"We're going to be rich," Brock said.

"Would you two stop talking to her?" He glared at Brock. "We wouldn't even be in this situation if you hadn't been so stupid. I never told you to cut anything." He balled up the business card Curt gave him and threw it on the floor. "The deal will never go through now, you idiot."

"But Uncle Grayson . . ." Curt winced. "I was trying to help."

"You've been a screw-up since the day you were born. You couldn't even join the army."

Curt clutched the dog tags hanging from his neck. "That wasn't my fault. I wanted to serve my country. I'm not a coward like those buggy-riders."

"I know all about your heart murmur, nephew. Your mother reminds me about it on a daily basis. You must be brain damaged too if you think kidnapping four people was a good idea."

Curt licked his lips.

Brock stepped back from his friend.

"I was helping those filthy buggy-riders who don't deserve that land and gas. What have they ever done for anyone? They don't even fight for our country. They'd happily let someone else do that for them." Curt trained the gun on Becky. I slid on my seat in front of her. "Don't think I won't shoot you, because I will."

"Grayson, you have to let us go. This is going to ruin everything you worked for," Scotch said.

"I don't need your advice," Mathews snapped and turned to his nephew. "Give me the gun."

"They don't deserve it. You do, uncle, and men like my father, who fought and died for this land. Amish scum." He spat.

"Curt. Give. Me. The. Gun."

Curt stared at his uncle with tears in his eyes. Slowly, he handed the gun to Mathews. "They don't deserve it," Curt whispered.

"I know," Mathews said.

A man stepped out from behind a huge hibiscus bush and aimed the jet stream of a water hose into Mathews's eyes.

I blinked. "Joel?"

Mathews covered his face and dropped the gun. The force of the water pressure forced the weapon to slide under a potted rose of Sharon.

Before he could dash after it, I donkey-kicked Brock in the knee, the same one he fell on the day I met Becky on the side of Route 13, the day I moved to Appleseed Creek. He cried out in pain and let go of my arm.

Then I ran to Becky.

"I think she broke my kneecap!" Brock rolled onto his side.

Curt stared at his friend.

Joel still had the water trained on Mathews, who struggled to his feet.

"Curt, you idiot, find my gun!"

Curt started to search the ground.

I grabbed a flathead screwdriver beside a stack of ceramic pots and tore through the duct tape around Becky's ankles. She didn't move. "Get up!"

She jumped up as if I'd electrocuted her.

Brock held his knee. Tears rolled down his baby face. He didn't appear nearly as frightening as he did before.

"Find the gun!" Mathews bellowed.

"I'm trying." Curt looked at his friend. "Should we take Brock to the hospital or something? He's hurt."

"I don't care about Brock. I want those girls and the guy with the water hose."

I pulled Becky along behind me. She gasped through her tears.

"Becky, you have to calm down. We need to think straight."

She hiccupped.

Heavy steps crept up behind me. I spun around, brandishing the screwdriver.

It was Joel.

I kept the screwdriver in the air. "What are you doing here?"

"Following you."

I pulled back. "Why?"

"I wanted to talk to you about firing me."

I heard more footsteps and whipped a glance in their direction. "Can we talk about this later?" I shoved them both into the building. "How do you close this door?" It was an automatic door.

Becky just shivered.

"Becky, where is the button?"

She stared at me and reached behind a shelf of fertilizer. Slowly the door closed as Curt ran at it full tilt. It settled on the cement ground. *Thud!*

Joel quirked a look in my direction. "Did he just bounce off the door?"

I shuddered. "Would someone call the police?"

The greenhouse's front door slammed open. "We don't have to," Becky said. "They're already here."

Chapter Fifty-Three

Joel stood alone under a hanging basket. A silver sedan sat parked on the other side of an ambulance.

I pointed to the parking lot. "Is that your car?"

He nodded.

"Did you follow me home from the Mennonite church Saturday night?"

He nodded again.

I dug a hand into my hip. "Why?"

"I told you. I want to know why you fired me."

"You weren't fired. You were laid off."

"As if that made it any easier." The usual bitterness in his tone had ebbed somewhat.

"I'm sorry, Joel. I made the best decision I could for the department."

He shook his head. His shoulders slumped.

What he'd done changed him. Much of the anger he'd harbored against me had dissipated. *Heroics can do that for a person.* Despite all of his failings, Joel was a hero. The fact was difficult for me to accept, but it may have been even more difficult for Joel.

I swallowed. "Thank you. You saved Becky and me."

He hung his head. "I did what had to be done." Then he wandered away.

Chief Rose sauntered up to me with her hands on her hips. "That looked awkward."

I grimaced.

"See, I told you, you were the key in this case."

I wasn't so sure about that. "What does this mean for your department, Chief?"

"Crime does pay." A sly smile spread across her face.

Timothy's truck threw gravel in all directions as he swerved around a police cruiser.

Chief Rose shook her head. "Apparently none of the Troyers know how to drive."

He jumped out of his truck. Becky, who stood with Cookie and Scotch, broke away from the EMT taking her blood pressure and ran into her brother's arms. He hugged her to him while scanning the crowd.

Chief Rose nudged me. "I think he's searching for someone."

Timothy's eyes locked on mine. He said something to his sister, and she let him go. I stepped away from the police chief and met him under the shade of the oak tree. "Chloe, are you all right?"

I ran my hands up and down my bare arms. "I'm fine."

Timothy's chest moved up and down as if he couldn't catch his breath. His big blue eyes searched my face. "When Great called me, I got here as fast as I could. I'm sorry I wasn't there."

I scanned the crowd. The police chief was speaking to a protesting Curt. Brock had already been taken to the hospital in Mount Vernon.

Mathews sat in the back of a cruiser not speaking to anyone. He stared straight ahead. His high-priced lawyer had taught him well.

Joel stood in the middle of a group of reporters, relating how he saved the day—which he had.

"Chief Rose called you?"

He nodded.

I bobbed my head, my eyes darting around. "I'm glad you're here. Becky needed you."

He winced. "Becky? What about you?"

I forced a smile. "I did too. You've been a good friend."

Timothy flinched. "A good friend?"

I stopped. "Of course. I could have never gotten through this without you. I've seen what a wonderful brother you are to Becky and the children. You're like the brother I never had."

His brow furrowed. "I'm not your brother."

I licked my lips, unable to meet his gaze. "I know that. You're like a brother to me."

He lifted my chin, the calluses on his fingers brushing my skin. "No, I'm not. I don't want you to think of me as your brother. I care about you."

"I care about you too."

His face flamed red. "I don't care about you like I care about my sisters." He took my small and freckled hand between his two calloused ones.

"Oh." The light was dawning. A smile began to form on my lips, but just as quickly it faded. "What about Hannah?"

"Hannah?"

"Isn't she—aren't you together?"

He barked a laugh. "She wishes."

"You are promised to her," I said.

"We dated. It was nothing serious, at least not for me. Hannah might disagree. I told her many times that it's over between us." He frowned. "I dated her because I knew it was what her father wanted. It's been over for a long time though."

"I can guarantee she doesn't think it's over. She pretty much told me the two of you were getting married."

He rocked back on his heels. "I'm not going to marry Hannah."

Inside of me, a little voice cried out with joy.

Epilogue

Tuesday morning, I sat in the second row of a small courtroom in the Knox County courthouse in Mount Vernon.

Even the fact that Becky had been kidnapped the day before wouldn't convince the Knox County judge to move her court date for sentencing. Becky sat next to Tyler Hart in the row in front of me.

Timothy squeezed my hand. "It's going to be fine," he whispered. He was the only one from the Troyer family to attend. He told me that the Amish want as little interaction with English government as possible, but I wondered if Becky was hurt that her parents weren't by her side for the verdict.

The bailiff faced us. "All rise."

A rotund man in a black robe climbed to the bench. The judge sat, and so did the others in the courtroom. There weren't many. Becky's sentencing was not a big draw.

The judge's bushy eyebrows knitted together. He addressed the prosecutor. "Do you accept the guilty plea?"

"We do." The prosecutor wore a suit that must have cost half of his monthly salary.

The judge nodded and glared at Becky. "I hope you understand the seriousness of your offense, young lady. I understand some of the circumstances leading up to this accident were no fault of your own. The vehicle was tampered with; however, that does not discount that you were an unlicensed and uninsured motorist. A more experienced driver may have avoided the fatal accident."

I shifted in my seat. That was a little harsh of the judge to say. Timothy touched my wrist, and I stopped squirming.

"I do," Becky whispered.

"I can't hear you," the judge bellowed.

Becky cowered, but then straightened. "I do understand, sir." She spoke in a clear voice.

"Good. It is the decision of this court to follow the prosecution's recommendation. You are forbidden to apply for a driver's license until your twenty-fifth birthday, you have one year of probation, and you must complete one thousand hours of community service." He glared at her. "Although I usually feel that it does a young person some good, I don't think in this case that prison time is needed."

Tears pricked my eyes.

"Thank you, your honor."

The judge slammed his gavel on the bench. "Hart, get yourself and your client out of my courtroom."

Tyler nodded and shuffled Becky toward the exit. Timothy and I hurried after them. We met in the rotunda outside of the room.

"Is the judge always that cranky?" I asked Tyler.

"Always." He grinned and patted Becky on the shoulder. "Well, kiddo, you're going to be okay." He shook my hand. "I'll call you later today with the information about her probation officer."

"I never thought I would be happy to hear about a probation officer," I said.

Timothy threw his arms around Becky and they hugged. "Me either."

Tyler tipped his head. "I have another case this morning, so I will let you all celebrate." His footsteps echoed as he hurried across the rotunda.

Timothy pulled me into the hug with him and Becky. It was our own little circle, our own little family. When I first moved to Appleseed Creek, all I thought about was moving away from it. Now I wondered if I'd ever want to leave.

Together, we strolled out of the courthouse arm in arm. Timothy released me and gave Becky another big, brotherly hug.

As he did, I spotted an Amish man across the street, scowling at us. It was Deacon Sutter. I bit my lip. Soon the Amish district will need to choose a new bishop. *Will it be Deacon Sutter?* If the deacon wasn't chosen, how will he react, and what were his plans for the disobedient Troyer family?

Becky tugged my arm. "Come on, Chloe, Timothy's taking us to breakfast to celebrate."

I pushed away thoughts of the deacon and smiled at Becky's glowing face. "Breakfast sounds perfect."

Dear Reader Letter

Dear Reader,

When I was twenty-four years old, my first real job out of graduate school was to be an academic librarian for a small college in rural Knox County, Ohio. Knox County is right next to Holmes County, which has the largest Amish population in the world, and Knox County has a small Amish population of its own. It was common for me to see Amish buggies when I drove to and from work or to shop beside Amish families in the local grocery store. That experience inspired me to write *A Plain Death* and the future novels in the Appleseed Creek Mystery Series.

There are so many wonderful Amish novels in bookstores and libraries right now, but I hope you find *A Plain Death* to be a little different. First and foremost, it is a mystery novel. The novel centers around the death of an Amish bishop, who is killed in an auto-buggy collision. The protagonist, Chloe Humphrey, and her new former-Amish friends, Becky and Timothy Troyer, decide to investigate the case because Becky was the driver of the car. They must decide if the crash was an accident or perhaps murder.

Also, the novel may reveal something new about the Amish to you. In my series, I hope to show you how different the Amish are from order to order and district to district. There are many different Amish groups, and each group has its own rules. However, the heart of their culture is keeping their communities together. Most Amish don't drive cars because they think it's wrong to do so. They are afraid that if they were able to own their own cars, the community would splinter because motor vehicles make it easier for community members to move away from each other. It's a difficult and sometimes peculiar balance that the Amish have with the modern world. I hope I captured the essence of that in my writing.

Above all, I hope you enjoy the story—that the characters make you smile, the mystery raises your suspicions, and the romance touches your heart.

Blessings & Happy Reading!

Amanda Flower

Discussion Questions

1. What was your favorite part of the novel? Why?

2. Which character did you identify with the most? Why?

3. What did you learn about Amish culture in this book that you did not know before?

4. What aspect of Amish culture do you most admire? What aspect do you disagree with?

5. The protagonist, Chloe Humphrey, has a difficult relationship with her father. How is that relationship similar to Amish shunning?

6. The author lived in Knox County for three years during her twenties. How do you think that influenced the novel?

7. What do you think of the author's description of Knox County, Ohio? Is it a place you'd like to visit?

8. The protagonist, Chloe Humphrey, has a cat named Gigabyte, and a central character, Timothy Troyer, has a dog named Mabel. Why do you think animal characters are so prevalent in mystery novels?

9. The novel shows that Amish differ from order to order and from district to district. How does that apply to Christian denominations in general?

10. Becky Troyer and her brother Timothy leave the Amish for different reasons. Do you think their reasons were believeable?

11. The author, Amanda Flower, considers herself a cozy mystery author. Do you know what makes a mystery "cozy"? What makes *A Plain Death* a cozy mystery?

12. Of the antagonists in the novel, which do you dislike the most? And why?

13. Before the end of the novel, who did you think the culprit was? Were you right?

14. What do you think about the conclusion of the mystery? What about it surprised you?

15. What do you think the future holds for Chloe and Timothy?